About

Jennifer Pierce is a writer and editor working in academic publishing. She is a graduate of Wheaton College (Massachusetts) and Oxford Brookes University. She currently lives in Boston.

Slow Motion

Slow Motion

Jennifer Pierce

unbound

This edition first published in 2021

Unbound
TC Group, Level 1, Devonshire House, One Mayfair Place
London W1J 8AJ

www.unbound.com

All rights reserved

© Jennifer Pierce, 2021

The right of Jennifer Pierce to be identified as the author of this work has been asserted in accordance with Section 77 of the Copyright, Designs and Patents Act 1988. No part of this publication may be copied, reproduced, stored in a retrieval system, or transmitted, in any form or by any means without the prior permission of the publisher, nor be otherwise circulated in any form of binding or cover other than that in which it is published and without a similar condition being imposed on the subsequent purchaser.

This book is a work of fiction and, except in the case of historical fact, any resemblance to actual persons, living or dead, is purely coincidental.

ISBN (eBook): 978-1-78965-140-9
ISBN (Paperback): 978-1-78965-139-3

Cover design by Mecob

Printed and bound in Great Britain by Clays Ltd, Elcograf S.p.A.

For George and Kathy McKendall, who helped make this book possible.

Super Patrons

John Auckland
Deyonne Bryant
Heather Cain
Jennifer Carnevale
Tom Crawford
Ernest Crivellone
Marlene Cutitar
Dr. Gary D'Orsi
Zachary D'Orsi
Marilyn DelDonno
Kaitlin Deveau
Nick Deveau
Ivette Fantasia
Kate Gibalerio
Cate Hackett
Dennis Hanno
Christine Hanson
Kelsey Lepore
Kaitlin Lozinski
Mary Anne McKendall
Maureen McKendall

Miriam McKendall
MJ McKendall
Ray McKendall
The McKendall family
Joan Melaragno
ML
Andrew Pack
Scott Pack
Bill Pierce
Kathryn Pierce
Lois Pierce
Marita and Rob Pierce
Robert Pierce
Karli Ryan
Beth Spradlin
Carolyn Tisdale
Creative Writing Wheaton College,
Massachusetts
Paul & Diane Yingling
Jim Zachazewski
Francesca Zunino Harper

1

It was golden hour over New England as Angela pulled out of her driveway.

She'd always thought this town belonged on a postcard, the words *Greetings from Westview* spelled out in cheerful letters designed to look three-dimensional, with little shops, church steeples and the brick clock tower fitted neatly inside them. Blue and green splashed against the background. Quaint, picture-perfect.

Ahead of her, long lines of light stretched across lines of identical white houses, with arches, marble pillars and gleaming windows, emerald landscaping and aquamarine pools. Mirror images that echoed all the way down the street and curved around a cul-de-sac.

One day this summer, she'd looked outside and realized how fake her neighborhood looked. She couldn't unsee it now. Hated the sprawling lawns and perfectly structured architecture that used to feel like home, the way the false flawlessness had somehow seeped into the skin of the neighborhood's inhabitants and crafted living copies of magazine photographs, all posed perfection and perfume-stale pages. Everyone hiding behind smiles and curtains, afraid of their secrets breaking free and floating through the air before landing on evergreen trees and sinking to the bottom of the water that billowed across town for miles. Whispers everywhere.

She glanced back at the sun-soaked street in her rear-view mirror as she drove away, wondering if anyone else felt like this behind all the gold. And then she realized where the map on her phone was leading her.

***

Summer was always Angela's favorite season. When she was five years old, she spent every day outside, squinting through rainbow-stained sunlight and blurry chlorine circles in the pool, soaring on the swing set in a magenta-ruffled bathing suit to dry off. One hot, cloudless afternoon, as Angela splashed and stared at the shimmering distortion of the pool's azure-swirled tiles, Madelyn, her babysitter, perched on a deck chair, talking on her phone.

"Can you keep a secret?" she asked after hanging up, and Angela pinky-promised in peach nail polish because she'd never had a secret of her own to keep.

The secret was the Emorys—a boy Angela's age named Owen, and his younger sister Haley. The family had just moved to Westview, Madelyn said as she drove to their house, Angela watching the town flicker by from the backseat, hair still wet. The Emorys lived in a neighborhood that she'd never been before, across a cerulean dam with a panoramic backdrop of evergreens. The house was smaller than Angela's, lawn overgrown. Owen was smiling the first time she saw him, in a red shirt, sliding toy cars across an uneven driveway adorned with chalk portraits that left colored dust on the soles of her shoes. His mother came running outside in blue jeans and messy hair, thanking them breathlessly as she got in her car for an appointment she'd forgotten about.

Angela liked Owen right away, because he was different from the children her mother made her play with in their own neighborhood, not afraid to shout or laugh too loudly or get dirt on his clothes. She spent the rest of that day running around the yard with him, Madelyn watching them from the windows as Haley slept. The next time Madelyn came over, Angela begged her to take her back to Owen's house, and then they were spending almost every day together.

He gave her a toy car to take home and she hid it under her pillow, racing the tiny wheels across her sheets when the lights were off and the house was quiet. She brought him things from her father's office, crisp notepads and tiny tins of mints, everything branded in blue with the name Witney Residential. They looked at newspapers and studied words they didn't understand, pretending to be adults before tearing the columns into strips for papier-mâché masks.

Once, she met Owen's father, and he was somehow scary but she didn't have the words for why. Around him, everything seemed quieter, more breakable. The only darkness in a sun-kissed summer.

Angela tried to capture every moment in her memory, bold and colorful. Spraying Owen with a garden hose, feet sinking into warm, soft mud. Cherry Popsicles that melted in the hot July sun, staining the cheap wooden sticks and their mouths bright red. Throwing handfuls of grass at each other, tiny slashes of jade and emerald spinning through the air. Scribbling bold oil pastel lines on construction paper and bleeding watercolors across the empty spaces and writing their names across the bottom with thick black markers. Owen and Angela. Curving loops and sharp peaks.

Angela wished that summer could last forever.

***

When summer ended and school started, she wore a new dress, navy with white polka dots and a wide white ribbon that looped into a bow in the back. The fabric was uncomfortable against her skin. Her shoes, white with cut-out flowers and a strap that buckled at the ankle, engraved swirling red lines into her feet. Her mother had painted her nails pale pink the previous evening, braided her hair in the morning. They drove to the elementary school with her Aunt Alex and cousin, Cassie. By accident, Angela and Cassie were dressed almost identically.

It was sunny and a white tent was set up on the front lawn. Angela wanted to be anywhere but here. Clad in dress pants and silk blouses, her mother and the other parents sipped lukewarm coffee from paper cups decorated with teal flowers while their children, Angela's new classmates, silently sat at their sides. As the parents wondered how long kindergarten orientation would take and whispered about a teacher's unstylish attire, Angela looked around for Owen.

The chatter in the tent quieted to a soft hum as the principal began speaking about the upcoming school year. Angela stopped listening. Through white beams of sunshine, she could see two latecomers standing hesitantly at the edge of the tent. Owen and his mother. The mothers seated at Angela's table began whispering behind manicured nails. One of the teachers ushered them to an empty table, Owen's mother keeping her head down as they walked through all the whispers.

"Is that *Valerie Emory*? Are they really back in town? I never thought they would actually go through with it."

"I'm almost embarrassed for them," Angela's mother whispered. "Did they really think that everyone would just forget?"

Angela smiled at Owen and waved, and her mother's gaze swiveled back to her.

"You *know* him?"

"He's my friend," Angela answered.

Her mother's thin brows became angry arches, lips

lines of disapproval. Quietly furious, she whispered something about *people like them*. Everyone at their table looked away, a masquerade of embarrassment, but it was obvious that they were hanging on to every word.

Angela hoped that she and Owen would be in the same class but they weren't. Her parents warned her to stay away from him, refused to explain why.

That year, her father was re-elected to Town Council and his company began to expand further and further beyond the East Coast. Angela became friends with the children of similar families who had lived here in Westview for generations. She accompanied her parents to receptions and charity functions, watched them cut ribbons and give speeches. And memories of Owen and their watercolor summer faded like an abandoned painting on a sunny windowsill.

***

Her senior year of high school was supposed to be fun, Angela thought now as she drove away from all those white houses, over a vast expanse of familiar blue, and down an old road. But it was Westview's tricentennial and the town was planning a series of events to mark the occasion. At her parents' request, she'd signed up for the volunteer committee, waiting until the last moment possible. A year of celebrating the past when she was supposed to be focused on a future that had been mapped out for her entire life.

Tonight was their first event, and she'd spent the afternoon picking up food and decorations. Her friends were all at the beach, going to the last party of the summer later. They'd been sending her pictures all day. She was supposed to want to be there with them.

She'd gone home to change for the event after dropping everything off at the community center when she got a phone call from Jan, the perpetually stressed coordinator, about another volunteer whose car had broken down.

"Can you pick him up?" she'd asked Angela, the address barely audible against all the noise in the background. Angela imagined her directing the alignment of beige folding chairs into perfect rows marked with straight tape across the floor. When she'd seen Jan earlier, her usually sleek hair was already frizzing out and her lipstick was smudged at the corner of her mouth. Anything was better than going back there right away, Angela thought.

And then she'd realized she was going to Owen's house. She hadn't been there since the summer they met.

The paint on the house was peeling, falling to the mix of dust and dying grass that was once a lawn. Dirty windows glinted gold in the fading sunlight. Her reflection was smudged, distorted. She pressed the doorbell once and Owen answered after a moment, phone pressed to his ear. He looked surprised but quickly hid it in a smile. He led Angela to the kitchen, indicated that she should take a seat at the table.

The scent of summer rain clung to the house. The lights were off. Plates with mismatched patterns were piled in the sink. Swirling blue lines and little red florets. The kitchen opened into a small living room, white walls with pink-flowered stenciling scrawled across the top. His sister was curled up on the couch in front of the TV. Her eyes widened for a moment when she saw Angela and she reached for her phone without saying anything as the bright flashing images of commercials lit up the walls and windows around her. Red-painted lips and high-heeled shoes and bodies sheathed in gauzy fabric. The light gave her face an eerie radiance, simultaneously bright and pale, her dark hair a shadow. The graceful, flowing accents and pitchy, short articulations and velvet murmurs coming from the TV blended with music playing in another room.

It was strange being back here. Angela felt like she didn't belong. She and Owen were too far apart now, stretched to the axes of different worlds, never colliding.

Even in a town as small as Westview, it was surprisingly easy to avoid people if you knew how. She'd constructed a social circle of people like her, one that never overlapped with his. She made herself shiny and bright so that everyone knew who she was, just like her parents, while he seemed to make himself invisible. Whenever they passed each other in the halls at school, they never spoke, never made eye contact, almost a silent promise between them that this way was easier. And until today, she'd never had a reason to return to this part of town.

Secretly, Angela had sometimes dreaded a situation like this, where being reunited with Owen was beyond her control. She ignored the part of her that knew it was inevitable here. Tried not to think about it, feeling a combination of guilt and discomfort that he somehow knew a side of her that she kept tucked away at the corners of her heart. Sometimes, in retrospect, the days they'd spent together in his backyard seemed like more than a simple summer friendship at five, but at other times she thought she was just remembering it as more than it was. Maybe it was because something about it felt unfinished, abandoned without clarity when everything else about her life had always been straightforward.

She glanced at Owen as he continued talking on the phone, pacing the length of the kitchen. It sounded like he was giving someone directions.

She remembered something she'd sometimes felt here. Something that somehow felt heavy and empty at the same time, a feeling that her five-year-old mind could only notice but never fully comprehend. And then she remembered all the rumors she'd heard over the years and wondered which ones were true because that was the problem with Westview. People here liked to talk. Anyone could become the target of the whispers in this town, and that was when the truth and the lies got tangled up, distorted by all the voices that decided what the real story was going to be.

If you wanted to play their game, you could hide secrets behind rumors that weren't as bad. Angela was good at it; she knew how to make people believe whatever she wanted. But the person she spread the most rumors about was herself.

Owen's voice cut across Angela's thoughts. He was off the phone now, addressing her as if they hadn't been ignoring each other's existence for years. "Sorry about that. Thanks for coming."

"No problem," Angela answered, trying not to think of all the places she could be savoring these final moments of summer instead. One last drive along the coast with her favorite songs playing, exploring tiny towns with their bright marinas and hydrangeas and shingled houses wind-worn stormy gray. On a rooftop in the middle of a skyline, watching sunlight turn into city lights.

For her last birthday, her parents had given her an expensive camera that she used to bring everywhere, snapping pictures of her friends and everything they did until they had a collection of everyday moments that once seemed so important. She'd stopped when each image started to look as fake as their neighborhood. Now that summer was ending, though, she wished she'd taken more pictures over the last few months. She felt a sudden, confusing need to capture everything about right now before it was gone, study them to find what was real, but it was already too late; she was here in this house she never thought she'd return to instead of all the places someone like her was supposed to be.

"To be honest, you're the last person I was expecting

to show up," Owen commented as if he could read her thoughts.

"Jan asked me to. My parents made me join the committee."

Owen smiled. "You'll have fun."

"I doubt it," she said, thinking of all those pictures of her friends at the beach. *Wish you were here*, they'd all told her. "So why are you doing this?"

"I like history," he answered. "I've been volunteering with the Westview Historical Society for a few years now. I think it's important to understand the place you're from."

Angela shrugged. Until a few months ago, she'd thought she understood Westview, or at least the way she belonged to it, perfectly. But lately she felt out of place in the little world she'd built herself here and she didn't think history was going to help it make sense again.

For a silent moment, they stared at the bright images on the TV.

"Alright, I just have to get a few things from upstairs before we leave," Owen said.

Angela didn't know if she was supposed to follow him or why she did. His room was messy, bed unmade, desk covered in crumpled papers with cross-outs and smudged ink. An entire wall was covered in maps, squiggling lines inked across crisp pages to detail the intricacies of cities and curves of continents, the earth's busiest squares and intimate corners sketched out in coded colors. A canvas of rivers and roads taped across blank space in a middle-of-nowhere town.

"Sorry about the mess," Owen said, extracting a backpack from a pile of inside-out clothing. He stuffed it with a stack of papers and folders from his desk.

"It's fine." Angela glanced at her phone, uninterested. She had a series of texts from Dillon, her boyfriend. She could imagine what they were—a picture of one of their friends getting buried in the sand, a story about someone they'd run into, plans for tonight, some hearts. She didn't look.

She wandered over to Owen's mirror to check her hair. He had postcards, photographs and ticket stubs tucked between the glass and its wooden frame. One of the pictures was older, more faded than the others. A girl, curly-haired and smiling, lips stained with Popsicle lipstick. She was wearing a bathing suit splashed with flowers in shades of coral and amethyst, hugging a shirtless boy in mud-splattered denim. The sprinkler behind them shot glittering jets of water into an arc across the cornflower sky.

"It's us," she said, surprised.

Owen looked embarrassed. "My mom found it a few weeks ago. She's getting sentimental about this being the last year of high school."

Angela noticed several other old pictures now—Owen at various stages of childhood—that his mother must have taken out to show him. He joined her at the mirror to look at them.

"Do you ever miss being a kid?" he asked.

"Sometimes," Angela admitted. She wondered why she was telling him this. It seemed like such an insignificant thing to confess, something everyone must feel on occasion, but she never would have told any of her friends.

"There are a few more of these, I can show them to you later if you want," Owen added, glancing at the picture of the two of them together. He immediately looked like he regretted saying it.

"Maybe."

Angela looked at their reflections. Her own appearance hadn't changed much; her hair was lighter brown and her curls had fallen into loose waves, but the shape of her face was the same. She couldn't remember the last time she'd really looked at Owen, though. He was so much taller than her now. Over the years, the brightness in his eyes had dulled to an almost sad shade of blue-gray. His hair was slightly too long, falling nearly to his shoulders in a messy way that was somehow graceful. His face was longer, barely shaven, jaw more structured.

Looking at him this close, for this long, made Angela feel uncomfortable. She hated being too close to anyone. She tore her gaze away from their backwards faces, breaking the connection their eyes had forged through glass and sunbeams.

"Let's go," she told him.

Owen called goodbye to his sister as he and Angela made their way downstairs.

Outside, the slowly setting sun was staining the leaves on the trees gold.

"This is my favorite time of year," Owen commented, clearly trying to fill the silence as they stood in the driveway, Angela fumbling for her keys.

Angela shook her head. "I want it to be summer all the time." She spent all the other seasons wanting to do something reckless, trying to recapture that feeling of freedom when the days were endless, warm, and nothing mattered but sunshine and wind in her hair.

Owen laughed quietly. "Look around, though."

Angela's hand brushed against her keys. She hooked her finger through the silver circle keeping them together, withdrew them from her bag. The keys chimed as they collided. She unlocked her car.

"The whole town looks different," Owen added as he opened the door.

The rays of light slanting across the driveway made the windows sparkle and the dying grass glow. Shadows blurred against the house, erasing the dirty paint, removing every flaw so that everything here was pretending to be perfect, too.

The sunset glared and gleamed against the windshield. As she pulled out of the driveway, Angela squinted through the light and looked back at Owen's house.

It was still gilded in sun.

2

There was something bittersweet about end-of-summer nights, Owen thought. Maybe it was the cold that crept in and stole the sun's warmth with waves of clouds, the darkness that splashed across the sky early, a feeling of absence as though something unattainable had slipped away with the sunset. The way people retreated inside to fill their homes with artificial lights and heat, an inside-out version of summer. But there was also something comforting about autumn approaching, the routine of early alarms and crisp air, the slow sway of power lines over cornfields on pale mornings and the clean scent of the freshly scrubbed school. Somehow, something about fall felt halfway hopeful.

Owen was optimistic about the start of school, something he wouldn't have thought possible a few years ago. Their schedules had been mailed out last week and he had most of his classes with his friends; he'd managed to coordinate his volunteer commitments with his work hours. He liked the structure of it all. It kept him motivated, made him feel like almost everything was falling into place.

And there were all the traditions to look forward to—Halloween movie marathons with his friends and driving up to the mountains with his family, admiring trees awash in colors stolen from dreams as they hiked their favorite trail, before sampling fresh maple syrup and sharp cheddar cheese from a farm on a dead-end dirt road on the way home.

All of those were good things, Owen kept reminding himself, listing them over and over in his mind every time something dark tried to creep into his thoughts.

The nights were beginning to cool down lately and as the event ended, he noticed that the slow shift into autumn had already started. People leaving the community center had replaced their light summer clothes with the heavier fabric of fall, swinging their arms into long sleeves as they ambled outside into the parking lot. Angela was the only exception, wearing a pale yellow sundress like she could defy the almost-autumn air if she dressed like summer sunlight. The other volunteers had begun cleaning up but she was standing against the wall, watching and clutching her bare, thin arms close to her body.

"Are you cold? Do you want this?" Owen asked, indicating his sweatshirt.

Predictably, Angela shook her head. Owen briefly wondered if it was because she didn't want to give in to the idea of autumn or because the thought of wearing his clothes repulsed her.

There was a bright red poster on the wall nearby, its bold white letters detailing upcoming events in celebration of the town's tricentennial. Owen pressed its curling corners back against the paint, trying to think of something else to say to her.

Part of him still couldn't believe she was here, even though it made perfect sense. Everyone knew that the Witney family could trace their roots in Westview to the town's beginnings and they were proud of their history. They were important and they let everyone know it. Angela's father spent his days in a beautiful old office in the town center, and his evenings in the white-painted town hall, just like the generations before him. Her mother was from another old, wealthy family with a legacy here, too. She was the president of her family's company and was involved in countless local initiatives, coordinating almost every event in town from weekend farmers' markets to school fundraisers.

All evening, people had been coming over to talk to Angela and he'd watched her light up with a smile that looked practiced. That was how it always was here. Owen knew, or at least wanted to believe, that the Witneys had good intentions for their hometown but they seemed to think of themselves as New England royalty, and frustratingly, most people here acted accordingly. It seemed like every reputation in this town was designed or destroyed by the Witneys.

It was like that at school, too. Almost everyone wanted to be part of Angela's group of friends. She was always surrounded by beautiful, smiling people. But it seemed so easy to fall from grace.

"Let's go," Angela said now as Owen started folding up a row of chairs. The way she spoke always commanded attention, quiet yet sharp-toned, and she sometimes abandoned the edges of words, clipped syllables short in a way that was more effective than shouting.

"We're not done yet—"

"It's fine. Look, they have plenty of people to help," Angela interrupted, already walking toward the door. "We're leaving," she called to Jan, who was popping balloons with a pair of scissors, shriveled rubber and coiled ribbon sagging to the floor.

"Thanks for your help! Have a good night," Jan answered.

They stepped outside together into the golden glow of streetlights. The town was quiet, the nearby stores dark inside. They crossed the silent street to where Angela's car was parked. Owen glanced over at her cautiously as she backed out of the parking space. A girl in yellow silhouetted against the town her family built, windows rolled down to let in summer air and the scent of evergreen trees, a soft breeze kissing her hair.

Last summer, in city archives, Owen had pieced together an almost century-old secret that could change everything but he couldn't imagine ever using it against her. Because the truth was that he'd been infatuated with Angela Witney since freshman year, when his life was falling apart and hers looked perfect. Every time they passed each other in the hallway, he'd look away but he'd memorized all the little details of her. The flower perfume she always wore, the way she twirled a strand of hair around her finger when she was bored in class. How when she laughed, you could see it in her eyes first.

She didn't talk on the way back to his house. Her phone was placed in the cupholder between them and Owen could see it light up with unread messages as the car glided across the dark curves of the town's topography. He hated driving at night here. Minimal streetlights made it necessary to know these roads like muscle memory. Last year, the town had made it even worse by permanently shutting off half the streetlights to save money, most of them in the northern part of town where he lived. All the lights in the center of town and neighborhoods like Angela's were still aglow. Late nights, on his way home from work, Owen always thought about how eerily easy it would be to veer off the street, careening into trees and darkness. Sometimes those thoughts brought back nightmares and memories that were further in the past than they seemed.

"Thanks for the ride," he said as Angela parked at his

house. The front lights were on, patterned with the faint flickering of moth wings. Crickets hummed against the late summer stars.

Angela was momentarily silent, eyes scanning her phone screen, and Owen thought he caught a glimpse of something like sadness but then she looked up and gave him the smile she'd been giving everyone in town all night. Curved lips with eyes that didn't quite mean it. "No problem."

"See you at school," said Owen, closing the door and leaving her with that strained smile and the glow of her phone in the dark. He walked toward the house.

"Wait," he heard Angela calling as he reached for his keys on the stairs. He could see her getting out of the car. "You forgot your backpack."

Her feet crossed the short length of the front walkway, rhythmic against the delicate stillness of country night and empty roads. She met him at the bottom stair like a shadow. Placed the bag at his feet.

"Thanks," Owen said. As he moved to pick it up, softly but sudden as static, she touched her fingers—pale with slim silver rings and glossy nail polish—against his hand. He looked down at their hands instead of at her. "Do you want to come in?"

Angela was quiet. Owen could feel the faint beat of blood pulsing in her fingertips as they stood there awkwardly with the innocent intimacy of not exactly holding hands. He wished she would say something. She seemed so distant, as if her thoughts were far away even as she stood there with him, so close, skin so warm.

"No," said Angela finally. "I need to go home."

She moved her hand away, erased the lines of her fingerprints from his palm. The sudden absence felt like ice. There was a strange expression on her face, unreadable. Something about her eyes right now reminded Owen of burned-out light bulbs.

"Drive safe," he mumbled, somehow startled by her abruptness.

He suddenly felt the heat of embarrassment in his stomach, on his face. Of course she didn't want to come inside to dim lights and dirty dishes like they were five years old again, not when she could get in her car instead and drive back to her picture-perfect life in her magazine neighborhood. She probably had a party to go to, friends whose nights wouldn't start until she made an appearance. She'd hold the room's attention the way she always did. She was the center of Westview's universe, glittering with a delicate balance of sunshine and poison, and that was the way it would always be. People like Angela had better things to do than sit around old houses with people from their past in forgotten parts of town. And he didn't even know what he would have suggested doing once they got past the doorway. She would have just stood here silently like she did earlier, probably quietly judging her surroundings, the windows his mother kept asking him to clean and he kept forgetting about, all the places where a new coat of paint was long overdue. Wishing she were somewhere else. Dreaming of all the places she could run away to.

He walked into the house. Turned on a lamp. It blinked, slow, filling the room with tired amber and shadows. By the time Owen looked back outside, Angela was already driving away into pitch black, headlights toward clean lines of cul-de-sacs with soft lawns and shiny windows.

3

The first day of her senior year was only half over and Angela already wanted to leave. She stood at her locker, watching her peers parade through the newly green-painted halls. This town was small enough that she knew everyone here. She knew that the freshmen waiting outside a nearby classroom and pretending not to look at her were from her neighborhood, located in the southernmost area of Westview. All her friends lived there, too, in pretty white houses, the main road blurring into other small towns and wealthy suburbs.

Owen, who she'd already had two classes with today and had awkwardly looked away from each time she walked to sit in the back with her friends, lived in the northern part of town. Those neighborhoods were separated from hers by miles of reservoir carved into Westview's heart and filled with water nearly a century ago, the reason this place was mostly blue and evergreen everywhere. The roads in northern Westview were narrow and winding, passing farmland and fields and crumbling stone walls that framed weathered, leaf-covered cemeteries. Anyone who had moved into town recently lived on the outskirts of those neighborhoods, in the Witney Estates, the luxury housing community her father's company had developed in an attempt to revitalize the area.

The two halves of town met in the west at the small, gated campus of Walcott College, and here at the high school in the east. In Angela's opinion, this building was the ugliest one in the entire town, long and brick with only one floor. Its newest feature was the auditorium that had been paid for by her family the previous year. Their names were engraved on a plaque outside its wide double doors and Angela couldn't help admiring it every time she walked by, watching light glint against the letters. Even though she wasn't a star student or athlete, her name was carved into the school in a way that no one else's was.

"There you are," said a familiar voice, startling Angela out of her thoughts.

Dillon was standing there, dressed in his football jersey, cedar-brown eyes bright. He kissed her and she made herself erase all the questions and doubts she'd had about him lately. She made herself remember when he felt like home, safe and warm. The quiet parts of small-town summers, citronella burning on patios while sunlight slipped behind the trees and secrets escaped to the space between stars.

"Are you going to lunch now?" she asked.

He nodded and they walked down the hallway holding hands. Angela could see people watching them like always. She threw her shoulders back, held her head high.

She'd spent more time than she would ever admit to anyone getting ready for today. Early this morning, she'd studied her reflection in the mirror wearing nothing, telling herself all the bad things they could say about her as she memorized the ways sunlight and shadows wrote on her skin and erased parts of her body. She'd tried on a dress she'd made herself but changed her mind. Instead, she'd made herself look as perfect as possible in a new designer outfit from her parents so that everyone watching her right now would show up in copies of her clothes all year. Extinguished all the bad thoughts and decided everything people in this town would say instead.

All the way to the cafeteria, Dillon kept pausing to talk to people, his football teammates, members of student council. That was one of the first things she'd liked about him. How confident and charismatic he was, how he knew all the right people here like she did. They'd known each other for years; their parents were lifelong friends, part of a close-knit circle of old Westview families.

They'd been together for just over a year now and it had been so easy. She'd fallen faster than she meant to, breaking the promise she'd made to herself that she would never get too close to anyone. She'd shared almost her entire world with him in early mornings of quiet sunlight and soft laughter in the parking lot before class, in words scrawled across late-night pages.

Now, though, part of her wished she hadn't. She didn't like that her words were all out there, tangible, folded up in his backpack, hidden in a drawer in his bedroom, and she couldn't take them back.

But at least he didn't have all of them. She'd kept some of her secrets for herself, just in case.

They walked outside through the open cafeteria doors. The sunlight was gold on the grass and beyond the cluster of picnic tables, the branches of the woods reached tall into the cerulean sky. Soon, the leaves would be vivid amber and ruby, the colors New England was famous for.

"Angela!" Rose was already sitting at their usual table, sparkly bracelets clattering on her wrist as she waved. She lived on the same street as Angela's cousin, Cassie, and she'd always been more Cassie's friend than Angela's. Since the last time they'd seen each other two weeks ago, she'd had her long red hair streaked with violet highlights—Angela knew she was waiting for a compliment, so she didn't say anything.

"I haven't seen you in *forever,*" Rose continued as Angela and Dillon sat down. "Why weren't you at Cassie's? Her parties are always the best, I can't believe you missed it. It wasn't the same without you, though."

"I was sick," Angela lied.

Cassie's annual end-of-summer parties were infamous, their tradition when her parents were out of town celebrating their anniversary. This year's had coincided with the tricentennial event. Angela had planned on going after she dropped Owen off at his house, but driving through the quiet darkness of Westview left her with a strange sort of loneliness that couldn't be cured by company. Instead, she'd gone home and spent hours watching old movies and saving pictures of styles she liked to her phone, blanket-wrapped while she inhaled the last breaths of summer from the open windows. She could see all the way down the street from her bedroom, all those newly manicured lawns and expensive cars. She always watched the street when she couldn't sleep but nothing ever happened.

"Did you hear about the fight?" Rose asked eagerly.

Of course she'd heard. Angela knew everything that went on in Westview, or at least the important things, but she let Rose tell the story anyway, only half-listening, all fake smiles.

"So Tessa's been secretly dating the captain of Logan High School's football team and when Cassie found out she asked her not to bring him to the party," Rose said. "You know how people get about the rivalry."

Angela nodded and glanced at Dillon, who was pretending to look offended. Logan High School had been their biggest sports rival for years and the rivalry had escalated since

last season, when Logan's football team won the state champi-
onship. Westview, who had been the winners for three con-
secutive years prior, was still bitter about it, blaming the refs for
bad calls and favoritism. Angela knew that Dillon pretended to
care more than he actually did, but Cassie's boyfriend, Adam,
took it seriously.

"Then Tessa got mad at Cassie and brought him anyway," Rose continued, looking over at the table where Tessa
was sitting alone, facing away from them. Her usually perfect
blonde curls were messy, shoulders slumped.

Something like this seemed to happen every year,
determining who got to sit at their lunch table and was invited
to parties, who had to find a new group. The one constant
had always been Cassie, who was walking toward them, long-
haired and blue-eyed like Angela, their strikingly similar silhouettes inherited from their mothers. She was smiling,
stopping to chat with people the way Dillon had in the hall.
Watching her now, it reminded Angela of their parents.

And then Angela saw who was following her. Paige
Clements, who had moved here last fall and had been trying
to join their group ever since. She was wearing the expression
Angela recognized from every newcomer to this table, excitement mingled with nerves.

"Hi," Paige said in a surprisingly confident tone, interrupting Rose's narration of the fight between Tessa's boyfriend
and members of the Westview football team. She and Cassie sat
down and took out their lunches. "Angela, I love that dress."

Angela gave her a small smile. "Thanks."

"Cassie told me we're all in the same photography
class," Paige added.

"That will be fun," Angela said, not really meaning
it. She could feel her stomach sinking. The class was new this
year and she'd signed up immediately, eager to learn how to

get better at photography. Then, at the last minute, Cassie had signed up to fill an empty space in her schedule. Cassie was the only deliberate exception to her rule about not getting too close to people and when they'd sat poolside comparing their schedules, late summertime shimmering, hazy around them, Angela knew she should have been excited that they had so many classes together this year. But every time she thought about it, she felt more and more uncomfortable with the idea of Cassie seeing critiques of work that actually meant something to her. It seemed like it would be easier with people who barely knew her, whose perception of her was only based on what she chose to show them.

She realized, looking at Paige, that this was the first time she hadn't been there when they all decided who to invite to join them. That feeling was unsettling. A reminder that someday they could all decide to replace her, too.

And now, everyone else was here. Adam, wearing his football jersey and talking animatedly to Cassie about something that had happened in their English class this morning. At the opposite end of the table, Naomi, the only junior in the group, impeccably dressed by old money with roots in this town that reached almost as far back as Angela and Cassie's. For now, all of them at the center of the Westview social universe.

Angela imagined what they all must look like from another table, blissful and beautiful in silk and linen. She could see Owen from where she was sitting, eating lunch nearby with his friends, tree trunk stripes in the background. He looked tired, dressed in faded jeans and a black sweatshirt. Angela wondered which table they would be sitting at if everything was different and they were still friends.

She could feel Dillon's arm around her waist, fingertips at her hip. Her friends were laughing, chattering around her.

Pulling her into the present. She was where she belonged. Where everyone else wanted to be.

***

As usual, Angela's mother looked like an image from a magazine. Dressed in crisp black trousers, a pearl-hued blouse, and a scarlet silk scarf, she matched the dark décor of the living room perfectly, as if placed there by a photographer. She was rearranging crimson roses in a crystal vase and it took her a moment to notice Angela's presence.

"Have you heard from your father?" she asked, then continued speaking without waiting for Angela to answer. "He's running late but he's in the city for a meeting anyway so he's going to meet us at the restaurant."

Angela's family liked traditions and this was one of them: dinner in the city of Cherwell after her first week of school. She felt a pit in her stomach, worried that her father might not be able to make it. He'd been working longer hours all year and she'd been arguing with her mother more than usual lately, both of them revealing all their sharp edges.

"Do you think you could change into something a little more appropriate?" her mother added, examining Angela's outfit critically.

Angela felt her stomach twist and she bit back a retort. It wasn't worth fighting, she told herself, especially if they were going to be alone for a while. She had a new dress upstairs anyway, and she'd imagined wearing it in Cherwell when she bought it. Dreamy larimar, floaty fabric. A dress that looked like it belonged to the city, to a girl with an interesting life there.

Twenty minutes later, they were driving to the train station a few towns over, the sky patterned with green and flecks of early gold foliage in the rear-view mirror. Her mother answered work emails on the train while Angela watched the suburbs scud by through the window, a seemingly endless time-lapse of beige neighborhoods and viridian harbors and dollhouse cupolas. Excitement bloomed in her chest when she finally saw Cherwell's skyline approaching.

The restaurant was located in the historic district of the city, where strings of gold lights twinkled from the trees and the streets were lined with elegant old townhouses swirling with ivy. Angela always wondered what they looked like inside. Sometimes she imagined all the shops and galleries and cafés she'd frequent if this was her life instead. Somewhere in this city were her people, she thought, the people she wanted to be.

Angela and Cassie liked to dress up and walk around like they lived here, fantasy versions of themselves. They ate at the newest restaurants and ordered drinks overconfidently to see how often they could get away with it. Before Dillon and Adam, they snuck into bars on the weekends and kissed boys whose names they didn't ask on rooftops, the sky swimming with city lights like electric stars around them. Blood buzzing with how thrilling it was, hands on her skin, drink at her lips while neon and moonlight collapsed into morning. She hadn't had that feeling in so long, adrenaline ocean-wild in her bloodstream, and sometimes she missed it. Lately, everything felt gray.

"I had lunch with Cheryl yesterday," her mother began as they sat down at their table.

Angela tried not to cringe. She hated how frequently her mother had lunch with Dillon's mother. The uncomfortable overlap of their lives sometimes seemed to be just for show, although she couldn't figure out who it was for.

"She said they loved having you at the beach house this summer. She thinks that you and Dillon are perfect together."

Her mother was smiling at her across the table like she always did when she talked about Angela and Dillon. She'd been so happy when they first started dating, almost proud in an unsettling way that made Angela feel like it was supposed to be an achievement.

"That's nice," Angela replied flatly. She looked at her phone, quickly replying to texts from Cassie and Naomi to avoid the rest of this conversation. She didn't want to think about Dillon right now.

Her mother sighed, drawing out the harsh edges of the sound. A server placed bread and water on the ivory tablecloth.

"It's nice here," her mother said after a few moments of taut silence.

Angela nodded. She sipped her water, cold with curled lemon.

"No one I know has been able to get a reservation for at least another month."

She knew how excited her mother was to boast to her friends about eating here. Her own friends were jealous too, judging by their latest text messages but today, their admiration wasn't making her feel any better.

"Maybe we can have your graduation party here," her mother continued, and from the way she was looking around the restaurant, Angela knew that she was already in party-planning mode, visualizing the rearrangement of tables and imagining flowers to match the hues of the room. As a child, Angela's birthday parties were always extravagant events that took months of planning, perfectly orchestrated and color-coordinated. Her parents both loved showing off the illusion of their perfect life under the mask of hospitality. Everyone knew that every party in Westview was not-so-secretly about the parents.

"Okay," Angela agreed, and went back to texting her friends with plans for the weekend.

They ordered an appetizer that neither of them was going to eat while they waited for her father, and Angela was reminded of the way she'd always wait up for him to come home when she was young, eager to fling her arms around his legs and inhale the scent of his suit. He'd pick her up and spin her around until the colors of the room blurred together and their laughter filled the house. She'd fall asleep in cotton pajamas to the soft cadence of his voice reading her favorite book, acting out different characters. That was back when they were all closer, when they used to make her blueberry pancakes with sweet maple syrup for dinner on the weekends and take her on trips to the zoo and aquarium. Somewhere in her closet was a box of stuffed animals from those trips, synthetic fur flattened and worn from too-tight embraces.

But somehow, they'd all drifted, when everything about their lives in Westview became about being perfect. The more they had to present the image of the perfect family, the further apart they floated. Angela's favorite part of the year became the week both her parents took off at the start of every summer. The three of them would go away on vacation, leave everything about Westview behind. They returned to the same place every year but she never got tired of it because they were always exploring, climbing narrow old clock towers for panoramic views of bright-hued towns painted across blue mountain backdrops, or driving through twisting cliff lanes framed by stacked houses and tangled wildflowers. In those blissful hours, no one had to be perfect because Westview wasn't watching. But as soon as they crossed the town line again, she could feel it, all those assumptions and expectations.

She saw her father in the doorway before he noticed them. He looked so much older than he had during their last vacation, those first days of summer, a long weekend instead of a week this time. Before she escaped to the ocean with Dillon, fleeing Westview for places where there was no distinction between the sea and the sky, everything blue for infinity.

Her father had touches of gray in his hair, slight creases around his eyes. He was talking to the maître d' with the practiced political smile he'd inherited from his family. And then he saw them, walked toward the table. He was wearing cologne and a scarlet tie.

"Angela," he greeted her, almost businesslike as if he'd forgotten to transition from his office persona to parenthood. She half expected a handshake. "I saw the dean of admissions at Walcott today. You need to schedule a tour and interview soon." His voice was enthusiastic now; it always was when he talked about Walcott.

Angela nodded and looked at her phone again. Her stomach hurt.

Walcott was one of her family's most important traditions, one that went back generations on both sides of her family. For decades, her relatives had retreated from their part of town to make a temporary home inside Walcott's bricks and ivy, a campus prettiest when it was dressed in autumn's scarlet and yellow. She'd heard all their Walcott stories dozens of times, how her parents, who had grown up on the same street, fell in love freshman year when they lived in the same hall.

At another restaurant in the city, Cassie was probably having the same conversation with her parents. Everyone important in Westview went to Walcott. It was a small school, typically selective, but Westview's connections to Walcott went back to the college's founding, intertwined with the history of the town itself. Angela and Cassie were related to the school's founders on their mothers' side and most people in their social circle were from legacy families.

For her entire life, Angela knew that she was expected to attend Walcott. She'd never questioned it until recently. She had a legacy to uphold there, a continuation of her family's legacy in Westview. After she got her degree, she would work for one of her parents and eventually take over the company, just like they'd done. She'd be involved in everything in Westview, just like they were. And Angela had been okay with that because she was proud of her family's reputation, their traditions. But at the end of last school year, while waiting for a meeting with her guidance counselor that she'd almost skipped because she *knew* she was staying in Westview and going to Walcott, Angela had looked through a brochure for a college here in Cherwell. And that day, for the first time, she'd imagined something different.

She'd always loved clothes and fashion. She'd started by repurposing old clothes a few years ago, finding ways to transform them even if she didn't ever wear those versions. She sketched out designs for dream dresses when she was bored, taught herself how to sew and follow patterns by watching videos online. Then she tried creating her own and it felt like magic, turning pictures she'd made in her mind to something real.

Harcourt College had a well-known, highly competitive fashion design program, and ever since she'd brought that brochure home and spent hours doing more research, she hadn't been able to stop thinking about it. And the fact that it was here, in a city she loved, made it even more appealing, while the entire life that was already planned out for her in Westview was slowly starting to feel stifling. Cherwell felt like an entirely different world. This place had everything you could possibly need. No reason to leave once you'd made it here.

She hadn't told anyone about it, not even Cassie. Harcourt might as well have been oceans away. She was never going there, simply because it wasn't Walcott and everyone knew that the Witneys didn't leave Westview, didn't deviate from the generations-long path laid out for them.

"Do you remember when we went swimming in the fountain?" her father was saying, and her mother was laughing, reminiscing about Walcott traditions. Angela had grown up hearing those stories, the unwritten rules that were part of her future. The secret room in the library that was reserved for seniors, the gate on the east side of campus that was supposed to bring you luck if you walked through it on certain days. She had a drawer full of Walcott T-shirts in her bedroom. In the living room, a black-and-white photograph of the college chapel, where her parents had gotten married. They both always spoke fondly about their time there and were still actively involved in the Walcott community.

This was the life she was supposed to want. Comfortable and safe, everything easy and familiar because it was already written for her. She just had to follow the rules, check all the boxes.

But what if there was something else?

The sky was dark when they left the restaurant. Cast in white and gold lights, the city seemed to have a different energy, full of endless possibility. Hopeful somehow, like everyone was on the brink of change, the swell of a crescendo. Angela wished that she could breathe it in, all the lights and traffic noise and color. On their way back to the train station, they walked past groups of laughing college students dressed up for a night out, a couple in stilettos holding hands. People in black ties and black dresses, on their way to someplace important. Everyone here seemed so defined and grown up and sure of themselves. Angela wanted that, too. To stop feeling so lost. She wanted something better than small towns. She wanted days fast-paced and people everywhere, rooftops kissing sky-lines and twenty-four-hour cafés for midnights when thoughts stole sleep.

Everything about this place made her life in Westview feel so inconsequential. Staying up late to make signs for pep rallies. Swimming in Cassie's pool at night while fireflies glowed in hazy moonlight. Watching Westview sports games under rented stadium lights after the sun had gone down, huddled on the bleachers with overpriced hot chocolate. For so long, her entire life had revolved around those things, moments that would pass by like a flicker in Cherwell.

Realizing that made Westview feel even smaller.

From the windows, she watched it all fade away, trading city lights for starlight on quiet backroads that somehow wanted her past and present and future to mean the same thing. It was almost dangerous, the way her family had made one place their entire world, the way they built traditions up around themselves like a fortress so tall it blocked out everything else. Everything she had was in Westview. She couldn't have anywhere else.

4

The town borderline closest to Owen's neighborhood was located on the top of a hill, where a white sign and miles of apple orchards welcomed him home after work. Westview was golden with pale fall sunshine as he drove through streets as familiar as heartbeats, slowed down on woodsy backroads where slight glimmers of blue were visible between the trees.

He parked his newly repaired car in his friend Max's driveway. Max lived at the opposite end of his street, just across from the place Owen always tried to pretend didn't exist.

Don't look don't look don't look he told himself now, like he did every time he passed by.

He forced himself to stop thinking about it and carefully lifted out the iced coffees he'd picked up for his friends on the way here. Focused on walking toward the house, his back to the road and the overgrown trees.

The living room windows were open. He could hear cheering inside as he approached the porch, long with old wooden rocking chairs and hanging baskets overflowing with tangled yellow flowers.

He knocked on the front door before opening it and stepping inside. He'd been coming here for almost two years now but he'd never quite gotten used to the way people flowed in and out of the house, coming and going without doorbells or curfews. Currently, the living room was filled with various friends and neighbors watching a football game on TV, cardboard pizza boxes open on the coffee table. His younger sister, Haley, was there in a blue jersey, sharing a chair with Max's sister, Sophia. Owen waved to them before heading into the kitchen, where his friends were sitting around the table.

"Hey," said Max, looking up from his laptop and taking the coffee Owen was holding out to him. On the screen was a draft of his latest movie review for the website he ran with Declan, who was sitting next to him in his usual baseball cap and TV quote T-shirt.

"Thanks for the coffee," Declan said, taking his. "How was work?"

Owen shrugged. "The usual."

He'd worked at Madison, a high-end department store in a neighboring town, since his freshman year and it was typical to see people from Westview there all the time. They'd always look directly at him, or maybe through him, faces unchanging, and he could never figure out if they were ignoring him or didn't recognize him dressed in his crisp work clothes, hair slicked back. He didn't know which was worse.

Owen took the last two coffees out of the cardboard carrier and placed one in front of Lucie, who was drawing something on a piece of paper with a focused expression on her face.

"What are you doing?" he asked.

"I'm working on a new logo for the site," she explained. She slid the paper over to him. "Which one do you like?"

Owen studied the sketches, little drawings of Max and Declan's faces, the site name written out in different letters.

He pointed to one where she'd exaggerated Max's glasses and Declan's baseball cap. "This one."

"That's my favorite," Declan agreed.

Max was leaning over now, pointing out his favorite design, and Owen sat down, feeling a familiar rush of gratitude toward all of them. He was lucky, he thought, that this was his life now, that these were the people he was going to finish high school with. Last weekend, they'd had an end-of-summer bonfire with people from the neighborhood and they'd stayed outside long after everyone else left, just the four of them, wrapped in shadows and sweatshirts around dying gold, echoes of their laughter against the woods. As they burned the last of the marshmallows, Lucie made them all promise to make this year memorable.

And now this was it, the beginning of the end. The last year of late-night coffees at the barn-turned-bar down the road and exploring the woods near Declan's house and afternoons by the water, things that had been tradition for all of them much longer than they had for Owen. He was glad he'd found this group, that they hadn't given up on him when it felt like no one else here cared.

He went into the bathroom to change out of his work clothes. When he came out, they were all waiting by the back door, bags in hand.

"Ready to go?" Max asked.

They followed him outside onto the lawn, footprints raising dust among strands of dead grass. Just behind an old swing set was a low fence and a yellow No Trespassing sign marking the transition into reservoir property, where thousands of trees protected the watershed.

It was almost impossible to go anywhere in Westview without seeing fragments of reservoir blue. It was everywhere, vein-like tributaries and smaller bodies of water like shattered hearts at the edges of neighborhoods, the biggest expanse of cerulean pooled like tears in the middle of town. There were two other towns in the state just like this, half-flooded in the early twentieth century, and another that was now completely underwater, a consequence of nearby cities growing faster and larger.

Once, Owen had seen a map marking all those towns, and others throughout New England and across the country. He'd seen lists of ones you could visit, some of their remains still visible in drought. They called them drowned towns, like a sibling to ghost towns, roadside attractions.

Everyone with memories of what Westview used to be had since died, but whispers about all this water and who to blame had been passed down through generations, names you weren't supposed to trust, grudges and rumors part of the town's pulse. And the pieces of reservoir land that weren't frequently patrolled for trespassers were an open secret among bored Westview teenagers. For most of them, it was just part of the landscape now, a story they'd learned once in school, the Witneys at the center of it all.

Stepping over the fence, they continued through the trees toward the water, crystal-blue and glass-smooth. As they walked, Owen thought of all those other towns like this, the same story.

He knew that history could be a lot of lies depending on who was telling it. And what he'd learned was that most of the story here wasn't true.

If he ever told anyone, he didn't know who would believe him. Because he was one of the names you weren't supposed to trust.

They'd reached the shore now. Owen and Declan took off their shoes, let the cool water trickle across their bare toes.

"You two are going to freeze," said Lucie. She spread out a blanket across the ground, then sat down with Max, both of them reaching into their bags for the snacks they'd brought with them.

"It's not that bad," Declan replied, splashing water in her direction. His phone chimed and he took it out of his pocket, scanned the screen. "Ava says the renovations at Insomnia are done so they're open again as of tomorrow. They're moving trivia nights to Thursdays at eight. Do you want to go?"

"Definitely," Max answered immediately; Lucie nodded in agreement.

"I don't know," Owen said. "I already have a lot of homework."

"School just started," Max protested.

"I need to keep my grades up. Make up for all the time I spent slacking."

"Come on, Owen," Lucie pleaded. "It's *one night* a week. It's not going to destroy your GPA."

"I know—"

"You can't let the mistakes you made before keep you from having a little fun now. It's our senior year … you *just* promised to make it memorable," Lucie continued. "You're going to need a distraction every once in a while. And we need you if we have any hope of holding on to our winning streak."

It had taken months of similar sentiments from Lucie for Owen to accept an invitation to spend time with the group outside of school. He still didn't know why she hadn't given up on him. He'd known the three of them since elementary school the way he knew everyone in Westview but even before he reached the age where parents stopped planning parties and playdates, he'd just let himself fade into the background. It hadn't been hard to do—Angela's family and their friends had already turned all the parents in their social circle against his family over what he now understood were longstanding resentments and an obsession with appearances, which quickly trickled down to his peers. All he had to do was drift away from the few people who didn't care what the Witneys said.

And then, for different reasons, his world imploded into nightmares and it was easier not to care about anything.

Sophomore year, around the time he decided he needed to reinvent himself, he'd worked on a Spanish project with Max and Lucie and without realizing it, he became part of their inside jokes and easy laughter. But at the time, academic success was his priority so it had taken him a long time to really let them in. Owen had never tried very hard in school before then but was determined to change that, filling the empty hours with coursework when he wasn't at work or volunteering for the Westview Historical Society. And when he started getting good grades, he'd surprised his mother and his teachers, but mostly himself.

When he found out that he'd been recommended for honors classes for his junior year, he'd almost thought it was a mistake because his own accomplishments didn't quite seem real yet. One of his teachers asked him to tutor a freshman student who was struggling and as they went over the material together after school in the library, as he helped him study for tests and create thesis statements, Owen realized he wanted to be a teacher. For years, he'd felt on the verge of falling apart, a frantic frenzy of *what am I doing?* beating in his head so loudly he just wanted to sleep it away. He'd felt like everyone had given up on him, let him fall through the cracks once he'd gained a reputation as a slacker. Proving them all wrong felt good, like he was on his way to putting the pieces of his life back together.

But it was really this group that made him whole. Westview had never truly felt like home, but they did.

"Okay," Owen relented. "I'll go."

Lucie looked triumphant. "Good. We need to make the most of this year." She sighed. "I'm already so tired of hearing about college applications. We've only been back in school for a week."

"How many people in our class do you think are almost guaranteed a Walcott acceptance letter anyway? Are you sure you don't want to apply there, too?" Declan said sarcastically, rolling his eyes.

He looked like he regretted it the instant he said it. They all knew it was a bad idea to talk about Walcott around Lucie.

"I'm not Vanessa," she said and her voice betrayed a little bit of sadness that made guilt flash across Declan's face.

"I'm sorry, I didn't mean—"

"I was right about her. As soon as she went to Walcott, I told you she was going to turn into one of those people," Lucie said bitterly. She looked across the reservoir in the direction of all the arches and cul-de-sacs, everything in white. "All she's ever wanted was to be someone like the Witneys—"

"Come on, Lucie, that's not fair," Max said.

"She acts like she's too good for our family. We used to be so close and now the only time she talks to me is when she needs help with the wedding. I'm surprised she even wants us there."

"You're her sister, of course she wants you there," said Max reassuringly.

"Anyway," said Lucie, "I could never get into Walcott. And even if I did, it's so expensive."

Over the summer, Owen had visited colleges near Westview and narrowed it down to three he wanted to apply to. Enfield College and Lenox University, both good schools, both affordable options, both close enough that he could live at home and commute to save money. Lucie had the same plan.

The third school was Walcott, which he'd been keeping a secret from his friends because if you grew up in Westview, you either loved Walcott or hated it, and they all fell into the latter category. He hadn't even thought about it as a possibility until one of his teachers suggested it, and even then, he hadn't really taken it seriously until he visited. He'd heard that Walcott had a well-known history department but it seemed so far out of reach. His grades were good but he wasn't a legacy student like so many of his classmates and his family didn't have the kind of money you needed to attend a school like Walcott.

But when he arrived on campus, he fell in love with everything. Tangled ivy and sun–kissed brick. The passionate way the faculty spoke about their work. The sense of community that permeated the whole place, the students he'd met that were proud to belong there. But mostly, he was determined to prove to himself that he was good enough. Good enough for Westview, good enough for Walcott. And a part of him he wasn't entirely comfortable with wanted to prove that to everyone else here, too.

"Speaking of people going to Walcott," Lucie was saying now, "I heard Angela Witney was at your house, Owen."

He felt all their eyes on him. He groaned inwardly. Haley, who hadn't said a word when Angela was there but barged into his room to ask questions later, had probably told Sophia because they both admired Angela. And Sophia told Lucie everything, even though Lucie and the rest of their friends had never liked families like the Witneys, who in their opinion, represented everything that was wrong with Westview.

He stepped onto the shore and sat down next to Lucie.

She narrowed her eyes at him and stretched out on her back, sliding on a pair of fuchsia-framed sunglasses. Owen could see sky and clouds moving lazily across the lenses. Declan emerged from the water to join them and sat, completing the circle.

"She gave me a ride to the tricentennial talk," Owen explained. "That was the day my car broke down. She's on the committee too because of her parents so Jan sent her over to get me."

Lucie looked at him for a moment without saying anything. She was so perceptive sometimes that he wondered if she'd figured out how he felt about Angela. He'd tried so hard to keep everything about her a secret—their long-ago friendship, the way he couldn't stop thinking about her now, the things he knew about her family.

"She didn't exactly seem thrilled about it," Owen added, feeling a little defensive.

Lucie sat up again. "You're not going to abandon us for her, are you?"

The way she said it was like a joke, lighthearted, but he could still see the hurt there, lingering from the way Vanessa had moved out of the house and out of her life to become someone like Angela. A girl with a life that looked perfect, leaving Lucie behind.

"Of course not. I promise."

He felt guilty saying it, like he was already breaking his promise with his Walcott application. The beginnings of the essay on his desk at home shouldn't have felt like a betrayal, but now, the half-formed sentences and scribbled thoughts seemed shameful.

"Good."

She was smiling at him now. It made his stomach hurt.

This time next year, Owen thought, they would have all moved on from Westview High School. He wondered if they would all be as close then or if afternoons on the reservoir shore would become a memory rehashed for tradition's sake, stolen hours between other commitments as they drifted further away from Westview and even each other. Over the years, they'd built jokes and memories into their language, certain words and phrases like codes that translated into laughter. He didn't want to think about that being undone.

He tried to picture it, all of them a year older. But all he could imagine was Walcott, the only place in Westview where you couldn't see the ripples of blue that whispered all over this town.

5

Join us for an open house! the email from Harcourt's admissions office read. Angela scrolled down to look for the date and suddenly heard the loudness of a car horn. She'd almost walked into Owen's car as he was backing out of his parking space. She glanced around quickly to check if anyone else had seen but the parking lot was almost empty.

"Sorry!" she called to him as he rolled down the window. He looked concerned but slightly annoyed. "So you got your car fixed?"

"Well, for now. There's always something wrong with it. I bought it from my neighbor. I thought he was being nice and trying to give me a good deal but now I think he just wanted to get rid of it." He paused, looking hesitant now. "I'm going to get coffee and try to do some homework before the meeting. Want to come?"

"Sure." She'd been planning on going home before the Tricentennial Committee met today but in the moment, this seemed like a better alternative. She looked around again, then got into the car. The inside was uncluttered and he was listening to music, soft and mellow.

"So what was so interesting back there?" Owen asked

as he turned left out of the parking lot. His driving was slow, almost cautious. It made Angela impatient.

"Just an email from a college."

He smiled. "Walcott?"

"No, Harcourt College."

The words sounded defensive. She knew that this was how every college-related conversation with people in Westview would go, commencing with the assumption that she was going to Walcott. That knowing smile, like there wasn't a possibility of her wanting to look anywhere else. People just expected her to stay here. She'd been thinking about that more and more since that night in the city with her parents, picturing herself away from here. The chance to be someone else, somewhere else.

"That's in Cherwell, right? Have you visited yet?"

"Not yet. I love the city, though." She hesitated. She didn't know why she was telling him this when she couldn't even tell her friends. Something seemed safe about Owen. This town was full of people judging each other, but it felt like he didn't judge her in the same ways that everyone else did, at least. "My parents don't know yet. They want me to go to Walcott. Everyone in my family has gone there."

"They're both good schools," said Owen, turning down the music, so quiet now it was barely audible.

"I know." Angela looked at her phone again. The email was still bright on the screen. She'd received a similar one from Walcott yesterday, filled with images of smiling students. She'd studied that message in the silence of her bedroom as nighttime sprawled over the neighborhood but she couldn't see herself at Walcott, couldn't place herself in those pictures.

They sat in silence the rest of the way to a coffee shop on the corner of a small string of stores. It felt like they were in the middle of nowhere. The coffee shop had dark red windowpanes, and a wooden sign with the name *Gracie's* painted in the same color.

"Have you been here before?" Owen asked as they got out of the car. Despite the afternoon's sunbeams, the sky had slowly turned gray and it was starting to drizzle.

"No." As small as Westview was, Angela had never been to this area before. She wasn't even entirely sure where she was.

"They have the best coffee in town. But don't tell anyone I said that because my friend's stepsister owns a different coffee shop here and she will never forgive me if she finds out they're not my favorite."

He held the door open for her and she walked into the dimly lit, coffee-scented room. The floors were scratched, the furniture old and mismatched, everything cozy. They took a table by the window and Angela looked around again. She recognized the young woman working behind the pastry-filled glass case—she had graduated from Westview High School several years ago. She still looked the same, with large glasses and her hair pulled back into a mahogany ponytail.

"What do you want? It's on me," Owen offered, standing up.

"Thanks," she said, smiling. "Any kind of tea is fine."

Angela looked out the window while Owen went to the counter to place their order. Across the street a woman wearing high heels carried a stack of envelopes into the post office, white paper kisses sent far away. Angela watched her walk out a moment later, then disappear into the blue-doored travel agency next door. She wondered where the woman was planning to go, and wished that she, too, could fly far away from here right now and land somewhere exciting, anywhere else.

On the wall facing her was a gallery of framed photographs, stolen moments snapped everywhere around the world, taken by someone who she imagined preferred wings over roots. Cobbled streets and flag-strung mountains and towers touching blue-drenched skies. Silhouettes of famous buildings and monuments she'd learned about in school. People and places with lives that seemed so much bigger and brighter and more complex than anything here. Angela wondered how people could sit here, gazing at these frozen windows into other places, and want to stay in Westview.

Owen returned, clutching two ceramic mugs, and placed the tea in front of her.

"Thanks," she said again.

"No problem."

She studied Owen as he ripped open a packet of sugar and stirred it into his coffee. She wished she could figure him out. She usually knew when people in Westview wanted something from her, but with him, she couldn't tell.

"Did you know that you were one of the first people I met in this town?" Owen asked, saving her from having to think of something to say. She wondered if silence would have been better than this conversation, though. She didn't want to dive into the past with him.

"That was a nice summer," she said, because she didn't know what else to say. She didn't want to tell him that the details of it were no longer perfectly painted in her mind but blurred together with other halcyon summers, or that she'd had better summers since. It seemed like their friendship still meant something to him, although she didn't know why. His eyes met hers, and she remembered how blue they used to be, bright with laughter as they splashed each other in a plastic pool.

Bells clattered and a gust of misty air swirled in as the door opened. Grateful for a reason to look away, Angela glanced over at the newcomer. He was tall, with flaxen hair and tired brown eyes. He'd graduated several years ago, she remembered. She recalled him playing his guitar in the hallways every morning before the start of class. And then she looked around yet again, realizing that she recognized every person here. She could feel panic rising in her throat at the thought that they might recognize her, too.

Days like this, she really felt how small Westview was, almost stifling to the point of dizziness. She used to love that feeling, the knowledge that wherever she went in town, people would know who she was. It used to make her feel important. Now she just felt like they were watching her. Judging, waiting to prove that she wasn't perfect.

She reminded herself that she'd gotten better at their game than anyone else. Even if someone did say something about seeing her here with Owen, she could find a way to make it untrue.

"Do you know what you're doing next year?" she asked, looking again at all the pictures on the wall.

Owen hesitated for almost too long. "I've narrowed it down to a few schools that I want to apply to. Enfield College and Lenox University both look like good options."

It sounded like a practiced answer, one he'd use politely on people because he thought it was what they wanted to hear. Confident and practical. She wondered what words were between the lines of his patient tone and almost-fake smile.

"Do you know what you want to study?"

"History," Owen answered immediately, and she knew he was sincere this time. "I want to be a teacher. What about you?"

It was the first time anyone had asked her that and she almost laughed. *I know what my parents want me to do*, she almost said.

"I don't know," she lied.

Owen looked at her thoughtfully. "What do you like to do?"

"I like photography. I don't think I'd want to make a career out of it, though. It's more for fun." Angela took a sip of tea, stalling for a moment before trying out the words she'd never told anyone. "Actually, Harcourt has a good fashion design program that I'm really interested in. I've been practicing designing and making clothes—"

"You know how to make clothes?" Owen looked impressed, which made her relax a little.

She nodded.

"Did you make that?" He indicated the dress she had on now.

"No. I don't wear them."

"Why?"

She shrugged, suddenly wishing she hadn't told him. Her stomach tightened as she thought of all the times she'd stood in front of her bedroom mirror wearing the clothes she'd made. Designs she loved and was proud of, but the moment she wore them out of the house, they'd belong to other people's eyes and all she could think was that everyone would hate them, even if they didn't know she'd made them. So every time, she changed her mind, changed into the outfits she'd already planned. She took another sip of tea so that she didn't have to say anything.

Owen had that thoughtful expression on his face again and Angela felt a swoop of fear that he somehow had her all figured out, which wasn't supposed to happen.

"Anyway, like I said, my parents are set on me going to Walcott," she said quickly. "But it would be nice to get out of here. It's so sad that people never leave."

The words sounded strange, like they weren't supposed to be spoken in her voice and the expression on Owen's face almost made her regret it.

"What are you talking about? Plenty of people leave."

The few people in her family's social circle who'd left had ended up back here, like something in Westview was magnetic. There was only one person she knew of who'd left for good.

"Most people I know go to Walcott," she said.

Annoyance flashed across Owen's face. "Not everyone can afford that option," he said quietly, his voice suddenly a lot less friendly, edged with irritation. "There's a lot more to this town than you realize."

"I know how Westview works," she said coldly. If she didn't, she wouldn't still be at the top.

"That's not what I'm talking about. I mean that people exist outside your bubble. Some people stay because they want to, some people don't have a choice. Not everyone can afford to go to schools like Walcott, and people do leave, for a lot of different reasons. If you just pay attention..."

Angela stared at the photographs on the wall beyond tables with all those familiar faces. Sterling cities on the water and castles bathed in sunsets. She could feel all the air disappearing from her lungs because she could see her future here so clearly: too intertwined in the town's life to ever break free, the same way her parents were. A neighborhood of white houses and stone facades, full of people she'd known her whole life. Forever defined by her family, by what she did and who she was in high school.

She stood up. "You don't know anything about me," she said. "I don't care that we used to be friends. We're different people now, or at least I am."

The bells clanged loudly against the wooden door as it slammed behind her. Outside, she texted Dillon, remembering how every time it felt like this town was out of air, he made it easier to breathe, or at least he used to. She waited in the rain for him to pick her up while Owen sat inside with cold coffee. As Dillon drove to his house, Angela glared at Westview through the windows. This place was only beautiful on sunny days, she thought. On days like today, it was just a gloomy stretch of winding roads and fenced-off water.

***

"Do you ever want to leave Westview?" Angela blurted against Dillon's lips. She should have been at the Tricentennial Committee meeting twenty minutes ago, but instead she was here in Dillon's room, the rest of the house empty, and she couldn't stop thinking about how mad she was at Owen, how she needed someone to tell her she was right.

Dillon moved away and Angela's vision was filled with the whiteness of the ceiling. Constellations of spackle, daylit stars.

He laced his fingers through hers. She looked at them. His nails were round, clean, hers pointed and painted the palest pink. "What do you mean?" he asked.

"Next year," Angela said hesitantly. "Have you ever thought about going somewhere else?"

"I'm going to Walcott. I already started my application," he said, and her heart sank because he wasn't going to tell her the things she wanted to hear.

"Aren't you?" he added when she didn't answer. "Everyone does."

There it was, that expectation, again. She was starting to regret coming here, trying to escape to him the way she wanted to run away to other places. She was mad at herself now, too, for lying to herself, pushing away everything she didn't want to admit about him so that she could feel at home here again. For wishing for a version of them that was long-gone, or maybe had never really existed.

"I don't know," she said. The mattress was hard beneath her back, the pillows too soft. Angela felt like her head was sinking into them, feathers and navy fabric. She sat up. She could see herself across the room in Dillon's mirror, makeup smudged dark around her eyes. Her hair was long, in messy waves. She felt lonely all over again, like she had that night driving back from Owen's house and she wished she were someplace dark where she couldn't feel the world moving.

She thought about summer. All her past summers had been miles of the bluest sky and bonfire sparks sending gold to the heavens. They were thunderstorms like dark watercolors. Ocean everywhere, sand stiff in her hair and dried in swirls on her skin. Those infinities between late night and early morning that smelled like spilled beer and firework smoke. This summer with Dillon had been perfect, because she needed it to be. It had to be everything, all those summers rolled into one. Something about that felt important, like the start of this school year signified a new reality and Angela just wanted summer in her veins.

For most of the summer, they'd stayed at his parents' beach house, where the rest of the world faded away. She took naps on the roof, watched the sky move above her. Inhaled the sun and the silence. She collected seashells in a glass jar for her bedroom at home and admired the ocean-honed perfection of their white ridges and dusky spirals. In the late afternoons, conversations congregated at the island in the kitchen as everyone prepared dinner, which they ate around a long table with the windows open so that their laughter leaked into twilight, and it was in those moments that Angela felt like she was part of something that her own family had been missing for a long time. And later, at night, she'd sneak out with Dillon, watching harbor lights, drinking on the dark, empty beach with nothing around them but the rhythm of waves. She'd been almost in love with him then.

"I guess I'd never thought about leaving before. Like, as something that I could really do," she continued without looking directly at Dillon. She could feel him watching her profile as he traced the outline of her fingers.

"Why would you, though? This town is in your blood."

That was exactly the problem, Angela thought. She imagined Westview's twisted roads as her veins, dark through her skin, all those lives moving and flowing inside the lines her family drew. She shuddered.

"Do you ever feel trapped here?"

She wanted him to understand. She could feel it burning in her lungs. Someone else had to feel this way, lost in a place they knew by heart. Alone when they were always surrounded by people who wanted their attention.

Dillon shook his head. "I like living here."

Their world was so small. Maybe they were different in a town ruled by a reservoir instead of saltwater tides. Because ever since they'd returned to Westview, she'd noticed a shift. When they went places together now, it felt like a performance for everyone else, Dillon all pretentiously polished and preppy, laughing with people Angela had been friends with first as she smiled along to hide her sadness. It made her wonder if she'd made a mistake. If Dillon was just another boy who liked the idea of her, the status of her, and for the first time, she'd let herself get too close, forgetting that playing this game required her to stay far enough away that she couldn't get hurt.

She was afraid her heart had read it all wrong, saw an anchor when he was really just a warning sign. If he knew almost everything about her, almost all her thoughts inside-out, she wondered what it meant if that wasn't the version of her he liked. If all he wanted was the Angela that everyone else in this town saw. She didn't understand how it had taken her so long to notice, how she could have fallen for him.

"Walcott will be fun," he was saying now, looking up at her with those eyes that made her wish for nights on starlit marinas and the euphoria of saltwater all over them as they jumped off docks, laughing. He ran his fingers through her hair, almost combing it. Turning her into the perfect girl she was supposed to be. "Like now, but better."

And for so long, that was how Angela thought her life was supposed to go. Until today, no one had ever asked her what she wanted to do. They just assumed she wanted Westview. That it was the only option. It was so much easier when she loved this town, when it felt like everything she needed was here.

But now that wasn't enough, not since she'd realized what she could have in Cherwell, where she could be part of something bigger than herself. All those city lights, art and inspiration everywhere, the freedom to discover the person she could be. Everything in constant motion, constant change, a place where stories weren't just written in high school. In Cherwell, if you listened to the rush of traffic the right way it almost sounded like the ocean.

The thought of breaking up with Dillon hurt more than it should. It meant running away, untangling herself from the strands of him that wrapped themselves around her words and thoughts and heart the heavy way sand-laced seaweed choked their toes on shorelines. So instead she kept running back to him, disappointed in herself every time.

He was still looking at her, pulling her back toward him now. She flinched away.

He sighed and reached over for his laptop to resume

the TV show they'd been watching earlier and Angela stayed where she was for a moment, sitting up, glancing at the girl in the mirror. Her chest aching, sadness stinging beneath her skin because neither of them could be what the other wished for.

Dillon smelled like summer. Like the color green and the sea. Angela closed her eyes, sank back into the pillows. She was drowning, drowning in her thoughts and his arms and miles of trees planted to protect the broken parts of small towns.

6

"Okay, you were right," Owen told Lucie as they got out of the car. "I'm glad I decided to come to these. I definitely need the distraction."

"Told you," she teased, then smiled sympathetically, concern in her eyes. "You're okay, though, right?"

"I'm fine," Owen assured her. She'd been there when he got burned out at the end of last year, the only person he'd ever let see him that way. She'd spent hours driving around with him to nowhere, helping him feel a little less alone in the wide, empty darkness after midnight.

He followed her into Insomnia, the old barn that had been transformed into a bar, café and performance space by Declan's stepsister Ava and her wife, Ines. It was cozy inside, dark with lights strung across the rafters and work by local artists displayed neatly along the walls.

Ines was at the bar, pouring out tastings of local wine for a group of people who Owen vaguely recognized from living in this town for most of his life. He and Lucie waved to her and she smiled back as she explained something about the wine's aroma.

"I'm going to find Ava," Lucie said as they claimed

their usual spot, a low table in the corner surrounded by chairs and a couch. She took out a bag of the newest bracelets she'd made to sell here. "I'll be right back."

Owen settled into the couch, trying to relax. Insomnia's trivia nights had become something to look forward to each week lately among a never-ending cycle of school assignments and mundane hours at work. He'd been seeing Angela a lot more, too, as they prepared for the upcoming Tricentennial Gala. Since that day at Gracie's, they'd come to a sort of unspoken truce, and they were almost formal now whenever they had to talk to each other. He felt uncomfortable every time he thought about what he'd said to her, playing it back in his head over and over, the expression on her face when she'd left. At the time, he'd been frustrated that her entire perception of this town seemed to be based on a few families in her privileged social circle. So he'd just blurted it out without thinking. Part of him wished he'd said nothing, because she almost certainly hated him now.

What he was most anxious about, though, was that he had an interview at Walcott coming up.

He'd gone to an information session there with his mother last week and when he saw how much she wanted it for him, he was even more determined to go. But then, they'd met with the admissions and financial aid teams and his heart broke a little.

They sat in the parked car in the lot across from campus afterward. He could see scraps of green grass and ivy through the gates. Sienna bricks and amber trees. He knew what she was going to say before she said it, her eyes jewel-bright with tears she was trying to hide.

He couldn't afford to go there. Even with his job and financial aid and a potential scholarship, it was almost impossible. And he'd be paying off student loans for years, something he couldn't afford to do either.

But there was one tiny glimmer of hope. The Westview Scholarship Fund had announced that they would be awarding one full-tuition scholarship to a graduating senior this year, a bequest from a wealthy community member who had passed away last year. It sounded too good to be true.

His mother had encouraged him to apply anyway and that made him feel guilty and hopeful all at once. He knew that financially, he'd be better off at the other schools he was applying to, and he'd be happy at either of them. But the more he thought about Walcott, the more he wanted it.

Max and Declan were walking in now, talking animatedly to Theo Hanover, one of their classmates whose trivia team had been their rival since they'd started coming here. Owen waved them over.

"Theo was just telling us that they're going to break our winning streak today," Max said.

"You say that every week," said Owen.

"And yet we've been undefeated for how long now?" Lucie chimed in, coming back to the table and sitting down next to Owen.

Theo glanced over to where his friends were sitting. "That's about to change. We finally convinced Sam to join our team."

"Are you saying you want to reinstate the bet?" Max asked. Last school year, he'd had an ongoing bet with Theo that the loser would buy the winner's coffee before class the following day, which everyone knew was just an excuse for them to spend more time talking to each other.

"You're on," said Theo, reaching over to shake Max's hand.

"Theo! Stop talking to the competition," Brooke

Marston called from their table across the room, grinning and waving at them.

"Good luck," Theo said, giving Max a quick smile before he walked away.

"I think this is going to be the year for you two," Lucie said once he was out of earshot.

"That means she wants to try one of her matchmaking schemes on you," Declan said.

"When was the last time that actually worked?" Owen asked, thinking of all the times Lucie's well-meaning attempts to set up various friends had ended disastrously.

"Beginning of this summer. Declan and Kira," Lucie answered immediately.

"They broke up," Owen pointed out. "After three weeks. Are you sure that really counts?"

"Whose side are you on?" Lucie said, pretending to pout at him. "I have an idea, though. What if we invite them all over next time we have a bonfire? Think about it. Fall weather, s'mores, stargazing…"

"I'll consider it," Max agreed. "But there are going to have to be ground rules because I don't think anyone wants a repeat of—what's wrong?"

Lucie was looking at her phone, irritation crossing her face. "Vanessa … I'll be right back."

She walked outside, holding her phone to her ear, and Owen and Max went up to the counter to buy snacks. Owen ordered a cup of coffee, knowing he'd be up late working on homework and his Walcott essay. They paid with the gift card they'd won last time they were here. As they waited for their food, he noticed one of the women from the bar examining the little brass jewelry stand holding Lucie's bracelets. She bought one and pocketed the card containing Lucie's contact information and the link to her online shop. He hoped that would cheer her up.

By the time their food was ready, Lucie was back, telling Declan about her conversation with Vanessa.

"She needs me to pick up some things for the center-pieces in Cherwell this weekend," she was saying as Owen and Max sat down. "I was planning on going there anyway because I need new supplies for the bracelets I'm making Haley and Sophia for the gala. Any chance any of you want to keep me company?"

"I'll go if you're going Saturday morning," Owen offered. "I don't have to work until later."

Lucie beamed at him. "Thanks."

He smiled back. Lucie had been working on the bracelets for weeks but refused to show them to anyone until they were perfect. Owen knew that she could easily make something that would pass for all the expensive jewelry people like Angela and her friends would be wearing that night. But he also knew she wouldn't. She'd been there when Owen took Haley to Madison so that she could use his employee discount on one of the clearance dresses from last season and when they realized they were still too expensive to justify, she'd quickly offered Haley her Homecoming dress from last year. She'd been there for every glance they got in the halls at school from the people in this town who seemed to have everything, seen the way pretty eyes flickered over their clothes and lips turned into snide smiles to make them feel small. So instead of try-ing to be like them, Owen knew she'd make Haley and Sophia something that was only theirs.

He tried not to think about Walcott or Angela as the first round of trivia started. Tried to focus on right now, the moments of his senior year that were supposed to be memo-rable, like they'd all promised.

When it was his turn to bring up their answer sheet, he glanced over at his friends in their little circle around the table. Declan, frantically searching on his phone for the answer to a question they hadn't been sure about. Lucie and Max, singing along to the song on the speakers. And a space for him between them. They were the best part of this place, all their reservoir days and movie nights, their expeditions to town fairs and fireworks. He was so afraid of hurting them, that his desire to go to Walcott and the way he felt about Angela would make them think he was leaving them all behind. Especially Lucie, whose feelings about Walcott were all tangled up with Vanessa. They were almost everything he had here, and he wondered why he was willing to risk ruining all of that.

***

"We're not going in there. This is too much," Lucie said.

Through the windows they could see a ceiling covered in chandeliers like an entire sky of crystal snowflakes. Gold lions and marble statues lined the floors. The store was small but so full of mirrors and gilded clocks that it looked like a downpour of glitter.

Owen could see their reflections in the glass, four teenagers in jeans and sweatshirts and sneakers with the letters from the window printed across their bodies, staring in at the chandelier snowstorm.

"Let's try Cherwell Lanes instead," Max suggested, and they walked away toward the bus stop.

As the bus staggered through the city, Owen could see why Angela liked it here. All the different neighborhoods, all those different worlds contained within its gridlines. You could be a new person whenever you wanted. Reinvent yourself as many times as you needed to.

He could understand that. He used to lie awake at night wishing he were someone else. And then he'd made it happen, or at least as much as he was able to in Westview. The only problem was that Westview never forgot.

They got off the bus at Cherwell Lanes and strolled through its maze of narrow alleyways with tiny, bright-painted shops and flowers bursting out of window boxes like runaway bouquets. Owen felt like he'd stepped back in time as they walked beneath pastel-striped awnings and tiny triangles of fabric that zigzagged gracefully from shop to shop on strings lit with bulbs as gold as pennies.

They turned around the corner to an outdoor flea market sprawled across the entire alleyway, old cameras and flowery porcelain and patterned boxes jumbled across tables. Lucie immediately gravitated toward a table covered in jewelry and Owen watched her sift through long strands of beads, delicate pendants, holding them up to sway gently from her fingertips. He knew she was picturing all the ways she could make them into something new. He wandered over to Declan and Max, who were looking through a box of old records.

They stopped at a nearby coffee shop after they found what they'd been looking for, and walked into the back garden, all whitewashed walls and light-laced trees.

"Do you want to go to the corn maze at Winthrop Farm after school next Friday?" Max asked once they'd pushed two small tables together and pulled up chairs around them. "It's the first day of their fall festival."

One of their traditions. Wandering through narrow paths of tall corn stalks, drinking hot apple cider on haybales. They'd go apple picking in the warm fall sunlight while bees buzzed around fallen fruit, buy tiny maple candies that dissolved on their tongues as they walked back to Max's house. Together, they would make a pie, filling the house with the smell of butter and cinnamon and afterward, they'd eat it outside with a fire crackling or in the living room, with the horror movies Max and Declan insisted on watching all season echoing against the walls.

Next Friday. The day of his Walcott interview. Owen suddenly felt jittery with nerves.

"I can't," he said. "I have to work."

It was the first time he'd ever lied to them. He could feel the guilt twisting at his stomach. He wondered again how he was ever going to tell them.

Maybe he should have just been honest from the start but now it felt like it was too late.

***

At work later, he rehearsed answers for possible interview questions in his head as a group of girls from school came in to buy dresses for the Tricentennial Gala. He could hear them giggling in the fitting room. Once they were gone, he hung up everything they'd left behind, black tulle and beaded satin.

Those girls all lived in Angela's neighborhood. Owen had classes with one of their brothers, saw their parents in this store all the time. They were the type of people everyone in Westview wanted to be, the type of people who went to Walcott. And the longer Owen lived in Westview, the further away their world felt.

7

"Smile," said Cassie, holding her phone out in front of them.

Angela did, and as soon as Cassie was done taking the picture, she slid her sunglasses on, turning the football field sepia. The breeze carried hints of early autumn, tingling against her bare arms.

"I'm cold. I'm going to get my jacket," she said. "I'll be right back."

Truthfully, she just hated the matching T-shirts Cassie had made for them, white with each of their boyfriends' uniform numbers in ruby rhinestones on the front. Last year she would have loved them. They would have stayed up late decorating them together, watching old episodes of their favorite reality TV shows and talking for hours. Back then, she would have never imagined keeping secrets from Cassie.

Angela stepped off the silver-striped bleachers and strode past a group of classmates selling red-wrapped chocolate and Westview sweatshirts. Her car was parked close by, facing the chain-link fence. The looped metal divided the field into diamonds of white-lined grass, the pattern broken only by a sign with her family's name on it. Her parents had paid for the field's renovation three years ago, her father telling the community how much he enjoyed his own days on the Westview football team. He still came to the games sometimes, sitting with his former teammates whose sons were now on the field, chasing their old championships.

As she locked her car and swung her jacket around her shoulders, Angela noticed Owen at his car on the opposite side of the parking lot. She watched him for a moment, then he glanced over and saw her.

Angela looked away quickly, pretending to check her phone.

Part of her, though, was determined to prove that all the bad things he probably thought about her were wrong. She didn't know why she cared. Or why she was walking toward him now.

"Hi," she greeted him and then the words were tumbling off her tongue, all messy and blurred together in a way that was unlike her. "Listen, I'm sorry for what I said to you at Gracie's, that wasn't fair..."

She could see in his expression that he knew she wasn't used to apologizing.

"It's fine," Owen said. "I'm sorry too. I shouldn't have judged you, it's none of my business."

She didn't want to admit that maybe he'd been closer to the truth than she was comfortable with. They stood there awkwardly for a moment, Owen smiling hesitantly, clearly waiting for an answer.

"What are you still doing here?" she asked instead.

"I just finished tutoring. What about you?"

"Football game," Angela answered. She saw him glance at her shirt with a strange expression on his face and she zipped up her jacket to hide all the rhinestones, hating that he'd seen it.

"You should come," she added without thinking.

He hesitated.

"Come on," she said.

She could feel everyone's eyes on them as they walked toward the bleachers. She smiled at them all.

She used to love giving people something to talk about. For a while it was fun, so easy to make people believe anything, then do something else to make them think the opposite. But now it was more about survival, the need to control her own narrative. People were going to talk anyway; she'd quickly figured out that she was two steps ahead of them if she spun the rumors about herself. That way, she could hide the truth if she needed to.

The bleachers were crowded now. The rows of parents, shoulders draped with fleece blankets, left little room between Owen and Angela as they squeezed into the space Cassie was saving. The angles of their bodies collided.

Cassie looked confused when she saw them together but she quickly rearranged her face into a friendly smile.

"I'm Cassie," she said, leaning over and holding out her hand for Owen to shake as if she was networking.

"Owen." He didn't even look surprised, like he'd expected Cassie to live in her own little bubble here, the same thing he'd accused Angela of. The truth was, she knew exactly who Owen was; she'd probably heard every rumor that Angela had. She was just trying to give him a blank slate, which she and Angela would only do for each other.

"We're on the Tricentennial Committee together," Angela said quickly.

Cassie nodded and turned her attention back to the game. Angela could see Dillon and Adam's red-clad silhouettes on the field, raising clouds of dust and grass blades as they ran.

She checked her phone as the game went on, starting to wish she were anywhere else. Cassie loved going to these games, but Angela always got bored quickly, even back when she'd wanted to be here to support Dillon.

She had another email from Harcourt. She opened the message, scrolled through photos of smiling students and a list of upcoming events. There was a link to book tours and information sessions. She stared at it for a moment, index finger hovering over the link.

And then her surroundings erupted in the shouts of people in red and white.

Cassie and Angela groaned. A man in front of them was yelling at the ref while a group of parents a few rows ahead hurled insults at the opposing team's supporters.

"This happens every time," Angela said to Owen. All the voices around them were now so loud it was impossible to understand what they were each saying.

"They always make our town look bad," Cassie added, frowning a little as she glanced at the group of people shouting the loudest, always the same group every game. "It's so embarrassing, all these other teams hate coming here to play."

"Who do you think is getting kicked out today?" Angela asked. This was a game they played every time.

"Nolan's dad, for sure," said Cassie, indicating a man who was now storming toward the sidelines, bellowing at the ref. "Do you remember when he got into a fight with those parents from Logan last year?"

"Probably Aidan's parents, too."

Angela looked back at her phone as the crowd began to quiet down. She deleted the message from Harcourt, and opened one from Walcott she'd saved. It was full of pictures of people playing sports, peering into microscopes, walking across the quad. She recognized some of them as Westview graduates. She tried, again, to fit herself into those pictures.

Cassie's elbow collided with Angela's arm as the crowd got to its feet, cheering. "Pay attention. Dillon just scored."

Angela clapped slowly, unenthusiastic. She tried not to make eye contact with Owen, who wasn't clapping. As the noise faded away, she focused on the fragments of conversation nearby.

"It's so disappointing that they cancelled the Homecoming dance," a woman was complaining to a group of parents.

"This is typical Westview," her friend added. "Nancy Tremont and I both tried to talk to the principal but he won't change his mind."

"At least they have the gala on the same day as the game and the parade," the man on her right chimed in.

"It's not the same. The dance is a Westview tradition, don't you remember how much fun it always was?"

"I honestly think everyone's parents are more upset about this than we are," Angela muttered.

"So what exactly happened with the Homecoming dance?" asked Owen. "I've heard so many different stories."

Angela rolled her eyes. "The rumors are a lot more interesting than the real story. A few people got caught drinking at Prom last year so they decided to punish everyone by canceling the Homecoming dance. Since the Tricentennial Gala is the same night and most of the town will be there, they're trying to spin it as a more supervised version of Homecoming. And an opportunity to take pride in our town's history. We'll probably have Prom as usual this year, though, because so many people have already complained."

"What they don't realize," Cassie said, leaning over, "is that no one really cares about a dance in the high school gym with a bad DJ. The fun part of Homecoming is the afterparties. Which we're still planning on having."

The parents' conversation had moved on now, into obvious attempts to one-up each other. Angela was used to it, the language of this town. Everyone trying to persuade everyone else that their life was something to envy.

When the game finally ended, Cassie sprinted across the field to congratulate Adam. Angela and Owen lingered behind, slowly following the crowd off the bleachers. There was something about the way he was looking at her that she couldn't figure out. She could feel the silence burning between them.

"See you later," was all she could think to say once they reached the parking lot. She didn't even wait for Owen's response, doubling back to meet Dillon. She gave him a long kiss in the middle of the field, where everyone could see them. Just to show anyone who felt like talking about seeing her with Owen.

"Good game," she told him.

"Thanks for coming," said Dillon.

He smiled and put his arm around her waist, pulling her close as they walked off the field together. Showing her off to everyone. She wondered how she could have ever thought any of this was real.

"We're going out for food now," he added. "Do you want to come?"

"No thanks," she said, imagining all of them crowded into the booth of a tiny fast food chain, the smell of salt and grease seeping into her hair while she acted like there was no place else she'd rather be. "We're meeting Rose at Bella to pick out dresses for the gala."

"Okay," Dillon said. He stopped. "Wait, let me see your shirt. Cassie told me about them earlier." He tugged her jacket zipper down gently, revealing the rhinestone numbers.

She smiled, the way she was supposed to.

"It looks good," Dillon said, smiling back. He kissed her again, there on the sidelines for the whole town to see. Hands in her hair, at her waist.

Bella was a ten-minute drive away on Main Street, but the inside looked like it belonged in Cherwell, where the most expensive shopping streets were all brownstone and ivy and curly wrought iron. Chandelier-lit, with sparsely filled racks lining the walls. In the center of the room, a thin mannequin wearing nothing but strings of crystal guarded a display of beaded clutches and trays of perfume in tiny glass bottles.

The store was owned by Rose's mother, Helen, and the dresses there rivaled Cherwell's best boutiques. Angela had been buying dresses here for dances and formal occasions since she started middle school. Last year she'd even modeled for their spring social media campaign in exchange for a free prom dress, a shade of soft summer blue. She'd loved that dress and the way it floated around her, cloud-like, as she danced with Dillon, happy and tipsy because they were almost seniors and everything in Westview belonged to them. They'd all jumped in Angela's pool afterward, still dressed up, and then the light, airy feeling of the dress was gone, the fabric all heavy with chlorine and water, her makeup running and her hair saturated. She'd felt free then, like the world was opening up for her instead of getting smaller. Everything about that night felt so far away now.

"Angela, I have the perfect dress for you," Helen said as soon as she saw her.

She was holding a dress that Angela immediately hated. It was red, the exact shade of scarlet found in their high school colors. She could see herself in it now, paired with a simple pearl pendant, Westview come to life with small-town topography all over her skin, reservoir water instead of blood.

"I want to take a look around first," Angela said. She

wandered to a rack of dresses against the wall, trailing her fingertips across slinky silk and shimmery satin, and there it was.

The dress looked like it was made of moonlight. Pale gold and silky with tiny beads that flowed across the fabric like waves. She would be the center of attention in this dress in the way she wanted to be. It was absolutely perfect.

She held it against her body and carried it carefully into the fitting room. Helen was on the phone and Angela could hear her gossiping as she took off her clothes.

"Did you hear that Trent Prescott is coming back for the gala?" she was saying to whoever she was talking to. "No, it's not a rumor. His mother told me, she was here looking for a dress earlier. She got the one I showed you yesterday, that pretty black one…"

Angela recognized that name. Trent Prescott was a writer and TV presenter, born and raised in Westview, the one person she could think of who had actually left forever. He had a new travel show now that Angela watched sometimes at home when thoughts of leaving Westview kept her awake, stunning shots of cities and countryside flickering against her bare walls until she redrew them in her dreams.

"Why is Trent Prescott coming to the gala?" she asked, stepping out of the fitting room. The dress was smooth and cool against her skin. Helen was off the phone now, holding up jewelry for Rose, who was wearing the red dress Angela had rejected.

Helen hurried over to help Angela zip up her dress. "Apparently he's working on something about New England so he's going to be in the area anyway." She led Angela to the mirror. "I don't remember the last time I saw him, it's been years."

"I didn't know you knew each other."

"We grew up together. He was good friends with your parents in high school, too."

"Really?"

She was surprised they'd never mentioned it before. She'd heard so many of her parents' stories from high school but she'd never really thought about what they must have been like back then, what they felt like when they were the age she was now. She wondered if they'd ever wanted to leave.

Cassie joined her at the mirror in a navy dress reminiscent of winter midnights. "You need to buy that dress. It's perfect."

She was right. The dress was perfect, just like Angela had known it would be, all glimmer and ethereality. Long, tracing all the right places like a silhouette. All eyes would be on her. That was essential.

Because this was the truth, taught in this town the same way as century-old grudges and shortcuts through backroads. Dresses like these were supposed to be armor for Westview women. Wear the perfect dress and words wouldn't hurt. Distract with sequins and sweetheart necklines and there would still be rumors—because there were always, *always* rumors about everything imaginable—but not loud enough to touch you. If you had the right dress, if you played your role right, if you smiled while wearing the prettiest lipstick, you changed the conversation. You weren't the target of pointed words and whispers that flowed like blood and wine. You were safe, at least until someone else waltzed in wearing something better.

8

It was raining when Owen arrived at Walcott after school for his interview, but the campus was just as beautiful as he'd remembered. The trees were ablaze with the brightest foliage, aglow in orange against the pale sky. The pathways surrounding the quad were a sea of bobbing umbrellas as students hurried to class. Through ivy-curtained windows, Owen could see classrooms that looked warm and inviting.

He stopped in the student center bathroom on his way to the admissions office. He looked in the mirror, wondering if his clothes were okay. He was wearing the black trousers he usually wore to work with a dress shirt and tie he'd found folded up in the basement from his father's better days. Last night he'd looked through everything in his closet but nothing felt right. These were more expensive. He'd thought about it for a long time before he changed into them this afternoon, debating if he really wanted a piece of his father here with him. The idea of that made him feel sick.

He reminded himself that they weren't the same person.

He wondered if he was overdressed, if everyone here would see right through him and know he wasn't the type of person who could afford these clothes. He had classmates at school who dressed like this every day. Lucie always rolled her eyes when she saw them in the halls.

Maybe he would have felt better in his own clothes.

His hair was a mess. He liked it long but it was getting scraggly at the ends and his mother had been telling him for weeks that he should get it cut. He wished he'd listened; Haley had even offered to do it herself this afternoon before he left.

He took a deep breath and told himself that even though he was still in Westview, he wasn't at Westview High School. People came from everywhere to attend Walcott. It was so easy to forget that, because this wasn't a typical college town. It seemed like everyone stayed here inside the gates, their whole world on this campus.

This wasn't going to be like another version of high school, he told himself again. He was letting Angela get to him with her insistence that no one ever left this town, that everything stayed the same.

The admissions office was small and warm. He sat down on the couch near reception and waited to be called in for his interview, glancing nervously at the other people seated around him. None of them were from Westview.

He relaxed a little when his name was called and he was greeted by Sierra, the admissions counselor he'd met with the last time he was here. It made him feel better to be recognized in Westview in this context. Like he belonged here.

He exchanged pleasantries on autopilot, then followed her into a small office with beige walls. He could see pictures of Sierra and her friends on her desk, a few familiar Westview faces smiling around her. She was an alumna, he remembered, and she'd come here from a different state.

"It's great to see you again," Sierra continued once

they were both seated. "How is your school year going? Do you have a favorite class?"

"It's going well," Owen answered. His mouth was dry now and his palms were starting to sweat, heart thudding. He tried to calm down and remember the answers he'd practiced. "I'm really enjoying my American government and sociology classes. I've lived here in Westview for most of my life and sometimes it can feel like a bubble. Both classes have really challenged my way of thinking about the world."

"So do you think you'll major in one of those subjects?" Sierra asked.

"I want to major in history," Owen said. "I haven't decided what my specific concentration would be but I've always loved history. Last year I helped reorganize and digitize Cherwell's and Westview's archives. I've been volunteering with the Westview Historical Society for about two years and our main project right now is running events to celebrate the town's tricentennial year, which just kicked off at the end of the summer."

Sierra scribbled some notes down on a piece of paper. "Have you learned anything interesting from that?"

He thought about the secret he'd found, the one that could burn down this entire town. "Mostly that there's more to every story," he said instead. "It all depends on who's telling it."

Sierra nodded. "So why Walcott?" she asked.

He told her all the things he loved about this place, and he found himself relaxing as the interview went on. He talked about his career goals, classes he wanted to take, the clubs he wanted to join. And when he stepped from the cozy warmth of the admissions office into gray ribbons of rain outside, he was even more determined to go here, prove that he belonged. He could feel it in his bones. The longing to be part of this place hurt.

He walked past the fountain, watched the pattern of the raindrops. Lights were starting to come on in the nearby brick dorm buildings as the sky dimmed and Owen could see through the windows. Strings of tiny silver lights on white cinderblock. Pictures and posters and flags. He could see people slouched over their desks, sprawled on their beds, silhouettes with unknown stories. They had everything he wanted.

Damp pathways shimmered in the lamplight. The rain soaked through his hair, made his shirt cold and heavy against his skin. In the distance, he saw Angela walking toward him in a black dress and he felt a rush in his stomach, but as they moved closer to each other he realized it was Cassie.

She didn't acknowledge him. Even though they'd talked to him at the football game, she and Angela had gone back to ignoring him—but he'd noticed that sometimes, Angela didn't avert her eyes.

Raindrops twirled off Cassie's umbrella, little globes of gold in the light. And they kept walking in opposite directions, shadows stretching further apart.

Everything smelled like fall. Groups of friends were starting to walk from the classrooms and dorms to the dining hall, cheerful chatter buzzing in the rainy air. Owen remembered it from his tour over the summer, a beautiful old building with tall windows and dark mahogany paneling inside, round lamps on the walls. If he attended Walcott, he'd be living at home so he probably wouldn't eat many meals here but maybe this was where he'd spend time between classes. He'd looked through the course listings online and created a schedule for himself, trying to figure out a way to fit in work and get involved in some clubs and activities. Maybe he'd try to get a job on campus so that he wouldn't have to drive all the way to Madison.

Haley and Sophia were watching TV in the living

room when he got home. There was some leftover spaghetti in the refrigerator from last night's dinner. Owen scooped it into a bowl even though he wasn't really hungry. He sat down at the computer and logged in to his Walcott application.

Haley and Sophia were laughing at something now and the rain was loud against the windows. Owen hoped that Sophia wouldn't mention to Max that she'd seen him since he'd told his friends he was working. He still hadn't told them he was applying to Walcott.

He felt strangely lonely now. He hadn't felt that way in a long time. The adrenaline and aftermath of nerves had slowly burned down as he walked around the rainy campus.

He should feel proud about how well the interview went, he thought, but he wanted someone to share it with. He couldn't tell his friends. He couldn't tell Haley because Sophia was here. Even his mother didn't know how badly he wanted this because he was afraid of letting her down.

He thought of Angela for a moment and almost laughed out loud at himself. She wouldn't want to hear anything about Walcott.

Owen scrolled through his application. He'd already completed the forms and asked his teachers for letters of recommendation. He just needed to finish writing his essay. He still had time before the deadline, a few weeks left to find the perfect words.

He shut off the computer and put his mostly uneaten food back in the refrigerator. He went to his room and stretched out on his bed. Stared at the ceiling, paint smeared in streaky arcs. There was a stain across them like a figure-eight. Little leftover specks of adhesive from the plastic glow-in-the-dark stars he used to have hanging up.

He'd taken a map of Walcott from the admissions office before he left. He pulled it out of his pocket and unfolded it carefully. Owen loved the wall of maps in his bedroom, these diagrams of places both real and fictional, all curvy lines and sharp angles that made him dizzy if he stared too long.

When he'd first started collecting them, he'd known that the places they portrayed were as messy and complicated as they were beautiful. He'd thought that maps were supposed to simplify places, strip them down to bare bones to make them navigable to anyone. But after months of staring at the wall in the dark as he tried to fall asleep, watching the patterns illuminated by occasional passing headlights, he'd realized that wasn't true. It was the complexities of places that made the maps the way they were. History and politics and privilege were what drew the lines on maps. Especially in Westview—where you didn't talk about politics because it wasn't polite, but this whole place had poison and politics in its blood.

He pinned up the map of Walcott with a thumbtack, corners overlapping a glossy map of Cherwell. Then he stepped back to admire his wall. Ceiling to floor covered in blue seascapes and deserts textured like burned vermillion lace and mountains where snow touched the clouds. Multicolored roads, ribbon-like, tangled and spooling and sprawling for eternity.

Sometimes when he looked at these maps, he knew they showed places he'd never see. There just weren't enough days in a lifetime. But that was a little comforting too, because it meant that there were infinite places that didn't know his name or his history, so if he needed to, he'd never run out of places to start over.

9

Angela was putting on lipstick when Cassie pulled into the driveway and started beeping her car horn, the sound echoing down the street. She waved to her from her bedroom window and went downstairs.

Her mother was sitting in the kitchen, drinking coffee and texting someone. "Have fun," she said, not even looking at Angela. "Make sure you're back by five. We have the Young Alumni Awards at Walcott tonight."

Angela didn't bother answering. She'd been thinking a lot about her family's traditions lately, and how Westview and Walcott seemed entwined in all of them. This was yet another, an annual reception her mother hosted to celebrate the accomplishments of young alumni. Her parents were both involved in selecting the honorees, and Angela had been going to the receptions for as long as she could remember.

She got into Cassie's car, where everything was familiar, almost a ritual itself. Cassie with her long, wavy hair and the turquoise bracelet she wore on her wrist every day like a tattoo. Her car, clean with a pine tree scent. She was scrolling through her phone, making a playlist.

Cassie had the most extensive music library of anyone

Angela knew. She listened to everything and knew how to match songs perfectly to every feeling or occasion. At the start of every year, she made playlists for all of their friends, carefully selected lyrics against the clean slate of a new calendar. A soundtrack for their memories. Angela always kept them and listened to them months, even years later. Music always took her back to a certain moment. There was an electropop ballad that reminded her of the coziness of winter snowfall even on the hottest summer day, of being stranded inside with the scent of cinnamon while the world whirled with white. A beat that fizzled like sparks in her blood and made her want to dance to city lights while rain crashed from the sky. A chorus that took her back to summertime, when she felt most alive with the sun on her face, wind dancing with her hair, driving with the windows down and ocean–blue everywhere. She felt like she could settle into the songs, breathe in bass lines and melodies until they were part of her bloodstream, the closest thing she had to going back in time.

"Look in the bag," Cassie said as they drove out of town to the train station, an upbeat song playing in the background. "I got us some things for Spirit Week. I was thinking we could all go shopping for everything else sometime this week."

Angela peered into the bag at her feet. Everything inside was red, rolls of tulle and long strands of metallic beads.

"I like these," she lied, holding up a set of sparkly bows she would have loved last year.

Cassie smiled. "I thought you would."

Everyone knew their friends always had the best Spirit Week outfits. They'd wear group costumes to correspond with each day's theme and Cassie was always the one to plan and coordinate them.

The pressure to be perfect, to be everything that

Westview wanted, never seemed to bother Cassie. She loved almost everything about this town the way Angela used to. She was in the crowd of every Westview sporting event and she always ran their annual class fundraiser. She was excited to go to Walcott next year and she was going to run for Town Council as soon as she was old enough. Angela wondered how their lives could be so similar but only she felt like she was suffocating here.

"Can you tell me where we're going now?" she asked once they were standing on the railway platform, waiting for the train that went to Cherwell. When they'd made these plans last week, all Cassie would tell her was that she had a surprise in the city.

"Okay," said Cassie. "Don't be mad but I've noticed you looking at emails from Harcourt a lot lately. They have a prospective student day today so I thought we could go. I know your parents are set on Walcott for you but it doesn't hurt to look at other options, right?"

Nerves erupted inside Angela's brain but she couldn't help smiling. "Thanks," she said, twisting the hem of her sweater with trembling fingers. She and Cassie had spent so many afternoons last year talking about being at Walcott with Dillon and Adam. They'd eat all their meals together in the old, wood-paneled dining hall. Spend hours on the perfect green quad, get all dressed up for parties. It made her feel a little better that Cassie was holding the door open to a future that was different from that.

"How was your Walcott interview?" she asked as they boarded the train and found seats together, feeling bad that she hadn't thought to ask before.

"It went really well. I'm so excited. I already submitted my application."

The train started moving. Patterns of rooftops and

power lines whisked past, quick glimpses into backyards and autumn-kissed town squares. Cassie took out her phone, showed her the rest of her ideas for Spirit Week costumes, the dresses she was still trying to decide between for the gala. Once in the city, sunshine all over the sidewalks, they took a bus from the train station to Harcourt's main campus and Angela realized that her nervous fingers had worn a tiny hole into the hem of her sweater. She took a deep breath and felt a rush of excitement as she took in everything she'd seen on glossy flyers and phone screens.

They bought smoothies from the café in the student center. Sweet and pink, flecked with crushed berries like confetti. They sat down and watched students filter through the building. Angela admired their clothes. So many different styles, showing off their personalities through colors and cuts and prints and the items they paired with them. Maybe here, she could wear something she'd made without being afraid of the way other people would see it. Maybe she'd spend less time judging her reflection, slide softer words onto her skin like silk.

She let herself imagine it: here, next year, surrounded by new friends, thoughts of Westview tucked far away. Getting lost in designing, the exhilaration of bringing pieces of her thoughts to blank pages and shaping spools of fabric into something to share with the world. There was so much opportunity. A chance to figure out who she was outside of Westview. She could be whoever she wanted if she could just get here.

Lately, she'd been dreaming so vividly about other places she could taste them. Every time she woke up, it took a moment to realize she was in bed in Westview at the end of a cul-de-sac surrounded by trees and the disappointment would hit her like a car crash. She built cities in her sleep, found all the secret corners of Cherwell and mapped out places across oceans. In the hazy space between dreaming and waking, Westview didn't exist but every time she opened her eyes all its shades of blue and green and white came into focus, jewel tones and muted hues saturating her cerebrum. She'd never wanted to hide in her dreams so much before.

"The tour starts in a few minutes," Cassie said. "Are you ready?"

Angela nodded, feeling more confident now. Cassie linked arms with her as they walked to the meeting point.

She knew this was what she wanted as they shuffled through buildings alongside eager strangers. And afterward, listening to presentations at the information session, those feelings persisted. A sense that this was a place she belonged. The way she used to feel in Westview on nights she'd walk into a party, gazes turning toward her, and over the smell of beer and crowded bodies, she could remember the house's soft scent from childhood summers and from years of sleepovers; she knew which steps would creak beneath all their shoes even if it didn't matter now because the music was loud and their parents weren't home.

"So what do you think?" Cassie asked later as they walked through the bookshop.

Angela paused to look at an endcap of faculty publications. "I like it here." She picked up one of the books, feeling its weight in her hands. "Thanks for doing this."

"Are you going to apply?"

Angela sighed and put the book back on the shelf before following Cassie into the apparel section. "I want to but I don't know what I'm going to tell my parents. I don't think they've ever considered anything other than Walcott."

"I know." Cassie unfolded a T-shirt with the word *Harcourt* spelled out in boxy collegiate letters. She held it up to Angela.

Angela looked in the mirror at their almost-twin reflections and smiled.

"Maybe if you just talk to them, they'll understand," Cassie continued.

"I don't know. You know how they are. Going to Walcott is such a big deal to them."

"Maybe they'll surprise you. Give them a chance."

Angela took the T-shirt from Cassie, folded it up. "Did you know I used to be friends with Owen Emory?"

Cassie looked confused. "When?"

"When we were kids. It happened by accident. They'd just moved back here and my babysitter knew both of our families, and one day his mom needed help while she was with me, so she just brought me over there. We ended up becoming friends and I spent almost every day that summer at his house. And then my mom found out. She told me I couldn't be friends with him and she didn't really explain why. But I've heard a lot of different stories."

She still remembered the weeks after that. A new babysitter, Juliet, tall and freckled with long hair that she always pulled back into a blonde ponytail. She was quiet, uninterested. While Angela played alone on the living room floor, crafting dream worlds in a dollhouse, Juliet sat on the couch, eyes fixed on her phone or the TV. Whenever she left, Angela watched her fold crisp new bills into the back pocket of her denim shorts, slide her feet into the white leather sandals waiting by the door. She didn't like her, but she didn't like when she left, either. Something about her reminded Angela of her own mother. Closeness that felt so far away.

It had taken weeks of pleading into late fall to convince Juliet to bring her to the local playground, a large area that stretched from the top of a tree-shaded hill to a track where yoga pant-clad mothers jogged in pairs. Angela liked running so that day she started with the track, footsteps uneven and joyful in the sunlight. She ran past a couple pushing a stroller and a group of chattering teenagers. Tired afterward, she slowly began to make her way through the playground, swaying from monkey bars and pretending that the swings could take her high enough to touch her toes to the sky's brightness.

She climbed up to the top of a canopied fort overlooking a group of picnic tables, and when she looked out between the worn wooden beams, she saw Owen seated at a table with a small group of chattering children. Her classmates, but not the ones she spent time with after school. The table was covered with a white paper tablecloth, edges fluttering, red balloons and curly yellow streamers taped to the corners. A plastic pitcher of lemonade sat at its center and a small stack of brightly wrapped boxes was positioned on the ground.

Angela wanted to propel herself down the slide in her sparkle-skirted dress to sit with Owen. She looked over at Juliet. She was inattentive as always, dragging her sandaled feet through the woodchips as she swayed on a blue-seated swing. Angela hesitated, remembering how angry her mother had been as she told her not to talk to Owen anymore.

She watched Owen's mother lift the lid from a container, revealing a circular cake. She poked candles into its smooth surface, lit them. The tiny flames flickered like tangerine teardrops.

She kissed the top of Owen's head and smoothed his hair, then moved to the opposite side of the table to face him and began to sing. The voices of Angela's classmates joined her, pitchy.

Owen closed his eyes, filled his cheeks with breath. He exhaled, extinguishing the dancing lights. His mother clapped; the light from her camera flashed golden.

"Angela!" Juliet called suddenly. "It's time to go home."

Reluctant but obedient, Angela moved toward the slide and released her grip, static clinging to her dress. The soles of her shoes left a set of black stripes against the yellow curve of plastic. She was standing in the woodchips, so close to the picnic table and Owen was looking at her.

"Angela!" His face was filled with excitement. Like she hadn't spent every moment of school recess ignoring him.

"Angela, come sit with us, have some cake," his mother said, smiling.

Angela froze for a moment, taking in the bright balloons leaping on curled strings against the evergreen background. And then she did what she was supposed to do: spun around in a whirl of glitter and tulle, and ran toward Juliet.

She found the invitation later, illustrated by Owen, crumpled among a stack of old magazines while her mother was on the phone planning playdates for her with people in their neighborhood, picking who she'd be friends with.

She'd gone upstairs, found the tiny toy car from Owen still hidden in her bedroom. Wished for summer all night as she slid it across her mattress, wheels spinning faster and faster like they were approaching places she could only dream of.

"I know it doesn't sound like a big deal," she said now, realizing that Cassie was looking at her, waiting for a response to whatever she'd just said. "Things like that happen all the time in Westview. But that's the problem. They're both so concerned about how everything looks to other people. They have this whole life planned out for me. That's the person I'm supposed to be. Doing something different isn't an option."

"I know what you mean," sighed Cassie. "But maybe they can change. Maybe they'll be open to you coming here."

"People don't change," said Angela. "Not in West-view."

She bought the T-shirt. At home, she'd bury it in the bottom of her dresser, under all the shirts she slept in.

She wished she could tell Cassie everything else. How she knew that Dillon didn't like who she really was, how even though today she wanted busy streets and city lights, she still spent so much time wanting to go back to last year. When Westview was everything and she hadn't noticed all its imperfections.

Everything about today was already starting to feel distant. It all seemed closer in her sleep.

***

The reception for the Young Alumni Awards was held in Kent Hall, Walcott's original academic building. Angela's parents immediately left her alone, her mother hurrying over to chat with the other organizers, her father greeting a colleague. Angela stood awkwardly by the doorway for a moment, then took a seat at the back.

Portraits of every former Walcott president hung on the wall, all men. Her mother approached the white podium decorated with the college crest. She looked like she belonged in a portrait herself, dressed in navy and pearls.

"Welcome," she said. "It's an honor to be here tonight to celebrate the achievements of our young alumni…"

Realizing that no one would notice if she left, Angela slipped outside into the main hall. There was a long glass case along one side of the wall and for the first time, she studied the objects inside carefully. Black–and–white photographs of students who were long gone and buildings that were still standing. There was a class banner on sun-stained fabric, a century-old campus map. Old objects stamped with the Walcott crest.

She walked until she reached the heavy front door and pushed it open to wrap herself in lamplight and October twilight. She walked past the fountain all Walcott students went swimming in the day before graduation, the same one she and Cassie had splashed around in as toddlers. Across the perfect stretch of emerald quad where generations of students had studied, played games and forged friendships, where she used to find shapes in the clouds from a picnic blanket. There was the white chapel where her parents were married, with a gold owl weathervane on its steeple. Every year, on the night before classes started, the seniors gathered there to tell ghost stories to the incoming freshmen. She knew the Walcott traditions she hadn't even lived yet as well as she knew her own memories here. This place had always been part of her, the same sort of familiar as the house she'd grown up in, the Westview backroads she could wander in her sleep.

It just wasn't the place that burned bright in her dreams.

When she went back inside, her mother was conversing with one of the honorees, a woman in her late twenties in black trousers and a white cardigan.

"Angela!" she said, gesturing her over as soon as she saw her. "Have you met Lila Newbury? Lila, this is my daughter, Angela."

"I've heard so much about you. It's nice to meet you," Lila said, shaking Angela's hand. She was one of those people who Angela recognized from around Westview but because of their age difference, their lives had never overlapped in any way.

"You too," she answered. She curved her lips upward, realizing for the first time how much her fake smile must look like her mother's. "Congratulations on the award."

"Lila founded a nonprofit for children's literacy," her mother said, looking at Lila as if she were her own daughter.

Angela suddenly imagined Owen here, smugly pointing out that Lila, despite not leaving, was doing something that made an impact. *Not everyone in this town is as bad as you think they are*, he'd say. She tried to get his thoughts out of her head.

Before Angela had a chance to answer, Nora Buckley, Angela's neighbor and member of the Alumni Committee, swept over in a swirl of honey perfume and champagne.

"You're growing up so fast," she said. "You'll be here too next year, won't you, Angela?"

They were all smiling at her. Angela's fingers toyed with the hem of her sweater, making the hole bigger and bigger.

"I will."

"How exciting! Have you submitted your application?"

"I haven't finished yet," Angela said, not exactly a lie. She'd opened the website once, wondering what would happen if she didn't fill out the application.

"Do you know what you're going to major in yet?"

"I haven't decided. There are so many great choices," she said brightly but it didn't even matter because Mrs Buckley had stopped listening. She was busy beckoning Angela's father over from where he was surrounded by people, somehow engaging with all of them like always.

"Scott, let's get a picture of all three of you. This will be perfect for the alumni magazine."

As Angela smiled between her parents, making sure the way she was standing would capture her best angles, she knew this would be the picture they sent out on holiday cards, posted to social media like an advertisement for a perfect family. All smiles surrounded by portraits of Walcott's past presidents.

No one would know that pretending to be perfect could slowly tear you apart.

She could still feel the hole in the hem of her sweater. In the final pictures, the ones slipped through mail slots all over town, it wouldn't be visible, either hidden by text or edited out. But she would know it was there, just like every other flaw she couldn't unsee.

***

Dillon was already a few drinks in by the time Angela arrived at Paige's party. He kissed her sloppily and she pulled away, making sure she smiled and didn't flinch in case people were watching.

"Do you want a drink?" he asked, shoving a cup into her hands without giving her a chance to answer.

"Thanks."

She put the cup to her lips, pretended to take a sip. She didn't feel like drinking tonight. She went over to talk to Naomi and Rose, who were making drinks with a group of their classmates. Everyone turned to greet her when they heard her voice. The music was loud, throbbing at her head.

"Angela!" Paige called her name eagerly from across the basement. She rushed over to give Angela a hug. "I'm so glad you're here."

The expression on her face was familiar. Part relief that so many people were showing up, part panic that everything would get out of hand.

"Here, have a drink," Angela told her, giving her the drink from Dillon.

She sat down on the couch and pretended to listen to two sophomore girls who settled in next to her. They were dressed exactly the way she was, like they'd seen a picture of her and tried to copy it. She hoped Cassie would be here soon; she was probably out somewhere with Adam.

When she couldn't pretend to be interested in all the conversations around her anymore, Angela went upstairs to the bathroom, looked at herself in the mirror. She frowned. Under the harsh bathroom light, her shirt was a little too sheer, lipstick too bright.

She shut off the light, erasing herself. She could hear laughter in the kitchen but everyone else was downstairs so she slipped out the back door.

Like the houses, every backyard in the Witney Estates neighborhood was identical. A fire pit encircled by teak Adirondack chairs, a patio area for grilling and outdoor dining. An inground pool and hot tub.

The pool was covered up until next summer but the lounge chairs were still out on the deck around it, so Angela stretched out on one, looking up. The sky was clear tonight, dark at its apex and fading to a bluish purple around the tree-tops. It was easy to locate the bright stars of the constellation she used to spend so many nights staring at from her bedroom window. The wide W shape of Cassiopeia, the vain, beautiful queen chained to the heavens.

Once again, she wondered what her life would be like if she had different friends in Westview. Her mind wandered to Owen. What was he doing right now? She imagined him in the corner of a late-night coffee shop, listening to music. Or maybe at a bonfire in one of his friends' backyards, orange embers floating up in glittery slow motion to join the same stars Angela was sitting under now. All of them breathing in the same early fall air that made her think of red leaves and cinnamon, fog on the reservoir. The way the air felt in her lungs made her sad that summer was so far away, like her body knew the difference in the way each season breathed.

Their social circles never interacted so she barely knew his friends. It seemed like the members of his group were constant, though, unlike hers. If Angela had to guess, it was likely that she would no longer be speaking with at least two people at this party by the end of the fall semester. That was how it had always been. It was so easy to fall from the top.

And if she wasn't perfect, everyone would have her all figured out and she would be the one falling.

Sometimes that was her biggest fear. And other times she wondered if all of this was still worth it. If falling really wasn't the worst thing.

If Owen ever thought about her, he would have never imagined that she'd be sitting alone in the dark by a closed pool while a party went on inside. And neither would the people downstairs.

Did he ever feel like this around his friends? He always looked so at home around them. The way she used to feel here.

She heard the door open and she recognized the sound of Dillon's footsteps against the deck.

"Angela? What are you doing out here?"

She lifted her face and smiled. Moonlight all over her skin.

"Hey," she said, keeping her voice light. "Just getting some air."

Dillon lit a cigarette and climbed onto the lounge chair with her, placing his cup on the ground. He exhaled and smoke filled Angela's lungs.

"Do you have to do that right now?"

He dropped the cigarette into the cup. Rolled onto his side and leaned in close, his voice at her neck. "You look perfect tonight," he said. The words were warm against her skin. She could feel his thoughts all over her. He pressed his smoky lips to hers.

She didn't say anything. Didn't kiss him back. Just stared at the starry **W** in the sky. He moved away and she missed when this all felt real.

"Come on," he said. "Let's go inside."

She knew nights like these by heart. After a few drinks, Cassie would start dancing out of sync to whatever song was blasting from the speakers. Adam and Rose would make up a new drinking game, their competitive streaks surfacing for a few minutes before they abandoned all the rules. Naomi and Paige would flicker back and forth between giggly and sentimental on the bathroom floor. The start of a new relationship between two of their other peers, the end of another. And then, somewhere in the dark with Dillon, their lips together again.

She knew who she had to be on nights like these. Tonight's thoughts didn't belong inside big, beautiful houses with beautiful people. So she left them outside, under the stars, and rejoined the party with Dillon, smile on her face.

10

When Owen arrived at work, he discovered that sometime in the twenty-four hours between his last shift and now, the holiday decorations had gone up, oddly coinciding with the first day of their annual fall sale. The backdrop in the store window was magnetic magenta and neon, the Northern Lights billowing over fresh fake snowfall like electric whirlpools, the inverse of sunshine. The only products displayed in the window were inexplicably high–heeled boots, a path of stiletto footprints across the snowscape. Inside the store, tiny mirrors shaped like snowflakes and stars waxed and waned their way across the ceiling to mimic the wild flight of aurora light. Fake evergreens threaded with delicate gold guarded the escalators.

He hurried through the faux Nordic skyscape and walked into the break room with only two minutes to spare before he was supposed to punch in for his shift. An after-school meeting for a group project had run longer than it was supposed to and he'd hit traffic on his way here. Judging by how crowded the store already was, he knew he was going to have a headache by the time he left tonight.

He pressed his employee number into the time clock

and left the break room just as his coworker, Liz, was walking in.

"Prepare yourself, it's a nightmare here today. I think the holiday decorations are warping everyone's sense of time," she said as they passed each other. "I've been getting screamed at since I got here and I'm *this close* to just not going back out there."

Owen was working on the floor tonight, which was better than the register because the lines were long and everyone was impatient. Here at least he could move around as he tidied up abandoned clothes and put things back where they belonged.

He refolded a table of soft cashmere sweaters and returned two racks full of unwanted clothes from the fitting room to their proper places. He was in the middle of rehanging blouses and thinking about his Walcott essay when a woman approached him, holding a dark green dress with a clearance tag.

"Excuse me," she said. "I'm looking for this in a medium. Would you be able to check if you have any left in the back?"

Owen put on his best customer service smile and took the dress from her. "Absolutely," he answered.

He knew that they didn't have any extra clearance inventory but headed toward the back of the store anyway to waste a few minutes and check his phone.

As he walked into the back room, his phone lit up with a text message from Angela. He felt his stomach freeze.

I'm going to pick up the donations for the silent auction tomorrow.

He stared at the screen. Why was she telling him this?

They'd barely spoken since the football game apart from whatever they had to say to each other at the Tricentennial Committee meetings. He'd initially been surprised by how quickly she'd offered to coordinate the silent auction but this week, when she presented the list of places that had agreed to provide donations, he understood—people in Westview would do anything Angela Witney asked.

Owen looked up from his phone, trying to think of how to respond, and he realized that he was surrounded by a galaxy of color and glitter.

Once the sale was over next week, all the holiday merchandise would be pushed out to gleaming floors. Dresses cut out of winter skies, smoky gray and ice–white, inky midnight and the fullest, purest blue like the world after snowfall. There were clutch bags encrusted in narrow red gems and round purple stones. Silk scarves with rivers of letters and gloves so soft it seemed that snow would dissolve them like sugar.

Want to keep me company?

He could have sworn he felt his heart stop.

Sure, he wrote back immediately, then cringed, hoping he didn't seem overeager.

He realized he hadn't even looked at his other messages, then saw that Lucie had invited him to go to Cherwell tomorrow. His stomach filled with guilt as he texted her back, lying that he was working.

On a table beside him, someone had laid out pictures and diagrams illustrating the layout of the store, the configuration of displays, outfits for the mannequins. It was all so calculated, everything carefully researched, tested and planned out to make people want the dream this place was selling. The mannequins were all supposed to be arranged in little scenes in their respective departments. Faceless bodies wearing party dresses sewn from champagne bubbles and candlelight. Child-shaped plastic in festive pajamas surrounded by cheerful stacks of wrapped presents.

He wondered if people really believed that if they bought those things here, they could have that life. The fancy party, the perfect family on Christmas morning. It made him feel a little sick.

He brought the dress back out to the customer. She was examining gift sets of perfume, displayed in patterned boxes and topped with shiny bows.

"Sorry," he told her. "Everything we have left is out here."

"Thank you for checking," she answered, then walked away to look for something else. He wondered what dream she wanted to buy. Sometimes when he was bored here, he'd walk through the men's section, imagining what he would purchase if he could afford to, what would make him look like someone who belonged in Westview.

Owen put away more clothes from the fitting room and tidied up a display of handbags. Then he took his fifteen-minute dinner break, quickly making a sandwich from the bread and peanut butter he kept in the break room. He looked at his phone. Angela had texted him to confirm the details for tomorrow. Lucie hadn't said anything.

He went to the registers afterward to cover a break, carefully folding and wrapping layers of silk and wool. He smiled until his face hurt, at Westview people who ignored him, at strangers who demanded to speak to the manager. Fantasized about walking away from this place and its glittery lies. People here and people in Westview made him feel so small sometimes, like he didn't matter.

He thought about that as he drove home, navigating roads where streetlights blinked like fireflies, all the way to his own part of town where everything was completely dark, lit only by his headlights and patterned with the shadows of trees. Past the stretch of street on his block that he always tried to avoid looking at so that he didn't have to think about what had happened there on a winter night all those years ago.

There were so many parts of this town he loved—his friends and their families, all their traditions. The coziness of places like Gracie's and Insomnia. But he hated the way Westview was ruled by secrets and status and appearances. He didn't like the part of himself that felt like he needed to prove something to other people. People who judged him, didn't even care about him.

And then, at home, he wondered, as he clicked *submit* on his Walcott application and thought about spending tomorrow with Angela instead of his friends, if he was really so different from all those people after all.

***

Angela was already there, waiting by her car when Owen pulled into the small parking lot behind the bank. She was dressed in dark jeans and a lake-blue shirt that matched her eyes and reminded Owen of summer afternoons.

"Thanks for coming," she said, holding out a cup of coffee from Gracie's.

"You remembered," he said, then wished he hadn't. "Thanks."

She looked at him for what felt like a long time and Owen had to remind himself that she couldn't actually read his thoughts right now, all the feelings swirling in his head. He took a sip of coffee.

They walked out of the parking lot to Main Street. He stole a glimpse over at Angela, who still looked deep in thought.

"I heard you're on Homecoming Court," Owen said, the first thing he could think of to break the silence. "Are you excited?"

Angela didn't say anything at first, playing with her

hair as they walked, looking like she was trying to decide how to answer.

"Not really," she said finally.

"Why not?" He was surprised she was telling him this. He'd expected that she would be excited, or at least pretend to be.

She watched the cars driving by for a moment. Exhaled. "I'm not really excited about any of that this year," she said quietly, like she was confessing her darkest secret.

Her eyes darted to Owen's face, watching for a reaction. When he didn't say anything she continued. "Spirit Week and Homecoming is always such a big deal for my friends. We always plan our costumes in advance, coordinate everything, go shopping together. We always have to have the best costumes. It was always so much fun. And I thought it would be this year, too, since it's our last year. But last week, when we went shopping, it all just felt like a huge waste of time and effort. And it feels even worse because everyone wants everything about this year to be special. We don't have another chance to top this one if it's not as great as we all built it up to be. And that takes all the fun out of it."

The moment she stopped talking, she looked like she regretted it. Like she'd said too much.

"I know what you mean," Owen said. "There's a lot of pressure on this year."

She seemed to relax a little. Gave him a small smile. "I'm glad I'm not the only one who feels that way," she said softly. There was something sad in her eyes.

"My friend Lucie made us promise to make this year memorable," Owen added.

"Cassie did the same thing. I appreciate the sentiment but sometimes it feels like a little too much," Angela admitted.

"She's been making us these playlists to commemorate everything we do lately."

She held up her phone and Owen could see a long list of playlists with labels like *October* and *Monday Morning* and *Paige's Party.*

"It's nice of her," Angela added quickly, almost defensively, as if afraid he was judging Cassie. "I just don't think every moment needs to be special."

A notification popped up on her screen. "Look. She just sent me a new one for tonight. We're going to a party at Walcott."

She pressed play. The playlist was titled *Walcott Party* and as the sound of upbeat pop music poured out, bubbling like champagne, Owen felt like he'd been pulled into her world. She and her friends were this song, the music playing on the radio with the windows down to let summer wash all over their skin, and on city rooftops where everything glittered, Westview in the palm of their hands and the world at their feet. He could imagine what it would be like to be part of her group, all those girls with their shiny hair and sparkly dresses, boys who dressed better for school than he did for special occasions. Their lives all looked so beautiful. He pictured them all crowded into one of the dorm rooms he'd seen on his tour of Walcott with cinderblock walls and narrow twin beds.

Sometimes he wondered how someone who had everything could seem so unhappy.

He wondered if Dillon knew everything she was telling him right now, things she didn't seem to be able to talk about with her friends. He felt a little guilty.

He tried not to think about what it meant that even though she'd opened up to him so quickly now, he knew she would ignore him the next time they saw each other at school and he'd feel that familiar stab of hurt, a sinking feeling in his stomach. At the football game, when she didn't seem to care who saw them together, he'd wondered if everything would change. But it hadn't.

Angela shut off the music as they waited to cross the street, that thoughtful expression settling over her face again. Owen wished he could think of something else to say to her but the silence between them felt more comfortable now.

Their first stop was a narrow shop filled with expensive cosmetics. The woman at the register rushed over to give Angela a hug, ignoring Owen. The two of them talked for a few minutes while Owen stared silently at the glass bottles of perfume lining the marble counter.

"Anyway, this is our new skincare set," the woman explained, producing a beautifully wrapped gift basket from under the register. She handed the basket to Owen, then presented a small bag to Angela. "And here are some samples of our new products for you. Let me know what you like and I'll set it aside."

"Thank you," Angela said politely. "And thank you for donating this, we really appreciate it."

"Anytime," the woman said, smiling. "I'm really looking forward to the gala. Say hello to your parents for me!"

"We should probably put this in the car," Angela suggested once they were outside. Back in the parking lot, she opened her trunk and Owen saw that it was full of other small bags from the shop they'd just left, along with a tangle of sparkly dresses and strappy shoes.

"One of your Spirit Week costumes?" Owen asked, indicating a bright pink wig spilling out of a large bag from a party store in the same mall as Madison.

She nodded.

"What are you going as?" he asked as they continued back onto Main Street.

"I'm sworn to secrecy."

Owen laughed.

"I'm serious," Angela said. "Cassie is always afraid that someone is going to steal our ideas. We all had to promise not to tell anyone."

"You're right, though, your friends always have the best costumes," Owen said, remembering all the elaborate group costumes they'd worn over the years.

"I don't think I've ever seen you dress up."

He wished that his heart didn't skip a beat when she said that. He was surprised she'd noticed. But maybe it wasn't difficult to notice one of the few people who didn't dress up for Spirit Week. He shrugged. "I'm not really into costumes."

Angela smiled. "Fair. But this is your last chance, you know..."

"That's one thing I don't think I'll have any regrets about."

"Do you really want to take that risk?" She was laughing a little, eyes sparkling.

All of Main Street was decorated for fall with amber hay bales and pumpkins in the doorways, plaid bows and red and white bunting strung across windows. Everything was yellow with autumn leaves, drenching the trees that lined the street and soaking the sidewalk like paint. It made him think of how Madison was ready for winter, his world all dressed up for two different seasons. Time felt strange now, somehow fast and slow at the same time. He wished he could speed up the bad parts like taking standardized tests and worrying about college, and slow down everything that was good, all the late-night conversations with his friends and digging through old archives for Tricentennial Committee projects, the feeling of holding history in his hands and discovering forgotten stories.

And today, with Angela, her smile, her hair in the breeze, con-fessing things like they were friends again.

They continued down Main Street, collecting the donations Angela had procured for the silent auction—gift cer-tificates from restaurants and boutiques, a basket of wine and charcuterie from Westview Wines, a necklace from the jew-elry store. Everyone seemed to know everything about Angela. They asked her if she was excited for the gala next week, con-gratulated her on being selected for Homecoming Court, told her to say hello to her parents. And Owen watched her put on a version of herself that didn't match who she was once they stepped back outside, blazing autumn all around them. The way she held herself around them was different. She was taller somehow. Her movements were slow and precise, almost cal-culated like she was picturing what the moment looked like instead of living it. They all looked at her like she was an entire world, oceans and constellations, and Owen could see in her eyes that she was miles away.

He stood off to the side while she chatted with the staff at Westview's new fitness club. Everything there was sleek, all soft-gray and white and it reminded him more of a fancy hotel than a gym.

The sound of laughter echoed along the staircase and a group of girls Owen recognized from school descended into the lobby. He could see them staring at him, and then they lit up as soon as they saw Angela. Immediately, they were at her side, laughing and chattering, and Angela kept that perfect fake smile on her lips the entire time.

As the girls left, one of them glanced back and looked curiously from Angela to Owen, eyes lingering on Owen. The door slammed and he could feel his face burning.

"That's almost everything," Angela said when they left a few minutes later, looking through a list on her phone. Her voice was tight and clipped now. "Everyone else I spoke with already brought over their donations so this is our last one today."

They were standing outside a dress shop. Three mannequins wore long red dresses in the window. Angela glanced from the shop to Owen.

"It would be better if I go in here myself," she said. "I'll drop everything off at Jan's office on my way home."

He felt all the hope and happiness from today drain away.

He'd read too much into all of this. There was nothing special about this afternoon. She just wanted someone to keep her company and there he was, because everyone in Westview did whatever Angela Witney wanted. Of course she'd told him how she really felt about all the pressure of this year because to her, he was just a nobody who wouldn't care. Who wouldn't tell anyone.

And even if he did, no one would believe him. One of those names you shouldn't trust. She gave him her secrets like a message in a bottle, tossed out to the ocean to forget, to turn into sea glass.

And as soon as people noticed them together, all her walls went back up because he didn't fit into her world.

He had to stop overthinking every moment he spent with her.

"I'll see you at school, then," he said quietly and walked back to his car. He drove home slowly through this postcard-pretty town. Old white churches. The red-brick clock tower. Gold fields and the stone bridge that crossed so much reservoir that all the blue seemed to go on forever.

There were so many secrets in Westview. Owen had plenty of his own and knew plenty of others. Some secrets weren't worth sharing; they seemed small and insignificant.

Others ached to think about, hurt even more to talk about so he drowned them deep within himself. And still others, like that one he'd discovered on a slow, sleepy summer day, could cause ripples. But there were so many reasons not to tell, he thought, picturing Angela as he looked at Westview and all its blue.

11

The senior class Homecoming float took up almost all of Jocelyn Tremont's driveway. The lights were on in the garage, with cardboard and newspaper spread out over the floor, cans of spray paint strewn everywhere. A group of Angela's classmates were already there, busy moving pieces of furniture onto the float, which Jocelyn's parents were helping secure to the surface. Music from a playlist carefully curated by Cassie spilled from the garage into the autumn air.

"Hey, Angela!" Jocelyn greeted her, all paint-splattered. "I'm so glad you could make it!"

"You know I'd never miss this," Angela answered with her practiced smile. "It's tradition. And it's our senior year."

"Don't talk about that, it's so sad," Jocelyn said with a dramatic sigh. "But just another reason to keep up our winning streak. We can't lose the float competition our last year."

"Definitely not."

"So there are snacks over there if you want some," Jocelyn continued, pointing to a table against the back wall of the garage. "And we have a few extra T-shirts if you need one so you don't ruin your clothes."

"I've got one, thanks though." Angela reached into her bag for her old Walcott T-shirt, pulled it over her blouse.

"Perfect. We actually don't have too much to do today since we finished almost everything earlier this week. You have to see what Skyler's doing, this is amazing."

Skyler Gibbs was sitting by herself at a small table, surrounded by boxes of craft supplies. On the table she had sculpted Styrofoam into a plump, slightly lopsided layer cake, thick paint strokes textured like buttercream frosting, heavy with little red and white roses and hearts. Tiny fake macarons the color of peonies and buttercups tumbled down the sides, interspersed with brightly striped candies. Beside it, she'd constructed platters of tiny desserts and tea sandwiches, all fake sugary pastel.

"Wow," said Angela. "These look great. Do you need any help?"

"Sure," Skyler answered cheerfully. She moved a box off of the chair next to her. "Here, sit down. I've already made all of the designs so we just need to finish painting and decorating them. Don't worry about making them look perfect."

They worked in silence for a while. She and Skyler had never been close friends. She was one of those people who had been part of Angela's larger social circle since middle school but had never made it into her and Cassie's smaller group.

As she worked, Angela felt herself relaxing slowly. She dusted fake cookies with pink glitter instead of sugar, topped plastic pastries with pom-pom cherries and whipped cream constructed from fluffy cotton filling. She made a spun sugar sculpture from starry gold wire. She felt like she was part of this now, not like she was watching the world she was the center of from a distance and wondering why she wasn't as happy as she was last year.

Angela belonged here, everyone knew that.

She took a break to wash the paint off her hands in the house, ducking into the bathroom off the kitchen and just managing to avoid Cooper Lyman, who was helping himself to a can of soda from the refrigerator. She'd dated Cooper for almost six months during freshman year and after she broke up with him, he'd spent weeks trying to convince Cassie to go out with him. That made her so angry looking back, like they were interchangeable.

Angela scrubbed her hands with lavender soap, washing away the drops of paint. Watched all the color swirling down the drain.

Cooper was standing in the doorway between the house and the garage when Angela left the bathroom. He was talking to Paige, who was looking up at him with her eyes wide, twirling a strand of her long, black hair.

"Look who's here," he said when he saw Angela, his tone mocking, fake-enthusiastic in a way that made her dislike him even more. "Help us settle a debate. I don't think our float fits this year's theme. *Alice in Wonderland* isn't a fairy tale. Paige says it is. What do you think?"

Paige flashed her a knowing smile as if she expected Angela to side with her because they were friends. Because they were together in the exclusive Westview High School social circle that everyone else wanted to be part of.

You're not my friend, Angela wanted to tell her. *You were just in the right place at the right time.*

"I guess it depends on how you define a fairy tale," she said instead. "But maybe you should have had this debate before we built the float."

She joined Skyler but as she picked up a paintbrush, the feeling of contentment was gone. It suddenly felt pointless to sit here making little details that no one was going to be able to see as the float made its way down sleepy streets that only awoke for this one day each year. She felt like she was trapped in a snow globe of color and sugar.

She and Skyler climbed on the float and set the table in the dark. The stars were bright above the treetops, the sky clear with a full moon staining the neighborhood silver.

"I think we're done now," Skyler called to their classmates, who had just finished cleaning up the garage.

Four autumns of painting little worlds onto platforms in Jocelyn's driveway and this one was their best. A long table surrounded with mismatched chairs they'd painted vivid colors. Teacups and teapots with stripes and polka dots. Patterned paper lanterns suspended from vines and rainbow lights. Tall potted plants along the sides, fields of cardboard mushrooms and tangerine tissue paper flowers. There was an ornate clock with its numbers jumbled and crooked signposts pointing to destinations in every direction. Cake stands piled high with Styrofoam desserts.

"Wait!" said Cassie, helping them both down onto the driveway. "We have to sign it."

On the side of the float was a sign that said *Seniors in Wonderland*. They all took turns signing, leaving little drawings and messages and their names in bold colors like they did every year.

When it was Angela's turn, she dipped her brush into red paint and paused. Then she just wrote *Angela* in loopy letters, paint glistening on the almost-cursive, a little flourish at the end. Her name was already all over this town.

***

She woke up on the day of Homecoming and the gala to the sound of her mother knocking on her bedroom door, swinging it open before Angela had a chance to respond.

"I thought we could have breakfast together," she said cheerfully.

Angela rubbed her eyes. After they finished the float last night, they'd all decided to celebrate by building a fire by the reservoir. She'd sat wrapped up in plaid blankets with Dillon and watched the water fill with reflections of flames and stars until her head was hazy with beer she didn't even like. As the small hours swept over them, black and blue, it felt like the whole town was silent and sleeping except for their voices, their laughter in ripples across the reservoir.

Now morning sun was shining in through the thin curtains and she could still smell the fire and autumn night in her hair, lingering across her pillowcase. Soon Westview would be filled up with the sound of laughter and cheers and chatter.

She sat up.

"I'll be downstairs in a few minutes," she answered.

She pulled her hair back and scrubbed the mascara and eyeliner from her face. She looked at her phone and saw that Jocelyn and Cassie had both posted pictures of the group last night. So she did what she would have done last year. She left comments, little pink hearts on some of them. *So excited for today!* she texted the other girls on the senior court. She sent Dillon the same message, too.

Downstairs, the kitchen table looked picture-perfect with bowls of yogurt and berries and a plate of flaky croissants alongside a pitcher of orange juice and a little jar of strawberry jam. Her mother brought over a mug of coffee for herself and placed a mug of tea in front of Angela.

"This brings back so many memories of my senior Homecoming," she said, sitting down and placing a spoonful of berries on her plate. "I'm so proud of you."

Days like today were when Victoria Witney was in

her element, days steeped in town tradition, when her perfect family and perfect life were on display. She was already dressed for the parade in a red dress and pearl earrings. On her wrist was a charm bracelet with a tiny silver W that every former Homecoming and Prom Queen in Westview had, a reminder even decades later that they were still part of an exclusive town tradition. She was energized and smiling, ready to mingle with their friends and neighbors.

Angela's father was away for work, but if he was here, he'd be the same way. He always remembered the little details of people's lives, their interests. He was an expert at small talk in a way that made people feel important.

Today, Angela had to be perfect. She could already feel the pressure building up inside her head like storm clouds.

"I think you should curl your hair," her mother continued as Angela took some yogurt. She was looking at Angela as if she was really looking at herself in a mirror. "It frames your face better. And curls always look so nice on you in pictures."

"You're right," Angela forced herself to say brightly.

"Did I ever show you pictures from my Homecoming?"

Before she could even answer, the pictures were there in front of her. A teenage girl who looked exactly like Angela, hair curled and lips red. On the football field with a crown on her head. In a simple black dress and the same crown with balloons and crepe paper taped to the wall in the background. The same group of people were in every picture, smiling like they had everything in the world.

"Who are they?"

"That's Helen," her mother said. Angela could see the resemblance between her and Rose, the same red hair, the same smile. "Trent Prescott, Laura Kent and your dad."

"You never mentioned being friends with Trent Prescott."

"It was a long time ago," her mother said. "We haven't kept in touch for years." She held up another picture, two girls smiling on a staircase. "Alex and me."

If Angela had seen it without any context, she might have thought it was a picture of her and Cassie she'd forgotten about. She smiled and took a picture of it on her phone to send to Cassie.

She looked back at one of the group pictures. She wondered what their lives had been like at that moment. Her parents, who hadn't fallen in love yet. She wondered if Trent had known then that he'd leave, that the rest of them would stay here.

"Did you always want to stay here when you were in high school?" Angela asked.

"I always wanted to go to Walcott."

The way she paused, just a second too long before the word *wanted* made Angela look up.

"Do you ever regret not leaving?"

"Of course not," her mother answered. Her voice and expression didn't waver but, for a second, Angela saw it. She saw beyond the pretty clothes and energy that infused the community's lifeblood. And she saw all of the roots and anchors that kept her in place. Something there that said that once, maybe more than once, Victoria Witney wanted to leave.

"You should start getting ready now," her mother added before Angela could say anything else.

Angela put on one of Cassie's new playlists while she shaped her hair into long, loose curls. She changed into a black dress and heels she knew were going to sink into the softness of the football field. Smoothed poppy-bright lipstick on her mouth.

She looked perfect, just like she was supposed to. But she imagined the changes she'd make to her dress if she could. Rip out the scratch of lace at the neckline, make the skirt flare a little more dramatically so that if she twirled, it would spin around her body like a storm-spurred sea.

"Beautiful," her mother said from the doorway.

Angela felt her heart sink. She turned her back on the girl in the mirror. Years ago, she'd figured out all the best ways to garner praise from her parents, from everyone in this town. She used to collect those words and hold them tight to her chest. But now, she wished that attention could be for something different. Not just for looking pretty or dating the right boy or following family traditions.

Wasn't she more than that?

And yet, when she saw the small black box in her mother's hand, she felt a glint of pride. A tiny, sickening sliver of validation.

Her mother was holding the box out now, her fingers warm against Angela's. "This is for you."

Inside, a set of diamond earrings shaped like teardrops. They'd been passed down by the women in her family for years, promised to Angela so many times growing up as she sat cross-legged on her mother's bed, watching her get ready for parties.

"They're gorgeous," Angela said, sad and thrilled at once. "Thank you."

Her mother smiled. "Put them on. You should leave soon so you aren't late."

She walked away and Angela hung the teardrops from her ears. In the mirror she could see all the little worlds of light they held inside of them, cities constructed of glitter and star-dust.

She stood there for a moment and practiced smiling until she almost believed it, because her own little world was made up of Homecoming parades and the colors of New England fall mornings, fireflies blinking all the way home on late-night drives and fireworks glowing over the town square on the last day of the year. It was made up of pretty diamonds and summers surrounded by the bluest water and those things weren't supposed to make you feel sad.

***

It was sunny out, and Main Street was closed off for the parade. The meeting point was already crowded when Angela arrived and something about it made her inexplicably nervous. Members of the marching band raced around in search of mis-placed music and a group of freshman girls dressed as fairy-tale villains in dark green and glitter and black were posing for pic-tures atop their float.

Cassie and Adam were already there, greeting the rest of the court as they arrived, iced coffee in hand. They looked just as perfect together as Angela and Dillon were supposed to and she thought for a moment that the two of them should win even though she knew they wouldn't.

"Is Dillon here yet?" Angela asked as Cassie took pic-tures with the sophomore court.

Adam shook his head. "I haven't seen him."

Angela looked at her phone and tried to hide her annoyance. With the whole town watching, everything needed to go right today. The pressure that had nagged at her temples all morning was intensifying. She could imagine the whispers rippling down the street if people saw her looking unhappy, if Dillon showed up late, if they saw her fighting with Dillon or if Dillon didn't show up at all. She'd be able to hear their voices all around her as she rode through this blue and evergreen town, down a street closed off for her and her friends.

If Westview was going to talk about her, it was going to be because she chose to put her name on its lips, selected the words they were saying.

"Angela, come here," said Cassie, pulling her into a picture with a group of their classmates who were waiting to get on the float, all of them in costume.

She posed for the picture and smiled like a summer day. She wasn't supposed to feel anything else.

Dillon came jogging across the parking lot as they were about to get into the cars. "Sorry I'm late. I slept through my alarm," he said, wrapping his arms around Angela. His hair was still damp from the shower and he was wearing too much cologne. "Are you excited?"

She nodded, stretching her smile as far as she possibly could. She got into the car and perched on the rear deck and suddenly as Dillon followed her, the thought of performing with him for this entire town was exhausting.

"Wait," she said. "I want to go with Cassie."

He looked at her for just a moment too long for her to believe that he didn't care, but then he glanced at Adam and shrugged.

"Go ahead," he told Cassie.

She climbed into the car, smiling. She draped an arm around Angela and made the world smell of berries and jasmine.

"I'm so happy," Cassie whispered. They took a picture together.

Angela and Cassie had been on Homecoming Court every year. This was exactly how this was supposed to go. She remembered how proud she'd always felt when her name was announced. It was always fun to dress up, to ride through town with everyone looking at her. Now she just felt sick.

The cars started moving, slowly following the floats. Her entire world was lining the street, watching. She could see some of her teachers standing together, a group of Town Council members, friends and former friends and neighbors and classmates. She noticed Trent Prescott watching with his parents. Behind them, Westview was a contrast of scarlet leaves and dark pine, and in the distance, Angela could see the glimmering movement of reservoir water. The eastern border was just a few miles up the road, and no part of her life existed beyond those map lines.

She made her face ache with her smile. She waved, waved, waved all the way down the street like royalty. She could see the reactions when they saw her. She was everything they all wanted to be.

Her mother was standing with Cassie's parents and their extended families. And for a moment, Angela recalled childhood dance recitals, squinting through bright-hot stage lights into an audience hidden in darkness and locating her parents sitting there with flowers, raising their hands in a wave.

"We're the last ones for a while," Cassie said as they waved to their families. Everyone was there—the older cousins Angela remembered watching in Homecoming parades down this same street, all grown up now with degrees from Walcott, beginning to start families of their own. Aunts and uncles with the younger cousins who were still in elementary school.

"Maya's next," Angela said, smiling at their cousin, who was taking pictures of them from the side of the road, red ribbons in her hair. "I can't believe she'll be in middle school next year." Her old self would have wanted to teach Maya how to dress, how to act like her and Cassie so that they'd be watching her in this parade someday. Just like their cousins standing there now had done for them.

There were so many little girls watching with their eyes wide and she remembered being that age, watching parades of perfect, glittery girls stream by. Now she was one of them.

She wanted to jump out of the car and tell them she wasn't perfect, that this was all fake. Save someone from suffocating in small-town whispers. There was a whole world outside of Westview and they could chase after anything they wanted there, she'd say. A whole world where they were allowed to be messy and flawed and make mistakes without everyone they knew watching all the time.

She wished someone had told her that, some runaway princess with torn-up maps. Instead of handing her a legacy of chasing perfection.

The parade ended at the football field. She and Cassie lined up with the rest of the court. She kissed Dillon because every eye was on them.

Brady Davis and Staci Lyman, last year's King and Queen, were there to announce their names and crown this year's winners. Both of them were studying at Walcott now. They were both wearing their crowns from last year and they somehow looked so much older than they did at graduation just a few months ago. She'd seen them both at Walcott parties in the meantime and she hadn't noticed that until now. And then she realized that if she won, she was going to have to come back and do this next year.

She watched the freshman court stride across the field as Brady and Staci called their names. She tried to block out everything around her, all the red and white and blue and green and cheers.

She didn't hear them say her name but they must

have because suddenly she and Dillon were moving. Her heels pressed into the field. Everything was blurry. *Perfect perfect perfect* singing across her consciousness.

The court stood there together, a row of picture-perfect people. Cassie reached over and squeezed her hand as they all smiled for photographers. Then Brady unfolded a square of paper and it was time.

"Westview, put your hands together for this year's Homecoming King and Queen," he said into the microphone, little echoes of his voice floating out toward all the shiny cars in the parking lot.

A drumroll, starting out slow like the prelude to a rainstorm, speeding up to the frantic pace of a downpour. Angela wished the sky would open up all over this field.

And then, for a moment, the entire town went silent, and Westview was just this: sunlight lingering across the slow curve of power lines. Quiet water and trees in jewel tones. And bleachers of people she'd known for seventeen years blurring into magazine cut-outs as they held their breath waiting for something else to talk about.

It was so quiet, and in a heartbeat, it wasn't.

"Dillon Winsor and Angela Witney!"

The town exploded into applause. It was like her name was up in lights, the way it always was here. She could hear the syllables flying around in the air, newspaper headlines draped all over the trees. She was drenched in words.

Dillon squeezed her hand and they stepped forward together to be crowned. She never stopped smiling as Staci put a plastic tiara glittering with rhinestones on her head and handed her a red bouquet of roses. She clutched them to her chest.

Someday she was going to wake up in the middle of the night with this smile still frozen on her face.

The whole town was lit up with whispers and camera flashes.

She thought about Cherwell, where she could be anonymous. She could stand in the middle of a street there and shout her own name to the sky and it would just drift away, unweighted by all the expectations of this place.

Dillon had his arm around her. For a heartbeat, Angela wished he could see the gray clouds crowding her mind, hear the torrent of twisted words in her thoughts. And in all the noise around them, she couldn't tell if what she really wanted was to pull him even closer or push him far away.

She let his arm stay, holding her here so she couldn't sink or float. She smiled and smiled and hoped she'd never see these pictures, the way the cameras captured this version of herself.

***

The seniors won the float contest and Westview won the football game.

And there she was, caught up in the moment with them all, a girl in a crown under small-town skies. The whole world was gone except Westview, a storm of confetti, the smell of popcorn in the air. The entire town celebrating. The mood infectious. The way this always used to be.

She wanted to keep this feeling from fading away. To be that girl made up of summer, the girl Westview wanted her to be.

She and Dillon went back to his house because no one was home and she tried to tell herself that today was different, that she wasn't running back to him right now.

At his house in the summer, there were ceramic pots of tall basil on the patio and flowers in the windows. On the few days they were there instead of the beach house, they'd play music she could hear when she swam underwater, her hair swirling long like kelp around her face until she emerged to fill her lungs with air and sunshine. On the deck, the sun dried her hair into curls like ocean waves. Sometimes they'd lie in the soft grass and watch the clouds chase each other across a sky bluer than the seas could ever imagine. Watercolor flowers blooming inside her eyelids when she closed them. Back then, she was in love with his lips and the feeling of his hands on her skin.

And now, in his bed. Sheets crinkled like newsprint beneath them. She could feel everything crashing down around her.

She should have known that feeling wouldn't last long, that the energy of this whole town would burn out when she remembered who she really was.

"You're so beautiful," he said, and she wished he would stop looking at her.

She stared at the ceiling. She could feel the weight of sunlight on her face.

"Why aren't you happy?" He was sitting up next to her now, frowning.

"I don't have to be happy all the time."

"You're Homecoming Queen," Dillon said, confusion in his voice. "Isn't that what you wanted?"

She didn't know how to explain it to him. At this time last year, she'd floated around this town, daydreaming about today. And when she'd pictured it, this was exactly what she had imagined. Her and Dillon, Homecoming King and Queen. Senior year, when everything was theirs.

But she wasn't that girl anymore. And he wasn't who she'd thought he'd been.

"You're right. It's what I wanted," she said, forcing herself to smile, because that was easier than telling him the truth. Less complicated. He only wanted the shiny version of her. A happy girl he could kiss and take pictures with and show off to everyone in this town.

"Good," he said. "I can't wait for tonight."

He kissed her and again, for a moment, the world stopped like it used to. But then it all came back and she could feel words all over her skin, pressing nerves and bones together. Letters in her bloodstream, the start of an implosion.

She picked her clothes up from the sunshine on the floor. Put them on her body, let the warmth saturate her skin.

"I need to get ready. I'll see you later," she told him and she drove home with tears in her eyes and the plastic tiara on the passenger seat.

***

Sometimes Angela liked getting ready for events more than actually attending the event itself. Even though she was dreading the Tricentennial Gala, she loved her entire outfit. She loved the process of putting together a look. Last weekend, she'd found the perfect pair of shoes for tonight while on a date with Dillon in Cherwell. She wore pink lipstick and they'd wandered around the waterfront, watching the sun sink behind the skyline and city lights glow gold against calm water and cobblestones. They ate dinner at a nearby restaurant, in the quiet conservatory with long mirrors that reflected infinities of blossoms and vines and galaxies of twinkling lights, a solar system of white flowers and manmade stars in place of a ceiling. Angela was in love with almost all of it, the city and the way the restaurant made her feel so grown up but she couldn't shake the feeling that she didn't belong there with Dillon. Even though that night he'd been the witty, charming version of him she'd fallen for. In the mirrors' reflections, they looked so perfect together from far away.

She'd spotted the shoes in a shop window after they left the restaurant, tall and shiny and strappy, the exact color of her dress. She tried them on, and they were, of course, perfect. She held Dillon's hand on the way back to his car but she didn't mean it when she kissed him. She'd felt that way at his house this afternoon, too, and she almost didn't want to see him again tonight.

Now she stood in Cassie's bathroom with Naomi, Rose and Paige, teasing her hair into the same loose curls she'd worn earlier to the parade. Loud music played from the tiny speaker on the counter, a collection of rhythms and lyrics that reminded her of the smell of summer thunderstorms and late nights driving through small towns whose names she couldn't remember but she'd memorized what they felt like. Sound pouring out of open windows and lighting up empty roads until the notes touched the trees. And now, the leaves fire-bright outside and a plastic tiara she didn't deserve.

"Okay, here's the plan for tonight," said Cassie, standing in the doorway between her bedroom and her bathroom with her hair curled like wind and lips lava-red. She was wearing pajama shorts and a cropped shirt that showed off the anchor tattoo she'd gotten on her hip over the summer when she visited the Winsors' beach house. Back when they were *Adam & Cassie* and *Dillon & Angela* and summer days were sand and saltwater taffy, sneaking into bars and sunrise conversations on old docks. "We'll go to the gala for an hour or so. We'll come back here and change, then go to Adam's for the party..."

Angela's party dress was waiting in Cassie's closet. Short and tight, all dark sparkles. She was so tired of changing in and out of all these different personas today, in and out of dresses that felt like masks. She walked away from the mirror, back into Cassie's bedroom and carefully lifted her gala dress out of its garment bag.

She put on the dress and stared at her reflection as

Naomi helped her zip up the back. Slid her shoes on while her friends finished changing. Then they all stood at the mirror together.

Five faces with red lips, dressed in metallics and jewel tones.

"Almost everyone I've talked to is wearing black. We're going to stand out," Rose said. "In a good way," she added, which they all knew was unnecessary because they only stood out in a good way. Everyone wanted to be them.

Angela studied their backwards faces. They all looked exactly the same, and so would everyone in Westview tonight, regardless of what they were wearing. A whole room of mirror images, everyone trying to keep up with everyone else to survive here. Rose and Paige even had identical earrings. The same lipstick.

She reached into her bag for her own earrings, the diamond teardrops from her parents, and realized she'd left them in her bedroom when she'd taken them off to shower this afternoon.

"I have to go home and get my earrings," she said.

"Are you sure? You can borrow some of mine," Cassie offered.

"No, I have to wear these. I'll just drive back and meet you at the gala," Angela said. "I'll see you soon."

Even though their houses were within walking distance of each other, just a few roads apart, she'd driven to Cassie's earlier with everything she needed for the gala and Adam's party. Careful not to step on the hem of her dress, she got into her car and backed out of the driveway. She'd walked home this way so many times beneath dusk and starlight she could trace her footsteps with her eyes closed. On summer nights to cricket harmonies and in snowstorms that made the road and sky blur together.

The house was empty but it smelled faintly of the white candle her mother had been burning earlier, extinguished pear and freesia still lingering in the air. She was probably out for a drink with her friends before the gala.

She wouldn't have admitted it to him, but Angela was disappointed that her father couldn't make it to see what she'd been a part of. He would normally never miss an event in Westview but this trip was essential to the company's latest efforts to expand internationally.

She thought about the Witney Estates in northern Westview, identical houses with tall arched windows and sleek backyard patios with reservoir views. Her father's last project here before the company had started expanding beyond New England, stylish apartments with amenities in up-and-coming cities, cozy chalets for mountain getaways, and long, low villas blooming among the colors of the deserts. Someday, her last name would join skylines in other countries. Her name would build skyscrapers on ground her feet had never touched. Someone was going to rent an apartment with a name like Witney Towers in a place so far away they wouldn't even know who the Witneys were. They'd look out their window to see their city spread out before them, all the lights that made it alive, the silhouettes of famous landmarks, while here, Angela Witney looked at a reservoir.

The earrings were on her dresser. She put them on and looked in the mirror one last time. Practiced smiling. She was shiny and sparkly tonight, a perfect girl with everything bright ahead of her.

She tripped going down the stairs and stopped in the kitchen to fix her shoe. The mail was out on the table—an invitation, some bills. The latest issue of a travel magazine her parents subscribed to and kept in the guest room upstairs.

Angela sat down, flipping through the magazine until

she found what Trent Prescott had written. She remembered Owen telling her that there were plenty of people who left here, she just hadn't been paying attention.

Lately she'd wondered if people who left forgot they were from Westview when they were oceans and skies away, if a place like this deserved a flicker of reminiscence as they were taking in the world.

She wondered how people remembered small towns. Maybe they carried around the worst of their toxins, exaggerated by years and miles apart, or maybe they romanticized their memories. She wondered if Westview roads and fields were still tattooed into their consciousness or if it was all hazy, everything out of focus.

Maybe it was just easy to erase places like these from yourself. Maybe when your world got bigger, the only place you'd ever known before was disposable.

But returning, she thought, couldn't be as simple. Different maps drawn all over your heart, insides full of pictures that no one else could see in a town that never changed and remembered everything. It must feel like getting hit with cold water. Stranded in a snowstorm.

Reading now, it was like his words were drenched in photographs. Paragraphs and pages describing beautiful places bursting with colors that could break hearts, every place so, so alive in ways she knew Westview could never be. Snapshots into lives and experiences she couldn't even begin to fathom.

Angela thought about how she'd just stood upstairs practicing smiles. And she understood why he'd written himself out of a small town that lived and dreamed in shades of blue and green. She imagined him inhaling the blaring colors of faraway places and scribbling all these words, sculpted into sleek columns in glossy magazines that landed in muted suburbs like paper airplanes. His face on televisions all over town, part of him always here, even when he wasn't.

She wondered if any part of this place was still home to him.

He wrote about places like people he loved. No one would ever write about Westview like that.

Angela could feel an ache to leave this place with every word, all the way to her bones.

The fabric of her dress felt heavy on her body as she went outside to her car. For a moment, she imagined driving anywhere else as fast as she could, a place where she hadn't memorized all the stoplights and none of the roads knew her name. But instead, she backed out of the driveway and followed the lines toward Main Street, stilettos shiny on the accelerator as she approached the last place in Westview she wanted to be, a glitter-lit gala loud with the sounds of clinking glasses and rumors playing like an orchestra.

12

In all the pictures from this morning, Angela looked stunning against the sea of red and white, her hair in loose curls. She was wearing a sparkly tiara and Dillon stood next to her, a fake gold and velvet crown on his head. They both looked absolutely perfect, the movie version of a high school couple.

There was something sad in her eyes, though, a contrast with her smile, just slightly too bright. All week, Owen had watched her parade through the hallways with her friends in their matching costumes. Hair streaked with red and faces painted for yesterday's pep rally. If he hadn't seen that expression on her face almost every time he saw her, Owen could have convinced himself that the camera had just caught her at exactly the wrong moment.

He wished he could stop thinking about her. Stop the way his heart sped up every time she was around, the way he felt when he smelled her perfume, because there was no way Angela Witney ever thought about him. But then there were moments like earlier this week, at the Tricentennial Committee's last meeting before the gala. She'd looked over at him as everyone else argued for too long over a detail so insignificant he couldn't even remember it now. Made a face like she was trying not to laugh, like this was their own private joke and for the rest of the night he was floating, everything painted gold and the same blue as her eyes.

"Owen!" There was a knock at his bedroom door. "Mom wants you to come downstairs."

He opened the door and Haley was standing there with Sophia, both dressed up for the gala.

"She wants to take pictures of us before we leave," Haley added.

He followed them downstairs. They'd both styled their hair like Angela's, he realized, and were wearing the bracelets Lucie had made for them.

His mother was in the kitchen, taking a pie out of the oven to bring to dinner with Declan's family tonight. He couldn't blame her for skipping the gala—he'd once overheard her talking about how she'd learned who to avoid in this town and thinking about that made him hate Westview just a little bit. Owen probably wouldn't have gone, either, if he wasn't involved, and he knew his friends were only going because of him. The Tricentennial Committee had made the tickets free for all students as a sort of peace offering after the complaints about the Homecoming dance; they were expecting most of their fundraising to come from donations from families like the Witneys anyway.

"Let me take one of the three of you," Sophia offered once they'd started taking pictures in the living room.

Owen and Haley stood on either side of their mother, smiling. He could feel the warmth of her arm across his back, hugging him close.

He'd gone on a run around the neighborhood with her this morning, which they'd done almost every day over the summer, both of them early risers. Owen liked to let air and adrenaline and the steady pace of his footsteps against the pavement calm his thoughts. He wondered if she felt the same way when she was running, a sense of power over the things that must have haunted her, too.

Sometimes he wished they could talk about it: all the things everyone in this town knew, the darkest secrets she didn't know he'd seen and heard, the way it all made him feel like he couldn't breathe.

But she'd rebuilt the world for the three of them and he was afraid to break it open again, to unleash all the pain and ugliness. It was easier to run. To pretend that now, everything was fine, because she seemed happiest when he was okay.

Angela was the first person Owen saw when he walked into the gala. She was wearing a gold-beaded dress, hair long and curled. She looked so elegant, he thought, all glitter and red lipstick in a lobby lined with mirrors and black-and-white photographs. She was mingling with the crowd, laughing and smiling but when he caught a glimpse of her alone for a moment as she turned to greet a newcomer, off guard, he could see it again, the hints of unhappiness on her face.

This room was like a white paper doll chain, almost everyone dressed in black and pearls and red ties.

"You're right, this is a lot nicer than Homecoming," said Lucie, coming up beside him in a shimmery teal jumpsuit, handmade silver bracelets stacked on her arm.

"Have you seen Declan and Max?"

Lucie shook her head. "Max just texted to say he's on his way but I haven't heard from Declan yet." She looked around. "Look, there's Theo and Brooke. Let's go say hi."

"Okay, I'll meet up with you in a few minutes. I should check in with Jan first to see if she needs any help," Owen said, scanning the room. He didn't see Angela anymore but he saw Dillon alone by the stairs and Jan was standing at the door, chatting with some of the other volunteers.

"Hi, Owen! You look great."

"Thanks. I just wanted to check if there was anything I could help out with."

"Yes, actually, that would be great. I think we're going to need some extra bid sheets for the silent auction. There should be some in my office upstairs. Would you mind getting them and putting them out? Then you're free for the night."

"No problem."

"Thank you so much. And thanks again for all your help setting up this morning. Everything looks perfect."

Owen had never been upstairs in Town Hall before. At the top of the sweeping staircase was a wide mezzanine with marble floors lit by carved sconces. The ceiling was deep blue, with a celestial map painted across it in gold, constellations and zodiac signs blooming from the glimmering lines of the ecliptic and the equator. From its center hovered a massive chandelier like suspended stars and frozen moonlight. Owen could see down into the gala as people started to move out of the lobby toward their tables in the main room. Everyone was glittering.

The loudness of the gala echoed up here but Owen felt like his footsteps were screaming across the empty floor. The doors all around the mezzanine were closed. None of them were labelled. The first two were locked. The third led to a bathroom. And then, the fourth.

One wall was all wide windows, filling the room with cloud-marbled pinks and orange-hazed sunset light. Angela was silhouetted against clean glass, looking out over the steeple-printed skyline. Her dress shimmered softly. She started slightly at the sound of the door and Owen's footsteps, then turned around and motioned at him to join her. He walked toward her, turning his back on the windows when he reached her.

The rest of the room was beautiful in the saddest way. Cream-colored walls, dark lines of paint stretching from ceiling to floor in remembrance of roads that no longer existed. Slanted script surrounded by dashed lines to mark vanished villages. He'd seen maps like this in the archives, Westview a century ago, before most of it was turned to water.

"It's hard to imagine all of this here now," she said, gazing at the walls. "I remember learning about this in school a long time ago. But no one in my family likes to talk about it."

Owen didn't know how to answer. He thought about everything he knew about this town but couldn't say, the hours he'd spent working in archives, looking at people in old photographs and wondering what their lives were like. The afternoon he'd realized the truth, slow summer rain outside, time still as he stared at those documents, almost too easy, too lucky. As if someone had wanted him to find them.

She was standing so close to him and she smelled like flowers and then she was holding his hand, soft lines of their palms pressed together. He thought of Dillon downstairs and that night on his steps in late August, the way Angela's closeness was cold. His skin was tingling like the worst clichés and as she led him closer to the map, he let go.

"There are actually a lot of towns with a similar story," he said, trying to focus his thoughts, remembering the pictures he'd seen of all those other drowned towns. Black-and-white then, blue and green now. All around the country, houses and streets turned into water, like lost cities without the legends.

"It's not just Westview," he continued.

Part of him hated himself for switching into history teacher mode. This was what so many people wanted, this closeness to Angela. He'd thought about it so many times. But something about the look on her face in this room made every-thing seem wrong.

"So the story they tell us is that in the early twentieth century, there was an increase in population and industrial growth in Cherwell and they needed to create new water sources to keep up with demand. The state decided to com-pletely flood one town and partially flood others for dams and reservoirs."

Angela was looking at the walls, not saying anything.

"Westview was the last town they chose, in the mid-1920s. People were devastated. No one ever thought it would happen here because they'd been told there were better places for it. So everyone—especially your family—tried to pre-vent it from happening. They knew people would lose their jobs, the homes they'd lived in for generations. They'd watched it happen in those other towns. But there was nothing they could do. And the same thing was happening in other places around the country—as cities developed, sometimes smaller towns paid the price."

Owen trailed his finger along a thin line marking a river. "They destroyed the mills that used to be here." There was one still remaining, close to his house, by a stone bridge spanning a section of reservoir. An abandoned building with a motionless waterwheel.

"This was all farmland," he continued, moving to trace the area. "Most of it was flooded. Some families burned their fields before they left." He imagined lush fields blazing amber and gold, smudging the sky with smoke. Scalded earth silenced by cold, still water, fenced in by trees and new roads.

He stepped back, pointed to the center of the map, and Angela's gaze followed. "The rest of the reservoir is there. Everything there was destroyed, then flooded—schools, churches, shops, hundreds of houses. All of those people had to leave. A lot of them moved here." He indicated a space on the adjacent wall.

"That's where I live."

"And that's why most of your neighbors are families who have lived here for years. They were able to rebuild most of the town there. But some people were forced to move out of town and find new jobs and places to live because they lost everything here. They had to start over completely."

Angela was silent. She stood there studying the map, all those lines.

"That's so sad," she said quietly.

He couldn't.

He couldn't tell her.

But the words were at the back of his lips now and Owen was going to burn this whole town down.

"That's not what really happened, though," he said quietly.

She looked at him. Eyes wide. He could almost see the map reflected in them.

"What do you mean?"

He took a deep breath, aware of every detail in the moment, the seconds of space between all those years of lies and the truth. The way the setting sun painted shadows and light across the walls, creating new roads and neighborhoods that would never exist. Glitter and gold all over Angela as she stood between an old map of an underwater town and its rebuilt remnants outside the windows. Little specks of dust softly spiraling in the air above them.

"That story isn't true. There was never supposed to be a reservoir in Westview. Your family is the only reason it happened."

The words were out there now, sharp and suspended in the air. He couldn't go back.

"What are you talking about?" Angela's voice was frantic. She grabbed his hand, nails pressing little moons into his skin.

"A lot of towns in this area were considered but Westview wasn't one of them," Owen said slowly. He couldn't believe he was saying this, especially to Angela, because as he sat there in silent archives, he'd known that he could never tell anyone.

She was staring at him and he felt like time had stopped.

"But then members of your family—a few generations back on your dad's side—threatened to expose a scandal that would destroy the careers of the people making the decision," Owen continued, trying to keep his voice from sounding bitter. "They orchestrated a deal to build the reservoir here, blackmailing them into buying their property for part of it and keeping quiet. And as far as everyone else here knew, Westview didn't have a choice; to them, it looked like the same thing that had happened in those other towns. Your family pretended they were trying to stop it. They led a campaign against it, but it was all for show. People trusted them and respected them, though, so they believed them. They didn't have a reason not to. They thought your family was standing up for Westview. So even when the reservoir happened, when it looked like they'd lost, they still got painted as heroes for trying to do something about it."

Angela let go of his hand and he could hear the sound of her inhale. Owen stared at the space on the wall where the center of town used to be. "It's part of so many families' histories. So even now, your family's version of the story is what everyone in this town knows."

The names of people not to trust were passed down like heirlooms here. That was how the Witneys had distracted from the truth. They'd made sure that everyone in Westview knew who to blame, everyone except themselves. And so for years, all the names of other people who had played a part in turning this place to water were repeated over and over by the powerful families here, a warning. Names like Emory.

"My mom grew up in Westview and left after high school," Owen said. "Her parents moved away, too. My dad wasn't from here but everyone knew who his family was because they'd been responsible for designing and constructing the reservoirs, here and in those other towns. When we moved back here, people who weren't even alive back then remembered. I still don't know if they expected that to happen."

At some point, he suspected it had become mostly about appearances. His family's life had never looked like the Witneys', all shiny and perfect. That, coupled with their history, made them an easy target. Easy to judge, easy to talk about because they didn't fit in here so the Witneys tried to keep them as far away as possible.

He remembered how so many people had treated his family like they were invisible. How no one had any idea what was really happening. He sometimes wondered if anyone would have bothered to help even if they did know. If they would have just looked away.

"Who else knows about this?" Angela asked. Owen could see it all washing over her. Panic in her voice.

"I haven't told anyone," Owen said quickly. "I'm not going to."

Her eyes on him. Blazing. "How did you find out?"

"Last year I worked on a project for the Cherwell archives. It's all there. Letters and photographs and documents. I don't know how they got there, if they're even supposed to be there ... Westview obviously did a better job covering it up."

Angela didn't answer. Maybe she thought he was lying.

She was going to ruin him now, Owen thought, like everyone else she got tired of, to protect herself and all the walls she built. His mouth felt dry, his words ringing in his ears.

He watched her cross the room, toward the windows and the sunset.

"This town is so small," she said after a moment.

He joined her at the window.

After what he'd just told her, some people might have said it like a threat. A reminder that they could just as easily find all his secrets, spread them across Westview like wildfire. But now she just sounded sad. Something in her face had shifted.

Looking outside, Owen could see that the shops were closed for the evening, glowing streetlamps shining shadows against pearl-draped mannequins in their windows. The streets were quiet, empty. Partly because so many people were downstairs, putting on a facade illuminated by candles and mirrors. And partly because people didn't travel to Westview to stay. They just passed through its sleepy streets on their way to glittering city destinations, all the places Angela wanted to run away to, because Westview was just a tiny dot on someone else's map. There were no hotels here. Just white-painted shops and rows of streetlights on roads with money and too-big houses and in the distance, lines of evergreen guarding inevitable blue.

This place was the entire world to some people, only small because of all the water.

Angela was quiet, watching him, and then, in the sunset-lit stillness of the map-painted room, she stood on her toes and her lips were on Owen's. Lipstick-smooth but sad-shaped.

Kissing her was almost like he'd always imagined, soft skin and the clean taste of mint, the spark of their lips together but something about it seemed wrong, like they were both trying to escape from themselves, lend each other knotted thoughts and loneliness, and Owen realized that this was everything he wanted and didn't at the same time.

He pulled away, trailed his fingertips away from the silk and beads.

Angela's cheeks were flushed and her hair was disheveled. There were so many emotions written all over her face and he wished he could think of what to say but none of this seemed right after everything he'd just told her. This shouldn't be happening, the truth still surrounding them like smoke.

And now she was stepping back, the sun draining away into an iris sky, room slowly gloomy with dusk, and without words he watched her leave.

13

Angela felt like that map was burned across her body as she stood at the top of the staircase. Her senses seemed oversaturated with so much glitter and the sounds of everyone she knew, so loud, so bright she almost couldn't breathe.

Her mother stood downstairs, dressed in obsidian. Smiling, holding a glass of wine like liquid garnet. Angela wondered if she knew. If her father had flown their secret miles away, folded up in his suitcase with expensive clothes.

They'd once traced their family tree, the map of who she was supposed to become. A legacy to be proud of in a town she was supposed to love. She had their stories, their blood, the diamond earrings her mother had placed in her hands this morning. Their lethal obsession with perfection. And now she had the truth. It made her feel sick.

For a moment, all she could think of was water, crashing in through the windows, shattering all the glass into splintered ice, seething over this entire town until it was nothing but blue.

And as she walked through the crowd, numb, there was Dillon, with an embrace that smelled like ocean and liquor.

Dillon, who she'd forgotten about until now because

for just a few seconds, all she knew was the warmth of Owen's hands, the noise of the gala and the sadness of maps muted by his lips on hers, and the way their bodies were close enough to trade heartbeats made her feel like everything and nothing mattered. Silence and stillness and the feeling that everything could change, until it didn't.

Dillon was everything she wanted to run away from right now. But instead, she drank from the glass he gave her, faked a smile. Became yet another person's version of Angela while she replayed the truth in her mind.

***

She couldn't sleep that night. Couldn't shut off her thoughts.

As she looked out at the dark, empty street, she thought of all the times she'd spun stories about herself so that she and her friends could write the narrative in this town. Stirred up speculation, let people scatter secrets everywhere, then proved them wrong and burned up their words.

She knew what to do now. And she knew it was selfish. For all the wrong reasons.

But she was so tired of this game, of trying to stay perfect in this town.

The house felt so quiet and lonely. Angela reached for her phone and started to text Owen, then at the last second, called him instead.

He answered almost immediately. "Wait a minute, I don't want to wake anyone up."

He was whispering, but he sounded wide awake, alert, his voice filling the darkness of her bedroom and she felt a little less alone. She could hear him moving around, a door opening, and then the hum of crickets.

"I'm sorry I told you like that," he said, his voice a little louder now. "I really wasn't going to tell anyone, though, if that makes it any better."

"It's okay."

He had every reason to tell people, Angela thought. If it had been anyone else, they would have already told this entire town.

"Can you help me with something?" she asked when he didn't say anything.

"Sure."

"Can you tell me where I can see everything you found about this?"

"It's all in the Cherwell archives, at the main library there. Or you can go to the online archive. You might need to make an account, though."

"Thanks."

They were both silent for a moment. Angela could hear the soft sounds of Westview midnights through the phone. She imagined Owen standing outside beneath October starlight in the fresh, cold air. Trees all around.

"I'm sorry for kissing you," she whispered.

Owen sighed loudly and she wished she knew what he was thinking. "I have to go. Good night, Angela."

She hung up and turned on her laptop. Typed in the website, hands shaking as she made an account.

Owen was right. It was all there. Letters and photographs and documents. She read them over and over again to make sure there wasn't a mistake, a hole in the story somewhere. Scanned-in newspapers, bold black letters screaming across wrinkled pages. Handwritten notes and typed letters and meticulous records. Everything. Right there in the Cherwell archives.

Afterward, she looked through the Westview archives and found the photographs.

Angela thought she knew this town like the lines of her hands but these pictures showed her a place she'd never seen, a place that now existed only under miles of rippling blue water. There were mills and white houses, small shops and farmland, old rural roads. There were pictures of the destruction, villages transformed into bleak landscapes with rows of dark, distant trees set against a gray sky. Everything gone.

The pictures here told the story of Westview since the beginning of photography, through the day most of the town disappeared underwater, continuing on to present day. Within the next few weeks, someone would probably upload pictures of the gala, bright images of people smiling and sparkling, celebrating three hundred years of a town that only half-existed, the rest of it gone forever because of someone like her.

And even though she was out of love with Westview, had watched it get less and less perfect every day, Angela hated what her family had done to it.

It was still dark out when she sent the email.

14

Owen couldn't stop thinking about Angela's lips on his. Her face caught in the last moments of gold before the sky turned dark, the room burning around them. The sudden coldness when she left.

He'd stood in that room for what felt like hours, but was probably just a few minutes, after she was gone. He'd found Jan's office and brought the extra bid sheets downstairs. And then he found his friends and they went back to Max's house like they'd planned.

They kept asking him what was wrong. He couldn't answer. And eventually, they stopped asking questions, but he saw the way they kept looking at him, wondering.

They watched movies in the living room with all the lights out, settling into the couches and air mattresses. Lucie fell asleep before midnight so Max turned down the volume on the TV, let the soft sounds and colors lull them into sleepiness. But Owen was wide awake.

He stared at the ceiling. Replayed it in his mind over and over. Wondered if telling her everything had been a mistake.

And then she called him.

Max was half asleep but Owen could see Declan's eyes follow him as he got up and stepped outside onto the porch. The neighborhood was quiet, just the sound of crickets that would go silent any day now, as soon as the first frost sparkled against front lawns, freezing fallen leaves into skeletons, delicately decomposed.

Now it was four in the morning and he still couldn't sleep. He looked at his phone. Everyone had posted pictures of the gala all over social media. Angela and her friends, gemstones clinquant across their collarbones, faces lit in painted smiles. Classmates in crisp suits and long dresses. An entire town engulfed in extravagance. Vines of diamonds like bloodlines and roadmaps and whispers. There was a picture of Owen with Lucie that he didn't even remember being taken.

He could hear splattering on the windows and he imagined long lines of raindrops turning the whole town gray. Rain-slick streets and muddy yards. Everything damp and dreary against the evergreens.

Some nights now when everything was almost perfect, when he'd had a good day at school or after he'd tried cooking a new recipe with his family in the warm kitchen or spent hours wandering with his friends, the memories would slip into the edges of his consciousness as he was falling into dreams. Just to remind him that they were still there, that things couldn't get too perfect. He didn't know which was worse, when they jolted him wide awake like a scream and kept his heart racing for hours or when they lingered quietly, stirring sleep and reality together so that he couldn't tell the difference. His father with his angry hands on his mother's face in bleached sunlight. Time distorted, sirens like heartbeats, everything covered in snow and glass and ice. And that sound he'd never forget.

Freshman year, he'd fallen for Angela like so many

people here had, enthralled by the way everything about her life looked so perfect, so effortless compared to his own. What he hadn't realized then was that she knew that, so she just played along with everyone. Made herself into everything they wanted to be, all those different versions of herself that people like Owen had crafted from what they weren't.

It seemed like very few people in Westview actually knew Angela Witney. She seemed so afraid of people seeing who she really was, scared of showing any flaws.

Sometimes, though, he watched her forget she was supposed to be perfect and for all her frustrations and contradictions, that was the girl he was falling for now, when she was just Angela, erasing the daydream version he'd drawn in his head.

And now he wondered if that kiss meant something or if it wasn't real.

Somehow, he managed to fall asleep for a few hours. Max and Declan were still fast asleep when he woke up again, but Lucie was awake, dressed in a sweatshirt and jeans.

"Do you want to go on a walk?" she whispered when she noticed he was awake.

"Sure."

He got changed quickly and walked outside with Lucie into perfect, classic New England fall, savoring the crisp morning air. The sky was clear now, the sun pale gold, but the roads were still dark with last night's rain and blood-red maple leaves.

They walked a mile to Winthrop Farm, trees on fire with color all around them. In the orchard, plump apples were still blossoming from stout, twisted trees. Tall cornfields stretched out beyond them into the horizon. There were big barrels of gourds in every shape and size, speckled and green-striped and goldenrod-yellow. Pots of neon chrysanthemums.

Inside the farm stand were fruits and vegetables in every color, sweet jams and honey and butter and fresh eggs. The brightest candy apples wrapped up in cellophane, stacks of perfectly-browned pies with lattice crusts.

Lucie bought pumpkins to bring back to the house and carve later. Owen bought them apple cider donuts, warm and coated with cinnamon sugar. They ate them at an old picnic table at the edge of the orchard. He loved that he could just sit in silence with Lucie. They were good at keeping each other company. Like when Hanna Cole broke up with her over the summer and they spent a whole afternoon swimming in the reservoir until she wanted to talk about it. And when Owen was stressed about midterm exams last year and she'd insisted that they take a break and spend a few hours wandering around the park in Cherwell, which turned out to be exactly the right decision to help him refocus on studying. Sometimes just knowing that someone was there for you was enough.

Lucie took out a pen and doodled designs for her jack-o'-lantern on a napkin. Owen inhaled the scent of the orchard. His thoughts were still racing. He wondered what Angela was doing right now, what would happen the next time they saw each other. He wished he could tell Lucie everything. He wished he could tell Max or Declan. But sometimes he felt like they were more Lucie's friends than his because they'd all been friends first.

They sat there in the sun, quiet for a while. And then, when he wanted to talk but couldn't say what he really should have, he filled the space by talking about things that didn't matter as much. The homework they were both putting off, a new show he'd been watching that he knew she'd like. Their plans for the rest of the day. He tried to take his mind off Angela, what that kiss meant or didn't mean.

Max's younger brothers were out in the front yard when they got back, playing football with some of the neighbors. Inside, the aroma of slow cooker chili filled the rooms. Owen started to feel more content as they carved the pumpkins and put them out on the porch steps. They roasted the seeds in the oven, golden and salty.

They'd invited Theo and his friends to join them when Owen was with Angela last night and they all settled in to watch the horror movie Declan had picked out. As the opening credits started, Owen thought again about all the secrets he was still carrying around. He wondered how long it would take them to break free. To rain all over the safe yet delicate world he'd been rebuilding, shatter all the glass from the inside.

15

On Monday, out of habit, Angela stood in front of the mirror, imagining all the things people in this town were going to say about her. She put on makeup, made her eyes look sharper as sunshine slowly filled her bedroom, red-gold.

But the only news that had spread across Westview were pictures from the gala and stories from the parties afterward.

She saw Owen as she walked out of class and their eyes met for a moment. She could feel the aftermath of kissing him, everything he knew about her blazing between them. She kept walking.

Angela checked the news on her phone as soon as she woke up each morning, then hurried outside with bare feet to snatch the newspaper from its red plastic box, fallen acorns pressing pain into her soles all the way down the driveway. Every day, her heart raced as her eyes roamed across fresh paper and glowing screens, and every day, nothing.

She didn't check the fake email account she'd made to see if Trent had written back to acknowledge receipt or follow up. Part of her was too afraid to know in advance what was coming or wasn't. She imagined he was still researching, verifying. Or maybe she'd been wrong. Maybe he just didn't care what happened here when he had better places to write about.

While she waited for words to make her world implode, she used silence as a weapon. Ate lunch in her car at school and ignored her phone, shut out everyone around her. She sat alone in every classroom and left as soon as every bell rang. Made herself as invisible as you could possibly be in this town.

***

"Angela, wait."

She pretended not to hear Cassie and kept walking to her car. But Cassie was faster than she was and caught up, grabbing her arm so that they were face to face in the middle of the high school parking lot, wind slinging their hair across their mouths and into their eyes.

"What's been going on with you lately?"

"Nothing," Angela lied, pulling away from Cassie's grasp and trying to walk away.

"You haven't talked to me since the gala and you didn't show up to Adam's party," Cassie said, catching up again. "Dillon said you've been ignoring him all week, too."

Cassie was wearing her Walcott scarf. Angela had the same one in her closet somewhere. They'd bought them together last year, dreaming of futures that felt so far away. She would have never imagined this was where she'd be right now, the weight of secrets in her bones, pushing away the one person who gave her second chances.

Cassie was safe. She could still have the perfect Westview life she was better at than Angela. The secrets were all on the Witney side so no one here could ruin her. The only thing that could was staying close to Angela.

"Did something happen?" Cassie continued when Angela didn't respond.

"No."

They'd reached Angela's car now and she dug through her purse for her keys.

"Can you just talk to me?"

She and Cassie rarely fought. Whenever they did, there would be silence between them for a few hours afterward, and then everything would return to normal, all forgotten. But Angela still hated fighting with her because those moments of silence were always so raw and loud, like the end of the world, and each time, she was a little afraid that maybe now they'd broken everything forever.

"Just leave me alone, okay?" she snapped, finally finding her keys and unlocking her car. She got inside and slammed the door. Lost Cassie's voice in the gusts of wind behind the glass. Her music switched on as soon as she started the car, one of Cassie's playlists like usual, this time from a night last spring, when she felt so beautiful in a new dress, so alive when she smelled flower blossoms in the air. She slammed at the buttons, trying to turn it off but that just made it louder.

She drove away, leaving Cassie standing there alone, confused. Promised herself this was for the best to dull the ache in her chest while white sun and gray skies glared against reservoir water, all of it screaming back at her.

***

Still nothing by November. Most of the leaves had fallen and all of Westview looked gray. Sometimes on nights like these, Angela's parents used to cook together, filling the house with the smell of herbs and citrus. They'd renovated the kitchen three years ago but Angela couldn't recall either of them using it to cook since then. The floors and counters were always gleaming like they were on display. Whenever she saw her parents in here now, they were always just cleaning, smoothing marble shiny and sterile. Everything smelled like lemon and chemicals.

Neither of her parents were home. Angela stared at the spines of cookbooks that probably hadn't been opened in years. They looked more like decorations now.

She carefully took one down from the shelf and opened it. Their favorite recipes were still bookmarked, corners of the splattered pages folded inward. Angela selected one she still remembered, flavors that used to make dreary evenings taste a little like summer, and wrote down the ingredients. She slammed the door behind her on the way out to her car, just to make the house less quiet, if only for a moment, then drove to the small grocery store off Main Street.

It was impossible to shop there without running into people she knew. In the produce section, Laura Kent, one of her parents' oldest friends, congratulated her on being crowned Homecoming Queen. As she picked out chicken, Jocelyn Tremont's mother pushed her carriage over and asked if she'd submitted her Walcott application yet. She smiled out of habit, just as brightly as she had on that field while the entire red and white-clad town cheered for her name, telling herself she didn't have to do this for much longer. Nolan Everitt, one of Dillon and Adam's friends from the football team, invited her to a party he was planning while they waited in line surrounded by tabloid magazines with screaming neon headlines. And Owen's friend Max was working at the cash register.

As he began to ring up Angela's groceries, she wondered with a cold shock of panic that spread all the way through her blood if Owen had told him about their kiss. They'd both been acting like it hadn't happened, back to their almost-formal interactions at the tricentennial meetings, the only time they ever spoke.

And yet, she kept thinking about him.

Angela's parents were both home when she returned but her father was still working, papers spread over the dining room table instead of tucked away in the tiny office he sometimes worked from downstairs, untidy and stacked with old books. He closed the double doors when he saw her and a moment later, she could hear him on his monthly conference call with the southwest team, chatting with the people already on the line while they waited for everyone else to join. The same friendly, attentive way he interacted with everyone here in Westview, remembering what sports their children played, the vacations they were planning, the hobbies they had outside of work.

But with Angela, he only seemed to be able to talk about Walcott lately, his eyes lighting up, always so genuinely excited about her future there that she couldn't bear to tell him it wasn't what she wanted.

She unpacked the groceries and turned on music, letting the sound wash through the kitchen. She remembered this song from the day she'd visited Harcourt with Cassie and felt a pang of sadness. Cassie had tried to talk to her again a few times after that afternoon in the parking lot but now it seemed like she'd just given up.

Her mother came downstairs as the chicken sizzled in lemon and white wine.

"I haven't seen Dillon or your friends around lately," she commented, as she sorted through a stack of packages on the kitchen table. "Is everything okay?"

"I'm fine. Just busy."

"You're happy, though, right?" But she asked in a way that didn't invite an answer. She unwrapped a dress from one of the packages and held it up as if picturing herself in it, frowning slightly. "This is supposed to be the best time of your life."

Angela wanted to scream. She wanted the sound to

resonate all over this town, to echo down all the winding roads and break the limbs off trees and sink into the water and shatter all the windows of white houses. She wished that people would stop telling her that. She imagined herself at Harcourt, meeting new people, working on projects she was actually passionate about. In Cherwell, exploring different neighborhoods, becoming part of the city. All the things that were supposed to be the best part of right now just felt like they were confining her to this place.

"I almost forgot I ordered this for you," her mother continued, holding up another dress. It was onyx-dark, flared at the waist.

"It's pretty. Thanks."

"Go ahead, try it on. I'll keep an eye on the stove for you."

Angela went upstairs to her bedroom to change. She stared at herself in the mirror, played with her hair, trying to decide if it looked better down or spiraled up into a tight bun. Found a perfect pair of shoes and long, sparkly earrings to match. She rummaged through her bathroom cabinets and painted black lipstick like ink on her mouth.

"It's perfect," her mother said when she re-entered the kitchen. "Not with that lipstick, though. Why do you even own that?"

Angela shrugged.

"Do you like the dress? I thought you could wear it to the Winsors' anniversary party."

She'd somehow forgotten about that. The invitation had arrived two weeks ago, swirling gold words like champagne on smooth cardstock. Everyone important in Westview would be there.

"Okay," she said, already dreading the party as she

helped her mother clear all the new clothes away and set the table.

They ate dinner in silence and Angela wondered again what her parents knew. If they were haunted by the ghosts of drowned towns and walked around Westview praying no one would ever find out. Or if she was about to break open their perfect world and fill it with a pattern of cracks shaped like every road in this town that had been submerged.

***

"I'm not feeling well," she told her parents on the night of the Winsors' anniversary party, and they believed her, because the way they saw it, Angela would never miss a Westview event.

Her parents left, all distant and dressed up, and she put on the onyx dress and took the train to Cherwell, then the bus to the Harcourt campus. From there, she walked down the street to a bar that was supposed to be popular with students. It was dark inside but not too crowded yet. The walls were all mismatched colors, layers of phrases and signatures scrawled over old paint. She almost wanted to add her own so that her name would be somewhere in this city.

As she looked around at what everyone else was wearing, she wished she hadn't worn this dress. She felt simultaneously childish and overdressed in clothes meant for an anniversary party at a restaurant covered in vines and little lamps and menus handwritten each day in neat calligraphy. She pulled her hair back into a low ponytail and took out her earrings to try to dress herself down as she pretended to look at the drink list even though tonight, she just wanted to observe, to see who she could be next year.

Suddenly a body collided with hers and waves of beer were sloshing all over her dress, the cheap smell all over the fabric like high tide. She stood there, frozen.

He was tall, blond-haired. "I'm so sorry," he said. "Let me get you some napkins."

He moved over to the bar with a surprising grace for someone who had just tipsily stumbled into a total stranger and returned moments later with a handful of flimsy paper napkins, which he gave to Angela.

She blotted her dress half-heartedly. She could feel the beer soaking through. All over her skin.

"What's your name?" he asked.

"Angela." It was always strange introducing herself to someone. In Westview, people always knew who she was, even if they didn't know her.

"Angela." He said her name like he was tasting it, stretching out the syllables, the lilt all over his lips. "I haven't seen you here before." He looked her up and down and she wished she was invisible. During summer nights on rooftops, this kind of attention had been exciting but now it felt like she'd slipped, drifting to the ocean floor while the sun blinked at her through every shade of blurry blue. "Are you from Westview?"

"How do you know?" she asked without thinking.

"You just have that look," he said, with a smile she didn't quite like. "All you Westview girls are the same."

There was something malicious and mocking in his eyes.

He touched her cheek, trailed his finger all the way down to her lips and she flinched away. She hated the way he was looking at her, like she was something shiny and new. Like she was all his. It made her stomach hurt, nerves fizzle.

For a moment, her thoughts spiraled. She could go back to Westview right now and she could stay there forever and everything for the rest of her life would be safe and familiar and warm. Everything planned out. It would all just be so *easy*. Nothing would ever have to be new or different or scary.

But then she focused on the people beyond him, laughing, talking, drinking, and beyond that, city lights bright like they'd stolen the starlight from the sky. She felt like she did whenever she had a fever, when her vision swam a little and her thoughts rambled like dreams and lightning.

He was still giving her that look. She stepped back, high-top table against her spine, and he moved closer, either oblivious to how uncomfortable she was or ignoring it. His fingers grazed her waist and she could feel his breath all over her face. Lips so close. Too close.

She knew how to handle people like him, how to destroy them with words. But the way he was looking at her, his hands, the way he was standing so close to her, made her feel like she was nothing, and all the things she could have said died at her lips. She could see herself the way he saw her—a girl in pretty clothes, here all alone. The noise of the bar and the stale scent of spilled beer pressed up around her, stifling.

She felt like her body was turning inside out and then she remembered how to move. She pushed him away and rushed toward the door, running the second she stepped outside.

She didn't slow down until she got to the bus stop, scuffing her stilettos on the pavement, breath cloudy in the chilly air. She slumped onto the bench, shivering. She could see groups of people walking toward the bars in the lamplight, blurry through the hot, angry tears in her eyes.

This was not how she'd wanted this night to go. She hated herself for running away. For having everything about Westview still written all over her in this place where you could be anonymous, a different person every day if you wanted to.

Soon, when the truth was out, she'd be dressed in different words—the most reckless part of her couldn't wait for that.

The bus was late so she walked to the train station because that was better than sitting there, alone in the dark. There were mountains of trash along the sidewalk. Pigeons and rats scurried from shadow to shadow and everything was so loud she couldn't think, a cacophony of sirens and car horns, a drunken argument on the corner as she waited to cross the street. The smell of the city burst from the grates in heavy gusts of hot stale air. A man walking by leered at her, slurred words that made her want to shrink.

Her shoes were making the backs of her feet bleed and she tried to avoid her reflection in storefronts, in car windows because she didn't want to see herself like this, hair messy and dress beer-soaked. Crying a little, because you could do that anywhere here and no one would care. No one knew who she was. There were probably people crying all over this city, on front steps and fire escapes and riversides, all the skyline lights reflected on their faces.

She spent the whole walk angry at herself, and on the train, she realized she should be mad at him, for the way he'd looked at her, the way he'd put his hands on her. For making her forget how to stand up for herself and feel like she needed to run away, all the way back to Westview, leaving Cherwell a little less in love.

You just have that look.

She thought about that all the way home, as she listened to loud music on quiet roads and got ready for bed in the empty house. She stared at herself in the mirror until her face was distorted and tried to see herself somewhere else. She changed out of the dress into pajamas and wrapped herself in soft blankets. Replayed the night in her mind as she tried to fall asleep.

All you Westview girls are the same.

And hadn't she thought that, too, at Cassie's mirror on the night of the gala? That they were all identical, because you had to be to survive here...

Her clothes all had memories, like perfume on the fabric. The silver sequined dress from the Cherwell New Year's Eve party she snuck into with Cassie, where they watched sapphire fireworks bloom across the skyline on a crowded rooftop. Lacy shorts from last summer with Dillon, when they drove without destinations and it felt like flying, car gliding fast on highways and beach roads, their shoes sandy and shoulders sunburned, everything painted in ocean–blues. A soft cashmere sweater from a February break with Cassie's family in a cold, red-roofed town with mountains in shades of snowy blue and still streets lit with white and gold and months-late Christmas lights, ice on the sidewalk. The fabric remembered the shape of her body, the inside of her thoughts.

In Westview, Angela wore designer clothes and smiled at parties. She didn't want to be that girl anymore.

She thought about those hands and eyes on her and wanted them gone. Wanted to tear up tonight's dress.

***

She went shopping in the morning and tried on clothes like new skin. Ink-black dresses so sheer and short and low-cut her mother would never let her leave the house in them. A sweater with little pearls and bows that almost seemed childish. Long, flowing skirts with screaming patterns and high heels like pretty weapons with tiny spikes and sparkles. Soft thrift–shop plaid and chain–store polka dots. She tried on gauzy trousers and combat boots and tight T-shirts with slogans across them.

Anything that looked like something Angela Witney would never wear.

She scoured flea market stalls with fake jeweled brooches and vintage coats and thought about the people who used to wear them. Modeled new personas in fitting rooms with sterile lighting and behind curtains in cramped corners. She bought everything.

At home, Angela tore apart her closet like ripping flowers from a garden, sleeves splayed out on her bed like roots. Hangers strewn across the floor. She filled the space with her new wardrobe, all mismatched styles and personalities. Cut them up, sewed them into something else so that she could be someone new. She stuffed the clothes she used to love into boxes. Piled them in the closet's corners. Left the old Angela there. Smiled at the mirror, closed her eyes and dreamed about the night of the gala, here in her bedroom when she cast off that gold dress, the words she'd sent away after midnight. In her sleep, she stitched those words, the truth, across chiffon skies and scribbled them over ribbon roads with sidewalk chalk.

When the weekend was over, she woke up early every day to avoid her parents before school. She drove around Westview waiting for the sun to rise, read books in her car in the school parking lot. At school, silent, she wore all her new clothes. Felt people watching her. Some of them, like Naomi, gave her looks somewhere between amusement and confusion as they passed each other in the halls. Others, like Rose and Paige and Jocelyn, tried to imitate her and she laughed to herself. They gave up by the end of the week.

She spent the hours after school in a tiny gym just outside of town, in the basement of an old office building with a musty smell and no air circulation and machines desperately in need of an upgrade. She knew no one from Westview would ever find her here; they all had memberships to the new luxury fitness club and spa on Main Street with tall windows and rosemary soap. Whenever she used to go there with her mother or Cassie, she was hyperaware of her appearance, how every movement looked. Here, she turned up her music so she couldn't hear anything and closed her eyes as she sweated out everything she hated about Westview. She made herself exist only in the space between songs so that she couldn't see that she was really just running in place. Let her limbs move fast, like the elliptical's rhythm had taken over. She felt like she could fly away when she ran. She left with her face red, hair curling from sweat, her eyes a little wild.

Angela wandered on the weekends. Went to Cherwell to make herself fall back in love. She brought her camera with her and took pictures of everything. She explored the esplanade along the riverbank for miles, where vendors with little gray carts made the air smell of walnuts and cinnamon. Listened to a violinist play pop songs slowed down into dreamy, aching notes that kissed the cobblestones and echoed along an underpass painted with leaves and vines.

She walked and walked, discovered alleyways bright with murals, blue lights dancing and blinking above her. She found bustling outdoor markets tucked away behind old churches and along slim sidewalks where the air was smoky with the colorful scents of sizzling food from every place she could imagine, serving paper platefuls of recipes passed down through generations. She went to the modern art museum by the water. Roamed through paintings and sculptures and photographs and took the elevator to the rooftop to watch the city glitter around her.

Every time she washed her hands in Cherwell, she knew it was water from Westview and those towns like it running over her skin. She collected it in her palms and then let go, stood there as it disappeared down the drain with clouds of soap.

Angela returned to Westview in the dark, snuck into the quiet house long after her parents had fallen asleep. She stayed up all night editing the pictures she'd taken, changing all the colors and angles into exactly what she wanted and erasing everything imperfect. Told herself that visiting Cherwell would never be enough. She needed to be part of its bloodstream, the rush of commuters in the morning, the revelers who sparkled past midnight and gave the streets a heartbeat. She wanted all the green lights that burned across the water. All the violet and neon, the words bright across the skyline in city gold. She wanted to know its streets inside out and understand everything that made you from a place.

It was still hard to believe that this entire world existed outside of Westview.

***

She was back in the city, browsing secondhand paperbacks for sale on long white tables along the riverbank when Dillon texted her about seeing a movie later as if she hadn't been avoiding him. She'd been ignoring him at school, never getting close enough for him to try to talk to her. Deleting his texts without responding. Trying to fade away.

She kept looking at the books, touching the covers and flipping through yellowing pages. Above her, the sky was the color of an oyster shell and little sparks of rain were starting to land on the concrete.

She knew she couldn't avoid him forever. He was one of the last pieces of the perfect Westview life she was no longer supposed to have, an anchor.

She picked up her stack of books and paid. And then she texted Dillon back as the rain fell harder and faster, agreeing to meet up with him in Westview later. She went home to a list of songs that matched the rainfall.

Her parents were both gone when she arrived. Her father's cologne still lingered in the air as if he'd just left and there was a mug in the kitchen sink, dregs of coffee coating the bottom. Angela used to love waking up to the smell of coffee, her parents' morning tradition. Sometimes, she used to wake up early just to sit downstairs with them while they read the newspaper and sipped from their matching mugs. When she tried it herself, she'd hated it, the too-bitter taste ruining the scent forever.

The newspaper was open on the table. They all used to revel in the calm of earliness, watching the sun rise over the treetops and glimmer on the dewy grass. Sometimes they would open the windows to let the clean, fresh scent of morning trickle in. Now they all performed their routines separately, like they were moving as fast as they could to get away from each other.

Angela went upstairs to her room. She curled up on her bed, wrapped herself in the warm weight of a blanket, buried her face in the pillows. Tried to fall asleep to escape.

Sleepiness blended her thoughts together into a collage of hazy images. Owen's face slid in and out of her dreams, but with Dillon's eyes. She thought of Westview people, interchangeable faces. Her mother, wearing Angela's clothes. A rainstorm of reservoir water all over Cherwell, skyscrapers regressing into trees, fir and pine, spruce and hemlock.

She woke up to the doorbell chiming.

Disoriented, she sat up and glanced out the window. Dillon's car was outside. She quickly scrubbed the smudged mascara off her face and pulled her hair back into a ponytail. Her dress was wrinkled from sleeping in it but she didn't care.

He was standing on the front steps, holding a bouquet

of roses and it made her inexplicably angry. He kissed her on the lips and she left the flowers on the kitchen table to wilt.

She made small talk in the car as if no time had passed, as if she hadn't been trying to build a version of herself that didn't include him. Westview didn't have a movie theater but there was one in the next town over, and she was relieved that the drive there was short so that she didn't have to keep pretending.

Angela didn't pay attention to the movie. As incandescent images flashed across their vision, Dillon laced his thin fingers through hers, rested his head against her shoulder. He smelled like the mint-colored soap his mother kept in all their bathrooms. His fingertips were calloused from playing guitar, his latest hobby. Angela thought of the stripes of sheet music on his bedroom floor.

And then she thought about Owen's bedroom and his wall of maps. How it felt to hold his hand surrounded by a painted atlas of their underwater town. How he smelled like shampoo with slight citrus undertones and just-washed laundry.

She used to take dance classes when she was younger and she'd always watch herself reflected in the mirrored studio, a prism of infinite little Angelas in fluorescent light, making sure her posture was impeccable, that her movements matched those of the lines of little girls dressed in black and pink. When she stopped dancing, she spent hours in front of the full-length mirror in her bedroom. Perfecting her facial expressions and making sure her clothes moved on her body the right way. She figured out the colors to wear to bring out her eyes, the hues of makeup that best suited her skin. Her signature eyeliner look, dark across her lash lines, pointed at the ends like inky daggers. And all those hours paid off because eventually she knew exactly what she looked like in every situation, how to make people react, just as if she was still looking in the mirror.

Then she'd learned that people liked her best when she was perfect.

It still made her sad that Dillon was one of them. That once, he'd known her better than anyone else in this town but when summer was over he wanted perfection instead of something real. The girl who would follow him to Walcott, not the girl who wanted to run away from white houses and reservoirs. He wanted Angela made of sunlight but when she shut her eyes she was the sea.

She had so many ex-friends and ex-boyfriends just like him. She never used to care. There was nothing they could do or say to hurt her because everyone knew that Angela Witney could destroy a reputation in an instant. She could make herself into everything they wanted and when she was tired of being used, she could whisper and weave doubts and confusion into their minds. When she was done, she'd carelessly fling back all of their words and actions, sharp particles of sand spiraling through windstorms into unexpecting eyes. She dressed herself like oceans and poison so that she was dangerous but everyone wanted to get closer.

She hated that for so long, she'd thought Dillon was different. Hated that it had taken her so long to notice that he wasn't.

Her break-ups always started the same way.

"Let's talk," she'd say, like it was a suggestion. A casual conversation. But they'd always look scared, like they knew what was coming.

Then she broke them apart, word by word. She knew the words that would hurt the most, how to string them together to knot around their hearts, embedding jagged shards of syllables. It used to make her feel strong, the way she could craft sentences that made boys want to crumble to the floor.

All those words were supposed to protect her.

Breaking up with Dillon should have been the same. In his car, on her street. There was something sadly romantic about it, she thought, the music and the melody of raindrops, the way her dress twirled when she walked away, a blur of blue against the saturated street and sky. All the way down the road, lights on in white houses.

When you perfected putting up walls, it was supposed to be impossible to get hurt. This time, though, it hurt a little to watch him go.

***

Monday was unseasonably warm and when Angela stopped in the cafeteria at lunch to buy a bottle of water, she could see her friends sitting outside at their usual picnic table. Cassie and Naomi appeared to be telling a story and everyone was laughing and Jocelyn Tremont was sitting with them. They were all huddled close together, the spaces between them closed to outsiders, and they were all completely painted in sunlight.

If everything was still the same, she would be at that table and Dillon would be the one looking in. He would have already been replaced by someone else Angela picked out, someone just like him.

She walked away through green halls with that snapshot in her mind. It stayed there longer than it should have. They were all gold and she was alone.

16

"Do you think this blizzard is actually going to happen?"

Max stopped in the middle of the street and tilted his head up toward the sky. Lucie snapped a picture. His silhouette against the bare, gray-brown skeletons of the woods and the wintery sky in the distance, almost a pale lilac.

"Everyone was panicking at work this morning. We were already sold out of bread and milk when I left," he said.

"I hope they cancel school tomorrow," Lucie said. "If they do, let's go sledding at Pembroke Hill. We haven't done that in years."

They moved to the edge of the grass as a truck rattled down the road, spreading salt all over the potholed pavement. Smoke drifted out of the chimneys. Owen could taste snow in the air. They continued to the edge of the neighborhood where the woods began, sipping coffee from the travel mugs they'd filled up at Declan's house. The ground was carpeted with fallen leaves, duller now than weeks ago when they'd glowed like jewels around gray roads and white steeples.

"Stop posing," Lucie called to Max and Declan, who had walked ahead of them and paused to pose, smiling, atop a pile of leaves. "I want these to look more candid."

They laughed and Lucie took a picture, catching them in the moment. Scarves and hair fluttering in the gusty air. All that faded color at their feet.

Lucie sat down on the remains of an old stone wall to look through the pictures she'd already taken as Max and Declan kept walking. Owen sat beside her, looking over her shoulder. Lucie was in the same photography class as Angela, he remembered. He wondered what she was doing for this assignment. They hadn't spoken since she'd called him after the gala.

He felt like he was still holding his breath, waiting for her to destroy him somehow. He'd heard that she'd broken up with Dillon and tried to stop wondering what that meant.

"You're quiet today," said Lucie.

"Just tired," Owen lied.

She looked at him, shut her camera off. "Is everything okay? You haven't seemed like yourself in a while."

"I'm just stressed about school and college applications," he offered, which wasn't entirely a lie this time. Just an omission. The Walcott decisions were due to come out within the next few weeks and he couldn't stop thinking about it.

Lucie gave him a sympathetic smile. "Did you apply to Enfield yet?"

"I did."

"Me too." Lucie stood up and reached her hand out to Owen, pulling him to his feet. Leaves crunched beneath their shoes as they started walking, following Max and Declan. "So there's nothing we can do now, right? We just have to wait."

"That's the worst part." That and keeping so many secrets.

"You put too much pressure on yourself," Lucie said, frowning a little. She'd told him that so many times but he'd never seen her look so serious about it.

"So you're just not stressed about this at all?"

"A little," Lucie admitted. "Who wouldn't be? But the way you're always pushing yourself ... it seems like it's more than that."

"What do you mean?" He didn't know if he wanted to hear the answer.

"Sometimes it seems like you're still punishing yourself for things that happened a long time ago," Lucie continued. "I know you made bad decisions and you're not proud of that but you also went through something traumatic. Everyone who matters understands that. You don't have to burn yourself out trying to prove yourself to anyone else in this town."

He wanted to believe her. He'd spent so much time trying to become someone who belonged in Westview and at Walcott. Sometimes he didn't know if he was doing it for the right reasons. If he was really trying to move forward, or if proving people wrong was just one small way of atoning for things he couldn't change. Maybe it was both. But sometimes, either way, it seemed like he'd never get there. Like he was grasping for something that just kept getting further away.

Lucie knew almost everything about him. She'd been the first person he'd ever told and she'd never judged him, even though so many other people here were. But there were still parts of the story she didn't know because Owen didn't think he could ever say them out loud. He could only think about it behind closed eyes in the dark. She didn't know how terrified he was that fragments of the person he used to be were still hiding somewhere. That he'd come back to haunt him someday, wrapping smoky fingers around everything that was good and tearing it apart. She didn't know about the other things he blamed himself for, the shame and guilt and sadness he felt when he thought about what he could have stopped if he hadn't been so afraid.

"I'm just saying that I know it's complicated but you should be nicer to yourself," Lucie added when he didn't say anything.

"I'm fine, I promise," Owen told her. He tried to smile.

He knew from the expression on Lucie's face that she wanted to say something else but she didn't.

"How was your meeting yesterday?" he asked, desperate to change the subject. She'd been planning a summer art show with a group of local artists and he suddenly felt a little guilty that he'd only thought to ask about it now.

Lucie narrowed her eyes like she knew exactly what he was doing but she told him everything anyway as they continued through the woods.

They'd reached the place where all the reservoir evergreens began. Ahead of them, Max and Declan stopped suddenly. Declan turned around, pointing. There were two deer drinking from the stream.

Lucie raised her camera and everything around them was silent, almost frozen until Owen stumbled and stepped on a branch.

It cracked in half, making a sound that reverberated on the water.

The deer looked up. Their brown eyes stared directly at the four of them. And then they darted away on skinny legs. Disappeared into the trees.

As they got closer to the reservoir, the first flurries of snow started to drift from the sky.

***

It was hot outside and he was building a kingdom from sand and he was thirsty.

There was sunlight inside and she was wearing a silver suit of armor and all of the planets in the solar system were shattered at her feet. Stardust all over the floor. A river of molten lead and mercury. Outside, the sky was howling with the color of wine. He covered his ears to shut out all the sound and color. Headlights everywhere and screaming shadows. His skin was covered in salt and diamonds.

The sun was rising again, exquisite jewelry strung across the horizon. He took a knife to the sky and tore up the sunrise. Let strips of pink and blue and soft orange fall away like wallpaper. Bird silhouettes dissolved into ink, dripped to the grass in rainy slow motion until the lawn was covered in letters and feathers.

It was nighttime and the sky was alive. Zodiac signs stitched together with pearls. Every face in Westview hovered above him, floating in the clouds, their voices shooting stars, and then all at once, they tumbled toward the earth in the shape of snowflakes. Buried all the sandcastles. Buried all the words. Everything was cold.

He was running and running and running, and above him the moon was falling falling falling from the sky and broke, golden at his toes. An angry voice everywhere and Owen knew who it belonged to but he couldn't find him. All the shattered moonlight left blood and jasper in his footprints. Red dust in his lungs.

She was stuck. Trapped beneath a crescent of glowing sun. He had to get to her. Why wouldn't his feet move in her direction *why why why why why...*

He was frozen by all the snow and the tides of that voice. The sky was sobbing in celestial watercolor. It melted the salt from his face, dyed the diamonds starry fuchsia, electric–blue.

He had to get to her. He had to get to her. He had to get to her. Her blonde hair was shrinking into stars her armor was wilting into pale wisteria and his voice was broken why couldn't he get to her why wouldn't his limbs unfreeze why was he swimming in siren light, siren song...

The frantic thudding of his own heartbeat woke him up. His body was soaked in sweat. Shaking, he stumbled into the bathroom.

He splashed cold water all over his face. Watched the drops slip down his skin, lingering at his chin. His face was so pale. Eyes red and bloodshot.

Owen stared at himself. He and Haley both looked more like their mother, except for the hair, people always used to say. He tried to see fragments of his father in his face. He could see him a little around the eyes, maybe in the jawline. But maybe his memory was lying.

He tried to slow down his heartbeat. Get his breathing back to normal. He tried to focus on the things around him. Bring himself into the present.

The cold laminate of the counter against his palms.

The mat beneath his feet, cloud-soft and petal-pink beneath his toes.

Two toothbrushes, purple and blue.

Haley's makeup jumbled in a plastic tray.

Green vines on the shower curtain, all twisted and tangled...

He had to get out of here.

He grabbed his keys and jacket and shoes from his room. He hadn't snuck out of the house in what felt like forever but he still remembered which stairs creaked, the exact slowness with which to open the door. He stepped outside. The reports of a blizzard tonight had been wrong. The ground was almost bare. In headlight gold, he could still see grass poking through a thin veil of snowfall.

He tried not to think about all the snow in his dream.

He hadn't had a dream like that in so long.

Owen could feel himself calming down slowly as he drove away, focusing on the dark road until he got to the one place in Westview that was always open when he couldn't sleep.

When he walked into Gracie's, he was surprised to find it so busy. The last time he'd been here this late, he'd had the whole place to himself.

He ordered a cup of coffee at the counter and brought it to a table by a window, watching the occasional set of headlights drift by outside. And then he felt a tap on his shoulder and Angela was standing there. She was wearing black leggings and a sweatshirt, her brown hair piled into a messy bun on the top of her head.

"Hey," she said softly and he remembered the last time they were this close, her lips on his. "Need some company?"

"Sure."

She sat down across from him with her cup of tea. Somehow her presence made him feel more disoriented, as if he was still dreaming.

"You look so tired," she said, a slight frown at her lips.

Owen looked at his coffee. He couldn't tell her the truth. That right now, everything he'd spent so much time running away from was catching up to him in his dreams and he couldn't go back to sleep because he didn't want to see how it ended.

He knew how it ended.

He gave her a small smile instead and repeated the lie he'd told Lucie earlier, for different reasons this time. "I'm just a little stressed about school and college applications. I don't think I was prepared for how much work this year is."

She sighed. Reached out and put her hand on top of Owen's and his pulse electrified at the warmth of her skin. For a moment, everything stopped and the night of the gala surged back to his senses in sharp focus. Her flower field perfume and sunset on maps, his hands on her curled hair and golden dress. Her lips. And then, just as quickly, she moved her hand away, up to her hair, briefly eclipsing her eyes. She tugged her elastic out, bringing her long hair tumbling down around her face, an avalanche.

"Where did you end up applying?" she asked.

"Lenox and Enfield for now," said Owen. He paused. "And Walcott."

"Good choices," she said but there was something odd in her eyes.

"You were interested in Harcourt, right? Have you applied there?"

"I did." She looked into her tea.

"I saw your cousin at Walcott," Owen blurted out. "After my interview. I thought she was you at first."

"I'm not applying to Walcott," Angela said quietly.

"Oh, I didn't—"

"Can I tell you something?" she asked, still looking down.

"Sure."

"I sent everything you told me about the reservoir to that writer from here, Trent Prescott. When you told me, I was mad at my family for what they did to this town and the people here. But that's not why I did it. I got so tired of having to act a certain way all the time, I thought if everyone knew the truth, I wouldn't have to try to be perfect anymore." Angela's gaze flickered to Owen's for a moment and then she looked away again. "I think that makes me a bad person."

Owen didn't know what to say. He'd been imagining every way she could ruin him since that night, waiting for it to happen. He'd never pictured her destroying her own family's reputation instead.

"You're not a bad person," he said finally.

"I'm not asking you to defend me," she said. "But what good is the truth if it's for the wrong reasons? It doesn't help anyone."

"The truth deserves to be out there."

"So why didn't you tell anyone? You have every reason to, after everything my family did to yours."

"I couldn't do that to you," Owen said quietly.

Angela sighed, almost like she knew he was going to say that. Owen wished he knew what she was thinking. The café was quiet around them, with the occasional turning of pages and clattering of dishes.

"So what are you doing here so late?" Owen asked when he couldn't stand the silence anymore.

"I can't sleep," she said. "Mostly because of what I just told you. This is the only place open this time of night around here. I've been coming here for a few weeks now. I've just been people–watching." She looked around the room. "It's weird … we grew up around everyone in this room, we think we know everything about them because it's a small town. But we really don't, do we?"

No one would ever imagine you'd be here with me, Owen thought. He shook his head.

"Sometimes you see a side of people here that you don't normally see, if you're just going by the Westview version of who they are," Angela said. Owen wondered what she'd seen, what she knew now that the rest of Westview didn't. But she didn't say anything else, like she was keeping their secrets safe.

They lapsed into silence again and Owen remembered that afternoon here with Angela at the beginning of fall. Back then, he would have never expected her to say what she'd just told him. He thought about how strange it was to be part of this group of almost-strangers who landed here when they needed somewhere to be someone else in Westview. He wondered if everyone in this town who had perfect-looking lives had places like this to go when they wanted somewhere to think at midnight.

He wondered if they ever woke up sweating from dreams where their entire world was falling apart, where all the lines between nightmare and memory were blurred. Outside, the sky was clear again and the snow in the parking lot had been erased by footprints and tire tracks. On his drive here, he'd kept checking, gaze flickering between the sky and the ground. Just for reassurance that the moon and all the starlight were safe up there in the heavens.

Across from him, Angela stifled a yawn. "It looks like we're not going to get a snow day tomorrow. I'm going to go home and try to get some sleep. You should, too."

They walked out to their cars together and Owen looked up at the sky again. He could still see the moon, the constellations intact high above the trees. He glanced over at Angela and was surprised to see her head tilted back, the moon in her eyes.

"Cassiopeia," she said, tracing the W shape with her finger. "I always look for that one."

Maybe tonight, if he wasn't tangled up in dreams where the sky was breaking, something could have happened. Maybe if she wasn't lost in cities and towns where reputations ran through generations of veins. Maybe he would have kissed her under the stars out here in the parking lot where there were no walls painted with the past, and this time it would be real.

Maybe if he were braver and told her the truth: that the only thing he'd ever known as powerfully as his feelings for Angela Witney was the sadness he'd carried around with him for so long. Feelings he couldn't even name. And all he wanted right now was the softness of her lips on his again because everything he felt about this girl could set reservoir water free and ignite fireworks high above this town to illuminate all the roads with burned-out streetlights.

Maybe if he did, he would go home and dream about every single moment of that kiss instead of lying awake waiting for the sun. And then he'd see her tomorrow and this time, everything really would have changed.

But he couldn't. So he looked away from the sky and unlocked his car.

"See you tomorrow," he said.

"Sleep well," she answered softly. The words left a cloud in the air. He watched it fade away as she got into her car. He could hear her music playing through closed glass. A woman's voice like a waterfall, cascading through late-night silence.

He drove through Westview slowly as usual, before stopping at an intersection where red light soaked corners of worn New England road that eventually left this town, the color shrouding potholes and picket fences and sprawling all the way to the old oak entrance of a church.

Owen didn't pray. He'd been taught to but he didn't believe in it. Couldn't remember if he ever had. He had a single memory of being inside a church. The sun through stained glass making rainbows and shapes on faces and the pages of paperback missalettes, memorizing every movement that light made to drown out floods of words and incense. The slow snake of rosary beads in twisted fingers. And those hymns that sounded haunted, their trembling melody lingering in stillness like smoke. That day, there were prayers at his lips like a fable but one he'd only overheard in whispers and wouldn't ever know by heart. That day, all the saints and holy water meant nothing.

Tonight from the street, he wished all the words he wanted someone to hear to the sky instead. All the way to the stars of an arrogant queen, a beautiful myth banished to the heavens in the shape of a letter that stood for all the places and people with the power to shatter his heart.

17

The article landed all over Westview on a Sunday morning at the start of December. It had been so long since she'd sent the email that Angela had been starting to think nothing would ever happen. But there it was now, the truth on the front page of the local paper, all over the Internet.

Angela could hear her parents' phones ringing all day, their voices behind closed doors, panic singing through their words. She snuck outside their room and tried to listen. Caught fragments of an argument.

"I still think—"

"I told you, we can't do that."

"But I just don't think people—"

"I know what I'm doing. I know this town."

"So do I…"

A sigh, the sound of pacing. She slunk away. In her bedroom, her phone was lighting up over and over and she let it die without looking.

She shut her door and drew dresses. Long skirts cascading with feathers, gold jewelry like broken cages. A waterfall, serene silk tumbling into frothy tulle, all of it burning at the edges. Short and clingy satin that almost looked black but if you were close enough, it was just words upon words, tangled together. She pulled fabric from her closet, splashed its colors over the floor until it hurt her eyes.

Eventually, her parents' phones and voices stopped. She heard doors opening, movement around the house. The fizz of an open can, a bright burst of television sound. The rush of water filling the washing machine.

Outside, Westview disappeared into darkness. A knock on her door.

Her mother was standing there. Hallway light spilled into the room, honey-colored. Her eyes swept over Angela, sitting cross-legged in the middle of the floor, surrounded by pages and fabric.

She walked in, sat down on the edge of Angela's bed and for a moment, it seemed like for the first time in years, they were going to have a real conversation. Her mother was quiet, her gaze lingering on a drawing of a gown with the outlines of continents distorted like pale marble. Angela wished that she could take it away, hold it to her chest so her mother couldn't see but it was too far out of reach.

"I know about—" Angela began.

"I just wanted to tell you that there's nothing to worry about," her mother interrupted. Her voice was calm, almost cheerful, no traces of the panic Angela had overheard earlier. "This is all going to blow over."

How can you say that? she wanted to ask.

This wasn't what she'd been expecting.

She wanted her mother to be angry. To feel the world burning, all the prettiest parts of this town glittering with furious flames, then that sensation of sinking, so cold and lonely. The same way Angela had felt when Owen told her the truth.

And the worst part was that she didn't care what made her feel that way, whether it was the weight of the real story or simply the potential threat to their reputation. She just wanted her to stop acting like nothing was wrong. For something in this house to be real. She should have known that wouldn't happen, that this time wouldn't be different. Her parents had always been this way, pretending everything was fine until that became the truth.

Maybe this was what happened when you planned your own downfall in the dark. When you played with wishes like matches, ignited too early and cast away carelessly, spread secrets for all the wrong reasons. She thought she knew this town so well but maybe she'd reacted too soon. Miscalculated.

"Are you sure?" she asked. If she were talking to anyone else, she'd make her eyes wide and unsure, lips turned down just slightly, a waver in her voice to weave those fine threads of doubt. But she knew that wouldn't work on her mother.

"Of course. You have nothing to worry about," she said again, smoothing out the wrinkles on Angela's bedspread.

"But—"

"Angela," her mother cut in, her voice tight now, irritated. It made Angela feel like a child. Her mother paused and when she spoke again, her tone was all smooth and glossy. "It will be fine. Just trust me."

Inside this house, behind the scenes, her family manufactured perfection. She thought her parents had known she was in on it. But now she understood that they didn't. They thought she believed the illusion they were selling to everyone else. And so even if they were worried, they would never admit it to Angela. They didn't know what she'd already heard, the panic in their voices behind closed doors.

She wondered if now, her mother was just pretending for her sake. Or if after their argument, her parents had a plan.

Maybe they'd found a way to keep their reputation safe, untarnished. And what would that mean if they had?

Angela wondered what would happen if she told her parents what she'd done. If she told them that the person who had figured it all out was Owen Emory, the boy they'd warned her to stay away from over a generations-old grudge, and yet he'd never planned to tell anyone else. She almost wanted to say it now, just to cause a reaction.

But her mother was already leaving, drifting downstairs to the kitchen where Angela could hear her father on the phone, placing an order for takeout like tonight was just a normal night. Leaving Angela alone on the floor with a pile of dreamed-up dresses. She wished she could wrap herself up in one, shield herself with something she'd created, but none of them were real and everything here felt the same.

***

On Monday, everyone at school whispered when they saw her.

Angela drew up a different world in her head to block them all out. A neighborhood in the city, little bars and brownstones, a cozy apartment full of new friends and new memories. Places she didn't know the names or details of yet but would become familiar as that life unspooled—coffee shops she'd study in, streets and stores she'd walk through for inspiration, restaurants that would become favorite dinner spots with people she had yet to meet. She walked through that world instead of high school hallways. Pretended their voices were just the sound of traffic.

In the bathroom after gym class, she stood at the sink with the other girls, reapplying makeup. Former friends and people who had once wanted to be like her. None of them spoke to her now. Some of their eyes met hers in the mirror, glinting. Others just looked away.

She could feel people watching her. It was almost rhythmic, choreographed. Their eyes stayed on her for too long, then their heads swiveled to whisper to their friends. She didn't need to hear what they were saying. Even people who had never seemed to have an opinion about her before were talking, even classmates who had always been polite. She could feel the coldness rolling off them as she moved, pretending she wasn't here.

And then she saw the crowd around her locker. Her insides froze.

They scattered when they saw her.

Her locker was scribbled with words in Westview-red. Every word she'd ever felt about herself, every bad thought she'd imagined across her body each time she stood in front of a mirror. Here in the hallway for everyone to see.

She could hear laughter all around her.

This shouldn't bother her. She shouldn't care what they thought. But her face was getting red, her heart beating faster and faster.

Their laughter was so loud, breaking through the ceiling to tell the clouds, raining down on neighborhoods just dressed in green wreaths and garlands.

Letters so bright, screaming at her.

Dillon and Naomi were standing there, watching, and they weren't laughing but they didn't say anything either and somehow that felt worse.

Angela turned around and walked away.

She imagined thorns blooming in her blood. Breaking through her skin. Making her sharper so no one could hurt her. Her boots tapped against the linoleum and she tried to concentrate on that sound, the staccato pattern they made. Focused on keeping that pace so it didn't look like she was running.

She went to the old auditorium that was only used to store things the school should have thrown away years ago. She and Dillon used to sneak in here during lunch sometimes. Now she sat in an empty audience, gazed at the dark, dusty stage littered with broken music stands and stacks of worn-out, too-blue gymnastics mats. She pictured all the people in her family who had walked through this school and sat here, too.

Had they known back then what all of Westview knew now?

She shut her eyes and leaned back in her seat, wondering what people were saying to her parents at work.

The door slammed and before she opened her eyes, Angela thought it might be Owen. Since the gala, he kept slipping into her thoughts, and then that night at Gracie's when he seemed haunted by something…

That night, in the parking lot, she'd wanted to kiss him again.

She wondered what would have happened if she had.

Instead, Cassie walked in, wearing a lapis-colored dress she'd bought in the city with Angela. She was carrying a stack of flyers.

Angela's mouth went dry. She didn't want to hear Cassie say the same things everyone else was saying, but she didn't want her to be nice either. She could still feel that reckless urge to burn up everything good about her life here.

"I thought you'd be here," Cassie said, acting like this wasn't the longest they'd ever gone without speaking. She was always the first one to break the silence when they'd been fighting but something about this felt different. She sat down.

"I told you to leave me alone." Angela's voice shook just a little and she hated herself. She looked down at the flyers Cassie was holding instead of at her, cheerful colors advertising the latest class fundraiser at a restaurant on Main Street. The same event they organized every year, the same Italian food served family-style, the same speeches and decorations.

Cassie sighed. "Listen, I really don't care what people are saying—"

"You should." Angela stood up and started to walk toward the door.

"I came here to see if you were okay. I'm just trying to help."

"I don't want help."

"So you're just going to push me away?" Cassie called after her. Angela turned around and she could see that Cassie was mad now. "It doesn't seem like a lot of people are on your side right now."

Part of her wished she'd never discovered anything imperfect about Westview. She wished she'd never imagined herself in a place beyond here. Everything would have been so easy if she hadn't.

"I don't need you on my side," Angela said, more disdain in her voice than she meant. She could feel resentment flooding through her like poison. It seemed so unfair that Cassie still had that unflawed perception of this town, that everything hadn't shattered for her, too. And before she could stop herself, she was saying the words to put little cracks in her cousin's world, the same feelings that kept her awake every night back when she first realized that she could want more than Westview but it was simpler not to. "All you've ever wanted is what's boring and easy here so don't let me stop you."

She pushed the door open and walked out so she didn't have to see Cassie's reaction. The halls were quiet now, everyone in class. The door clanged shut behind her, loud, an announcement.

She wished she could talk to Owen. He probably

wouldn't judge her but he wouldn't feel sorry for her, either. He was the only one who knew that she'd ripped up her world herself. He'd barely been able to hide his surprise when she told him.

But he wasn't here today, she learned as she slipped into class to the sound of the late bell, overhearing one of his friends saying that he was out sick. She wished she hadn't left her phone, dead, in her car. She sat down, pretending she couldn't feel everyone staring.

***

Angela didn't go home after school. Instead she went to Cherwell and watched the skyline from a rooftop, brighter and brighter as the sky got darker. Any other night, she would have taken pictures.

She tried to forget about everything that had happened today. All those eyes on her, the words on her locker, fighting with Cassie. Here, she was anonymous. She could pretend none of that had happened. No one in this entire city knew; every window and avenue stitched into a web of light as far as she could see, filled with strangers and eternal glitter on the horizon. It was never fully dark here. Not like in Westview, where a certain time of night stole each dimension and texture, making all the trees and roads and skies the same, the color of endless black almost aching.

On the way back to the train station, every time she saw her reflection in garland-framed windows, in the spaces between perfect plastic mannequins, she didn't care that her hair was windswept. Didn't care that makeup was smudged at the corner of her eye. She inhaled cold, almost-winter air and it electrified her. Its iciness stung, sang in her lungs.

As she walked, she saw the city get cleaned. She watched people sweep long brushstrokes against glass to make it gleam. She saw them polish ornate gold rosettes and letters that stretched across old facades. Watched the trash disappear from sidewalks. Everything would be perfect when the city woke up. Everything shiny and new. A place you could be anyone in.

But later, home in Westview, that brief feeling of freedom was gone and she couldn't sleep. She felt trapped, a pit of worry in her stomach as she thought about going to school tomorrow.

Angela opened her window to make the room cold and looked outside, down the street. The neighborhood was quiet as usual. Occasionally a light turned on or off, a breeze scattered fallen leaves across the lawns. She didn't know what she was watching for. Nothing ever happened here.

A car pulled into the driveway next door. She could hear a snippet of music blasting from the radio as the door opened. The passenger got out and immediately leaned back in, lingering for one last goodbye kiss. Drawling lyrics about summer starlight and old roads haunting the December night. Then the door closed and everything was silent again. The car backed out of the driveway, disappearing down the street.

Angela wondered how many people were inside their houses, talking about her family. She wondered how many of them were afraid of seeing their secrets in print, too.

***

"Which shoes?"

Angela looked up. She should have been finishing her calculus homework but instead, she was sifting through a pile of clothes, visualizing the ways she could repurpose them.

Her mother was standing there in a dress the color of saffron threads, holding up two pairs of shoes that looked almost identical.

"The ones on the left."

Her mother slipped the shoes on. "Why aren't you ready yet?"

"For what?"

"The PTO fundraiser is tonight. I told you about this."

"Oh. We're still going to that?" Angela asked hesitantly.

"What are you talking about? We go every year. Why wouldn't we go?" her mother said, striding over to Angela's closet.

It had been three days since the article was published. The words had been scrubbed off Angela's locker but she could still picture them every time she closed her eyes. People still laughed, whispered when she walked past.

Angela knew that if people at school were talking, their parents were, too. She'd overheard so many rumors she was starting to lose track of the truth, wondering if someone had discovered even more secrets or if the story had spiraled into lies.

And yet, her parents still seemed to be ignoring this, going about their lives as normal.

"Did someone say something to you?" her mother asked when Angela didn't answer.

Even now, after days of wanting a reaction, Angela couldn't tell her. Couldn't tell her about her locker, the laughter, the way everyone looked at her. Couldn't say that she was too afraid to turn on her phone, to see the perfect-looking pictures she'd posted on social media months ago saturated with angry new comments, text messages worse than anything people would say aloud.

"No, I just thought ... is it better to just keep to ourselves for a while?"

"I told you, this will all blow over. People will move on."

Angela could feel frustration rising in her throat. Whenever she drove past the reservoir now, she remembered those pictures and maps of places long gone. She imagined them coming back to life and bursting through the water. Every time she saw her last name in this town, sick shame crashed through her veins. The signs at school, outside the auditorium, on the football field fence. A road that intersected Main Street and one of the old brick dorms at Walcott. The Witney Estates, that whole fake-beautiful neighborhood they'd built to make people want to live here. It was everywhere, just like the names of the other old Westview families, on buildings and landmarks and hills.

They'd all made sure that certain names were on nothing but people's lips. If you weren't careful, you'd earn a place there among everyone else with bad reputations, people you shouldn't trust because of who they'd wronged here.

And that's what they were now. Angela couldn't believe her parents were acting like this was nothing.

"We need to leave in fifteen minutes," her mother added. She took a dress out of the closet. The first one Angela had ever made herself, following a simple pattern she'd found online. She'd felt so proud when she tried it on, the fabric glacier-blue, soft on her skin, and even though she saw all the imperfections right away, it made her want to keep trying. Her mother was looking at the dress with an expression Angela couldn't figure out and it made her stomach feel cold.

"I think you should wear that blue dress from Madison. I haven't seen you wear that yet ... where is it?" She hung the dress back up.

"One of the boxes in the back."

Her mother dragged out the closest box, lifted the lid. "You could have at least folded them. Everything's wrinkled."

She sighed. "Never mind. We don't have time. You can wear one of mine instead."

Angela always loved looking through her mother's closet. She had so many beautiful clothes, fabric that felt like luxury, almost enchanting. Growing up, she'd stand there while her mother got ready, gazing up at all those garments that could make a statement or transform you into whoever you wanted to be.

Tonight she picked a simple black dress she thought would make her invisible.

She undressed in her parents' bathroom, shrinking her stomach in. Watched the lines of her ribs emerge like earth in drought. She frowned at the purple-gray moons beneath her eyes.

"How are you wearing your hair?" her mother called through the door. "I think you should pull it back ... do you remember how you wore it for Dana's graduation?"

Angela did. Her hair looked dull now compared to her cousin's graduation from Walcott last spring. Her skin was beginning to break out along her jaw. She smudged on some of her mother's makeup.

Westview Country Club was decorated in red and white. She'd almost expected the room to go silent when they walked in but instead, the voices got louder. Angela felt everyone's eyes all over her as she stood there, dressed in her mother's clothes. She could still smell her perfume on the fabric, violet and mandarin.

"I can't believe they showed up," she heard someone say, and from the slight, sharp sound of her mother's inhale Angela knew she'd heard it, too. All around them, voices drenched in the same disdain her parents and their friends reserved for the people in Westview they disliked. That same breathless disgust she'd overheard threaded through years of gossip on pool decks and football bleachers and around kitchen tables, all directed at them now. Like every single unkind word the Witneys had ever uttered was here in this room, echoing back.

And she finally saw it, the panic she'd overheard Sunday morning, all over her parents' faces now as the people who would have normally rushed over to greet them turned away.

She felt like she was back in the high school cafeteria, watching her friends shut out the rest of the world from their usual table.

If Cassie were here—if she and Cassie were still speaking—they would have made a game of guessing who would come over to offer their support in hushed tones, who would make a loud show of ignoring the Witneys. There were the Marshalls and the Mertons, who'd known her parents their entire lives, always trying to gain access to their Westview inner circle, now acting like they didn't exist. They were whispering to each other, eyes darting, lips narrowing.

Laura Kent was the only one to hurry over. She murmured a reassurance to Angela's parents, and briefly, something about it reminded Angela of those Homecoming pictures she'd seen that October morning. Three old friends, years ago, with Helen and Trent. But now, Helen was standing on the opposite side of the room, avoiding their eyes. And Trent wasn't here, most likely long gone from Westview, someplace far away as the sentences he'd crafted screamed in his absence.

Her parents were looking around as if they were expecting people to follow Laura to where they were standing. But no one did.

"Don't worry about them," Laura told Angela, eyes flickering across everyone who was staring.

Angela made herself smile and walked numbly to their table. She could hear speculation following her. The latest rumor, that her parents had known everything all along. The same thing she'd been wondering lately. She kept her eyes down, memorizing the pattern on the carpet. Black and gold vines.

This was exactly what she knew was going to happen, what she *wanted* to happen when she sent that email, so why were their words tearing at her skin? She thought she'd been better prepared, that every fake secret she'd sown about herself made her stronger but it was different when it was the truth.

Her parents were looking around; she could see they were trying to gauge how people were reacting. Trying to predict where loyalties lay. Nausea rolled in Angela's stomach.

She needed to escape from this room. From the expressions on her parents' faces.

She pretended to go to the bathroom and instead walked outside to the gazebo she used to sneak out to with Dillon every time their parents made them come to events like these. They'd watch the sun spread fire and violet across the sky, sneak sips from the sparkly flask she hid in her purse. They could see inside the country club from there and Angela loved the feeling of watching her world from the outside, the fact that all her people were in that room together. Back then, she didn't need anything else. This was who she was.

Now it was like looking into a kaleidoscope.

She still couldn't understand why some days she would give anything to go back to a time when this was her whole world and nothing else existed. And why the rest of the time she wanted to make her life so large somewhere else that it would erase Westview from her blood and body.

Her hands were red with cold now. Angela closed her eyes and inhaled, trying to talk herself into going back inside.

She remembered that feeling of thorns blossoming from her, making her stronger. She exhaled and willed the sense of dread to leave her body with her breath. Left it there to dissipate in frigid air.

Angela could see her mother through the windows as she walked toward the building.

If you weren't from Westview, looking at her now, you would never know something was wrong. You'd see a woman in deep red, lipstick on her mouth and diamonds in her ears. Maybe you'd want to know how to make your life look like hers. She'd been teaching Angela for as long as she could remember, how to look perfect even when everything was falling apart. Because if you looked the part, everyone else was supposed to believe it. Maybe you'd even believe it yourself.

Angela walked into the lobby. Past red and white balloons, past a group of classmates who'd laughed at the words on her locker.

She was standing in the doorway when it happened.

She could see a group of her neighbors and classmates' parents chatting animatedly among themselves. Normally, they'd all be surrounding the Witneys.

Phil Everitt, whose son Nolan was in Angela's class, broke away from the group and walked toward where Angela's parents were still talking with Laura.

Her father turned, smiling. Angela was too far away to hear what he was saying but she could imagine it: a congratulations on Nolan's first college acceptance, a question about how their home renovations were going. Always remembering what was important to people, even now.

His smile faltered when he saw the anger on Phil's face.

If you weren't from Westview, Angela would have told you the three things everyone here knew about Phil Everitt: He wasn't from an old Westview family but liked to pretend he was. He was one of the football parents who was frequently kicked out of games for getting too aggressive with the refs. And he was notorious for causing a scene at events like these, usually after he'd had too much to drink.

She could see now from the way he was moving that he'd already started drinking and even though she should have guessed what was going to happen from the moment he walked over, she didn't believe it as she watched.

He started shouting, words slurring.

And then he lunged at Angela's father and they were stumbling across the vine-patterned floor, fighting. Their movement was a hurricane, collapsing a table and its careful settings, water and flowers bleeding across white linen. Glass breaking.

Everything stopped except them.

And finally, what seemed like an eternity later, the room was a blur of motion, a flurry of expensive suits and elegant dresses rushing to pull them apart. Angela watched people raise their phones around the room like glasses for a toast, recording to send this moment all over town.

There was blood on her father's face as he stood.

Everyone was yelling, their voices all tangled together. So loud it seemed like the sound might be too much for the windows and walls and they would all collapse into dust on the endless green of the golf course.

Angela's heart was beating so quickly she thought she was going to be sick. Her mother's eyes met hers across the room.

She didn't move, didn't want everyone looking at her again. She wanted to turn around and run in the opposite direction without stopping until she found someplace void of reservoirs and evergreen trees, somewhere the color red didn't exist.

Her parents were extracting themselves from all the noise, all the chaos. Walking quickly toward her now.

"We're leaving. Let's go," her mother said, putting her arm around Angela like she was trying to protect her from something. The expression on her face warned Angela not to say anything. But it didn't matter. All her words were lost anyway.

She remembered the fight at Cassie's party she'd heard about so many times and she knew that tomorrow, everyone at school would be talking about this the same way. Each moment leading up to it analyzed and embellished, a play-by-play of every detail.

They were silent all the way home, all the way into the house where Angela turned on all the lights, the heavy yellow harsh against the depth of winter dark outside. This was the way her family had always been. Every time there was something wrong, the house got more and more silent, more and more tense while they walked around Westview pretending everything was perfect.

But they couldn't do that anymore, now that everyone knew, and as soon as her parents' bedroom door closed, she heard their voices and phones again.

Angela washed the makeup off her face then changed out of her mother's dress and left it on the floor.

She knew she wouldn't sleep tonight. She watched the street again, most of the houses outlined in gold Christmas lights. A cul-de-sac of trophy cases. She saw her neighbors' cars return home from the fundraiser and imagined their conversations, looked for all the familiar constellations in the sky.

All the worst parts of the last few days slunk into her mind and it felt like she couldn't move; her head was heavy and dizzy at once. She was burning once again with how badly she wanted to escape from everyone here.

The closest she could get to that tonight was Gracie's, where everyone seemed to have an unspoken agreement that you could be whoever you needed to be there, all those people alone together in the middle of the night. So when the cadence of her parents' conversation faded, Angela found her keys and crept into the garage. On the way to her car, she walked past the recycle bin and there were all the magazines that used to be in the guest room upstairs. Pictures and Trent's words, all torn to shreds. All those places he'd sent to towns like this, nothing now but paper and ripped-up letters.

18

"How do you feel today?" Owen's mother asked, coming into his room as he finished getting ready for school. Her face was pink from running in the cold and Owen could hear the pitch of podcast voices still playing from the headphones she was holding.

"Better," he said. It was mostly true, if he ignored the aching in his head, the feeling of exhaustion that wouldn't seem to go away even though he'd spent most of this week sleeping.

She walked over and put her hand on his forehead. "You still feel a little warm," she said, concern crossing her face. "Maybe you should stay home again today."

Owen shook his head. "I'm fine." He hated giving her any reason to worry about him. And he'd already missed enough school this week—he'd gotten his notes and assignments from his friends but he still felt like he was falling behind.

"Are you sure?" She was frowning a little and Owen felt the familiar sense of guilt, that instinct to prove that he was okay.

"I'll be fine," he insisted, trying to make his voice

sound cheerful. In his mind, he gathered up every bad feeling and crumpled them together, cast it all far away so he could smile at his mother. He pretended he didn't feel sick anymore, that he hadn't spent the last few weeks afraid that he was starting to unravel and didn't know what to do.

He told her all the latest news from his friends instead as he packed his lunch. Lucie's art show, Declan's volunteer project with the animal shelter. The celebration they were planning this weekend for Max, who had just received his first college acceptance. Hearing those things always made her happy.

And even though he hated hiding the truth from her, it was easier this way. He could see the relief in her face. He didn't make bad decisions anymore, they didn't fight anymore. He was so careful not to talk about anything that might hurt. Because even though he couldn't protect her all those years ago or change his own mistakes, maybe he could atone even in the smallest way by keeping all the pain and bad memories locked away. By doing his best to hold up the world she'd pieced back together.

He used to be angry but now that had faded into sadness, fatigue.

Outside, everything was gray. Stripes of salt down the street, hardened slush along the gutters. Owen turned his car on, scraped the frost off the windows. The cold and the color of the sky made his eyes water. The air was harsh at his throat, bitter with a hint of snow predicted to fall this evening.

He turned on the heat in the car and looked at his phone while he waited for Haley. He'd texted Angela earlier in the week when he'd heard that the story about her family was out but she hadn't responded. The last time he'd talked to her was at Gracie's, weeks ago. She'd quit the Tricentennial

Committee since then and she seemed even more distant from everyone at school.

He typed out a new message now and sat there staring at the words, trying to decide if he should send it.

He thought of the pictures from Homecoming, the day she seemed to have everything but still looked so sad. A crown on her head and the whole town cheering at the sound of her name. He wondered how she felt now. He'd heard from his friends that the Witneys were all anyone could talk about.

Maybe Angela hated him now and that was why she hadn't answered.

Haley opened the door and dropped her backpack on the floor. Owen jumped, startled.

"Why are you making that face?" Haley asked, sitting in the front seat and placing her clarinet case carefully on her lap. She leaned over and tried to look at his phone. "Who are you texting?"

"No one," Owen said quickly, moving the phone away so she couldn't see it, leaving the message unsent. The car was taking too long to warm up. He turned the heat up higher, the sound sea-like across all the gray. He waited for Haley to put her seatbelt on, then backed out of the driveway.

It was Haley's turn to pick the music and as soon as it started, Owen recognized the song Angela had played for him that afternoon on Main Street. Buoyant and bright, a song that sounded like glitter. It seemed like so much had changed since then.

"Did you hear about the Witneys?" Haley asked as they drove over the bridge where for exactly thirty seconds, everything was reservoir, city-silver this morning with a thin sheen of fog swelling across it.

"A little," Owen said cautiously. "What are people saying?"

"Most people are upset. Almost everyone thinks that the family has known all along and were trying to keep it a secret."

Owen had wondered the same thing ever since the day he'd pieced the truth together. He thought about the expression on Angela's face in that room of maps, the sound of her voice when she'd asked if he'd told anyone else. And the way her eyes were a storm that night at Gracie's when she confessed that she'd sent all those secrets to Trent Prescott. She'd wanted those words to rain all over Westview.

She couldn't have known.

"Anyway, there are so many different rumors going around that no one actually knows what's real anymore," Haley added.

She started listing all the rumors she'd heard and Owen couldn't help feeling guilty, partially responsible for it all.

But the part of himself that he wasn't proud of, the same part that wanted to prove himself to Westview, felt like the Witneys deserved this. Because if their secret belonged to anyone else in this town, they would have never let people forget. That was how they'd gotten to where they were. They let grudges run deep and whispers run wild.

And that was why downfall was inevitable here.

He still remembered being five years old, not understanding why suddenly so many of his classmates didn't want to be friends with him.

Eight—overhearing whispered words about his family he didn't recognize, wondering what was the truth.

Fourteen—knowing exactly what people were thinking every time they looked at him. The moment in a dark apartment, beer sticky on the floor and heavy in his stomach, when he realized it didn't matter what was true because they'd already made up their minds. Didn't matter if he spent the rest of the night there, drinking until the stars were gone and he stopped being able to remember, or if he transformed into someone perfect. They'd all decided to think the worst of him.

All that because of the Witneys.

The way this town wrote their story, Owen shouldn't have liked Angela. And yet, every detail of each moment they'd spent together was so committed to his memory that he couldn't open his eyes without seeing something that reminded him of her, planting wishes in his heart. Moonlight, fall colors swirling from the trees. That shade of fiery gold that reigned as the sun fell, transforming infinite blue to riptides of pink and purple. Cricket song and constellations and every red light they'd stopped at driving home in her car. All of those things had her painted all over them now.

But that part of him he didn't like whispered that although both of their families had designed the reservoir in different ways, until now, only his had faced consequences. That part of him, harsh and ugly, felt a tiny bit satisfied that the Witneys were finally experiencing what they'd made so many other people here feel over the years.

He tried to silence it. At the intersection ahead, the light blinked from yellow to red and he slowed down.

"So last night Angela and her parents showed up at a fundraiser like nothing had happened," Haley continued as Owen stopped. She held up her phone. "Look at this, her dad got into a fight with Phil Everitt…"

Owen looked quickly at the video and cringed. He tightened his grip on the steering wheel, feeling his stomach clench. He glanced at Haley, who was now changing the music.

"I don't understand why they'd act like there's nothing wrong," he said. With the way the Witneys always seemed so concerned about how they were perceived, he'd expected some sort of response, damage control. Anything but silence.

"I know. You'd think they'd at least pretend to care. But I guess they know that there are people here who will support them no matter what happens."

He wondered what Haley thought of Angela now. If she still wanted to be like her. If she could separate Angela from her family and their secrets or if they were all too intertwined with who she was. He didn't ask. He didn't even think he could say her name without exposing the messy, complicated feelings running through his mind.

First period, he traipsed into study hall with Max. Normally, Angela sat at the back of the room with her friends, talking and laughing. Now she sat alone in blue, motionless, like she was trying to disappear.

He'd planned to use this time to finish catching up on all the work he'd missed but his head hurt and all the words blurred together on the page. He gave up and watched TV with Max on his phone, stress knotting in his stomach again. He tried not to look over at Angela but she wouldn't have noticed if he did.

"Did you hear what happened now?" Lucie asked later as they sat down at their usual lunch table by the window, overlooking the empty picnic tables and naked trees. She held out her phone.

"I already saw the video," Owen said, trying not to let his irritation show. "Everyone's been talking about it all day."

"No, look. Angela's dad resigned from Town Council."

He took Lucie's phone and skimmed the apology statement on the screen, carefully-calculated words that seemed too late now, almost insincere in the wake of the Witneys' initial silence. Reading between the lines, it looked like he'd been forced to resign after everything that had happened this week.

That had to hurt, he thought. There had been someone from the Witney family on Town Council for years; Angela was probably expected to run someday, too.

"Don't you think people are overreacting?" Declan asked, reading over Owen's shoulder.

Lucie reached for her phone. "Why are you defending them?"

"I'm not. But what are they supposed to do? Angela and her parents aren't responsible for what happened."

"They still benefitted from it," Lucie countered. "And depending on who you believe, they've been lying to this entire town for years. People like the Witneys think they can do whatever they want because they're powerful. Shouldn't they have to deal with the consequences at some point?"

Before Declan could answer, there was a flurry of sound and motion from the table where Angela's friends were sitting.

"Walcott decision letters," said Max. "I heard they were supposed to go out today."

Owen's mouth went dry and his heart started racing. His entire body felt like it had been plunged into ice water. It took everything not to reach for his phone to check the admissions portal as he watched their reactions, joy and relief on their faces.

He wished he could be part of that. He wished he could open his letter surrounded by his friends instead of feeling like he had to hide it from them, shouldering all the anxiety and anticipation alone.

Rose and Cassie were hugging each other, but Cassie didn't look as happy as Owen would have predicted for someone who had been proudly wearing Walcott apparel for years.

He looked away and shoved the rest of his lunch into his backpack, no longer hungry. His hands were shaking.

His entire life could change right now and he just had to sit here and act calm.

"We should hear back from Enfield soon," he said to Lucie, trying to remind himself that there was more than Walcott. Just in case. His voice sounded strange.

The moment the bell rang, Owen rushed out of the cafeteria. Down the hall, he could see students filtering out of the art room for their lunch period and he pushed past them into the now-empty room.

Self-portraits hung all over the walls around him, some sketched in shadowy charcoal, others made up of hundreds of miniature photographs, a few painted in neon. He felt like all those faces were staring at him, watching as he logged into the Walcott decision portal on his phone. Judging.

Every second the page took to load felt like an eternity. He felt sweaty and shaky, his jaw clenched.

And then, the only words in the world that mattered in the moment, there on the screen.

Congratulations! We are pleased to inform you…

It was floating and fireworks all at once. Owen felt some of the weight of the last few months disappear. All the color on the walls was blurred together and the panic was gone now, replaced with a new energy. He started to text his family but decided to wait until later to tell them in person.

He thought about all the nights he couldn't sleep. About all the mornings his alarm went off and he didn't want to open his eyes and see that he'd woken up in a town where all the color had been erased. All the midnights he spent aching to be someone else, somewhere else, wishing everything was different. He kept right now bottled up, a flame to keep him warm, all his own as he walked to class through the busy halls, people chattering and slamming locker doors. Everything here looked the same but now, he had another reminder that despite what he used to think, he could make things change.

19

As soon as she heard that her father had resigned from Town Council, Angela knew that her parents would already be home when she got there.

She drove around Westview for an hour after school, around the reservoir over and over. Watched the clouds on the water. She tried to map out the town's past across its surface but every contour she imagined reshaped itself into blue-gray ripples. Houses and churches collapsed into skeletons, foundations, nothing.

She didn't want to go home. So instead she drove into another town that looked just like hers with less water, stopped at a vintage shop she'd discovered back in the fall.

"Welcome back," the woman at the register greeted her.

She felt a sense of relief that here, she was only a returning customer, the girl who sometimes stopped in to study the collection of jeweled rings behind the glass and buy everything dark and glittery. Not Angela Witney.

She wondered how many people in this town knew what was going on just a few miles away in Westview. They'd probably heard; they probably knew the names but not the faces. It was strange how everywhere in Westview was a storm, her world imploding, but here, nothing. They all had their own stories she didn't know about either.

Her phone chimed with a text message from her mother as she tried on a dark dress that felt like city nights.

Where are you?

She didn't answer. She was tired of the way they kept shutting her out, like her name wasn't part of the story, like she hadn't been standing there watching while her father brawled across a ballroom floor.

And today, she'd probably been the last person in Westview to learn about his resignation because he hadn't bothered telling her himself when they briefly crossed paths in the kitchen this morning, his features swollen and discolored from the fight. She'd been sitting in class when the new wave of whispers and glances started and she'd had to find somewhere to charge her phone, turning it on for the first time all week, watching all the comments and messages she'd been afraid of fill the screen in rapid succession. She'd deleted them all as fast as she could without reading them, then searched her family's name to see what everyone was talking about now. Shame and loneliness, hot through her blood.

"Special occasion?" the sales associate asked, smiling, as Angela brought the dress to the register.

She started to say yes, then realized she had nowhere to wear it. She bought it anyway, dreamed up a glamorous life for the woman who wore it before her. She wondered how it had ended up here, in this town, on a girl who burned bridges and didn't know what home meant anymore.

In the living room, Angela's parents were waiting, smiling eagerly.

Were they really still pretending?

Frustration surged against her lungs and she wanted to scream.

"Did you get some good news today?" her father asked.

Angela stared at him blankly.

"I heard Cassie got into Walcott," her mother added when she didn't answer.

She froze.

This wasn't how she wanted to tell them; she'd been hoping to break the news with a Harcourt acceptance letter but she hadn't heard from them yet...

Angela hesitated. Took a deep breath. "I didn't apply to Walcott," she said, looking at the floor so she didn't have to watch them react.

"What?"

"I didn't apply to Walcott," Angela repeated. "I don't want to go there."

"Where is this coming from?" her father asked, the disappointment she hadn't wanted to see still all over his face. "You've always been so excited about going there."

Her mother was reaching for her phone. "I'm going to call them. It's only the early action decisions, I think you still have time to apply for regular—"

"Are you even listening to me?" Angela demanded. "I just said I don't want to go there."

"Then where do you want to go?"

"I want to go to Harcourt. In Cherwell. I applied for their fashion design program."

Her parents exchanged a glance.

"I thought that was just a hobby," her father said. "Like your photography..."

Those words, the dismissive way he said them, made

her want to cry. Her throat stung and she willed the tears not to move.

Her parents tried so hard with everyone in this town. They knew every detail that mattered to everyone else but they didn't know what was important to Angela. Didn't see that every time she sketched out an idea for a design or started sewing, she was alive in a way nothing else in Westview made her feel. It was her entire heart and soul on every page, in every stitch. All the colors, the feel of fabric, shapes and structures, the way she could send a message, make you feel beautiful.

She'd felt powerful when she realized that she had the ability to create something all by herself that could maybe take her far away from Westview and they were acting like it didn't matter.

"Angela," said her mother. "Do you have any idea how competitive that program is? Do you know how hard it is to make it in that industry?"

"So I just shouldn't try?"

"You have everything you need here. You're guaranteed to succeed. And Walcott is a tradition—isn't that what you wanted?"

They'd never asked that, just expected it. They didn't seem to understand that years of Walcott football games and Westview fundraisers wouldn't make that what she wanted.

She knew she was lucky, that there were people who wanted her life and the opportunities she had. She knew people would say she was throwing it all away.

But this was someone else's dream.

"No," she said. "It's not." And now, after everything this week and so long pretending to be perfect, she was angry. The words were spilling out, poison filling the magazine-perfect room, all over the fresh flowers on the mantle, fogging up the glass on old photographs. She couldn't stop. "I don't care about traditions. I don't want to stay in this town for the rest of my life, making sure I don't do anything that might make people talk about me and pretending nothing's wrong like you always do. I'm tired of trying to be perfect. And I want a life that's more than here."

Her mother was looking at her like she was watching something familiar and then Angela remembered the little flash of truth she'd seen the morning of Homecoming and realized what it was. She was watching her own past play out, words that were once hers leaving her daughter's lips.

Maybe now her mother was happy with her life here. She'd never given Angela any reason to believe that she wasn't. Maybe she was good at pretending and still wished she'd left.

Either way, she should have understood.

And Angela should have stopped then, but the words kept coming. "You wanted to leave, didn't you? But you never did so you're making sure I don't, either."

"Angela, that's enough," her father said, and she threw him a betrayed look.

She couldn't be in the same room with them, with all those words she'd left hanging in the air. She held the dress she had nowhere to wear close to her chest in its plastic bag and walked away.

Waiting on the kitchen table was a cake. White frosting, with the words *Congratulations Angela!* scrawled out in green. A brand-new Walcott sweatshirt folded up beside it with a perky bow on top. She imagined grabbing a handful of cake and flinging it all over the kitchen, covering all the shiny surfaces with sugar and crumbs.

She needed to get out of here.

She thought of Cassie and Dillon and all her old friends, probably having celebratory dinners with their families right now. It made her stomach hurt. For a moment she was angry at herself that she couldn't just be like them.

She used to be. It was easier that way. But from the moment she'd seen what a life outside of Westview could look like, she hadn't been able to look away.

She drove to Owen's house and she thought about that evening in August when she didn't realize she was driving to him.

He opened the door and he looked just as surprised to see her now as he did then.

"Hi," he said, almost like a question, and then he looked concerned. She could imagine how imperfect she must look right now, eyes red, face pale, a side of her she hated ever showing anyone. "Are you okay?"

She couldn't even pretend. "I needed to get out of my house and I didn't know where to go ... I'm sorry, I should have—"

"It's okay," said Owen quickly, stepping aside to let her in. "Come in."

"Owen, who's at the door?" a voice called and then his mother was there. She looked like Angela remembered her, long blonde hair and the same eyes as Owen.

"Mom, this is Angela. She's on the Tricentennial Committee with me," Owen said cheerfully, as if he was trying to hide Angela's sadness for her.

It occurred to her what a strange context that was to introduce her in, here in this house where she still had faint memories of running free through golden summer. There were so many more memories here that weren't hers. She could almost feel them in the air, smell them seeped into the floorboards like spilled perfume. This whole street was full of old houses that had escaped the reservoir destruction but eventually lost their value when the town was re-established on the southern side, and even more when her family built the shiny new Witney Estates nearby.

She thought again about all that water, cursed cobalt erasing old stories. She'd once heard a rumor that on certain days, when the water was low enough, you could see chimneys and weathervanes rising from the reservoir like skeletons screaming from the depths of the manmade spring. She knew it wasn't true; everything in those now-underwater villages had been razed to the ground on long summer days. Nothing but dust. But it still gave her chills to imagine houses like this, drowned.

"Angela. I remember you, it's nice to see you again. I'm Valerie," Owen's mother was saying warmly. Angela wondered what she was really thinking and wished she could disappear, because Owen and his family had no reason to like her, especially now. "Are you here to celebrate with us?"

"Celebrate?"

Valerie smiled, pride lighting up her face. "Owen just got his first college acceptance."

"Oh, I didn't realize ... I'm so sorry. We can talk later," Angela said, feeling even worse for showing up here and interrupting when she hadn't talked to Owen in weeks.

"No, it's fine. Stay for dinner. We were just about to start cooking."

"At least let me help out then," Angela answered, looking apologetically at Owen. "I didn't know you'd already heard back from colleges."

"He got into Walcott today," Valerie said. Next to Angela, Owen was motioning frantically for her to stop talking. He looked away when their eyes met.

"You're going to Walcott?" Angela said, realizing a moment too late that she should be congratulating him.

He was looking at the floor. "We'll see," he said. "I'm

sort of keeping it quiet for now, though ... don't mention it to anyone..."

Angela almost laughed. He had to know that every secret was safe with her now that barely anyone in this town would speak to her. But she wondered who he wanted to hide this from.

His sister was in the kitchen and her eyes widened when she saw Angela, gaze darting between her and Owen.

"Haley, this is Angela," Valerie said and Haley looked inexplicably mortified.

"Hi," Angela said, trying to smile. She flashed back to those sunlit days here, Haley just a toddler then.

Haley smiled back shyly and said something about Homecoming, the way people who didn't know her well always did. That day felt like miles away now. The day everything had changed.

Owen set a cutting board on the counter and started slicing vegetables for a salad, tomatoes bleeding and collapsing against the knife's silver blade. Standing there with all of them in the kitchen and the hum of the radio in the background, Angela was reminded of last summer and evenings in Dillon's beach house. Clattering dishes and sizzling on the stove and the smell of freshly shredded herbs. She had the same feeling here. It was like a ritual: Owen and his family, their easy conversation, stirring and slicing in graceful choreography. Angela almost felt like she belonged here too.

It didn't seem like any of them were pretending.

She caught a glimpse of herself in the window over the sink as she helped wash the dishes. Something about her face looked different but she didn't know how to explain it. Outside, it was snowing.

***

By the time she pulled into her driveway later with a container full of leftovers, it was dark and the snow had stopped, white lawns glittering under the streetlights. Through the front windows of the house, she could see her parents with the lights on in the living room.

The TV was on, and neither of them heard her walk inside. She stood there silently for a moment, watching a model glaze plum lipstick over her parted, pouty lips. Her mother was typing her credit card information into her laptop. Her father snored on the couch, holding an open book loosely in his hands. Not wanting to continue their fight, Angela backed quietly out of the room and went into the kitchen. She rearranged white cardboard boxes from restaurants in the refrigerator to fit her own container inside, then shut off the lights and went upstairs.

She had the entire top floor to herself, the biggest bedroom at the end of a hall of empty guest rooms. Her bedroom was the only room in the house she particularly liked. She'd redecorated it herself last winter—black and white with aubergine accents, glimmering gold lights and silver mirrors. The windows stretched from floor to ceiling, wrapped in gossamer curtains. While patchworks of photographs covered the walls of her old friends' bedrooms, Angela didn't have a single picture on her walls anymore. She liked the look of the blank paint.

The house was silent as Angela washed her face and changed into her pajamas. On nights like these, when it seemed as if three strangers were residing in the same space, she wished that she had someone else here to fill these rooms with noise and laughter. She sometimes used to imagine having siblings, someone to share the weight of every expectation. Someone to compete with, someone to be like her. But maybe it wouldn't be like that. Maybe they'd be just as far away as everyone else in this house.

There were too many rooms, too much time and space for all her thoughts. Even Cassie wouldn't have understood if she'd ever tried to tell her because there were no words to explain the emptiness, the way she felt the absence of sound. The way loneliness seeped into uninhabited corners.

She looked at her phone. Cassie had just posted a picture of herself and Adam with their Walcott letters. Rose posed with a Walcott pennant. Dillon, his parents and grandparents all wore the same Walcott T-shirt Angela had somewhere in her room. For a moment, Angela considered what would happen if she typed out the truth in the safety of the screen's soft glow instead of the usual carefully crafted conversation that barely sounded like her.

Instead, alone, she opened a new text message to Owen. Tried to figure out what to say, typing and deleting for a few minutes before settling on the simplest words.

Thank you.

She shut off the phone and turned on her TV, erasing silent space with unfamiliar voices. She thought about Owen's house, how even though there were flaws on the outside, inside were evenings like tonight that felt warm and whole. From the street, her own house looked clean and perfect but here, inside, everything was like glass, cold and breakable.

***

She found the smiles and memories from days and nights past hidden in a shoebox in her closet that weekend. They all had small holes in their ragged corners, from the years they once spent tacked up, then torn down when she was tired of them.

They took her back to what she'd forgotten. A sky glimmering with diamond stars they wished on and lying in dark green grass and swimming in cold water while bats flitted like shadows across the moon. She remembered the lyrics of songs turned to full volume. The sting of a curling iron against her fingers in a room that smelled like hairspray and pomegranate perfume, a dark gym with red and yellow and purple lights that cast shadows of dancing bodies against the walls. Watching dazzling fireworks paint the stars green and gold at night. The feeling of being full from laughter.

She couldn't remember every conversation but she could remember how it all felt. Some moments didn't need to be captured with the flash of a camera. They were still present in that box somehow. Like ghosts.

Some of them were so vivid she could have closed her eyes and sworn she'd landed back there. To when they were smiling girls on a staircase wearing light-colored dresses. Jewelry that made them feel grown-up shimmering in candlelight, sprinting in high heels through a sudden rainstorm, whispered secrets in the dark. Glitter stuck to the seat of the car. All the little moments that came together to form one image frozen forever into glossy rectangles, somehow meaning more in hindsight than it did at the time, when the light glinted against the mirror in the background. It was more than pictures, a single second, it was all the time around them.

Some people would have given anything to relive the life she had there. Anything to recreate and reconstruct those moments, bright on paper.

This was a box of when she loved her life in Westview. It held everything that used to matter. People here could be your entire world and now they were nothing, like ripping a photograph in half.

***

It was going to snow forever. Even though the sun was out, the same sun that used to watch and warm her on summer rooftops. Now the snow reflected it, stinging her eyes.

Angela lay on her back in the cold and made a snow angel the way she used to when she was younger, letting the frozen water falling from the sky crystallize on her skin. Back then, she'd never noticed how much winter hurt.

She watched the snow turn this entire town white. Freeze all the streams that led to the reservoir.

When it got dark, she worshipped all the winter stars from crystal snowbanks, the way she used to on the beach, until she couldn't remember the difference between sand and snow. Then and now, the whole galaxy was filled with glitter and salt and tears.

Inside, she tried to recreate summer. Slept under layers of blankets to make the room hotter. She closed her eyes and remembered neon green inflatable rafts, her chlorine-scented hair dark and wet on her skin, the humming of the pool filter, and the way the sun sparkled on the water when she jumped, the sky in slow motion, friends' voices distorted into currents when her ears submerged. Body burning through layers of greasy sunscreen. On the beach, a thin cotton sundress, beaded bracelets, a watercolor-striped silk scarf tied around windswept waves. Sand all over her feet. She remembered a hand in hers, empty shorelines, dark sea, gray sky. Rain. They ran back to the car, laughing, and stayed there, watching the sky darken and lightning glitter on the ocean.

***

She loved the historic market building in Cherwell with its cyan skeleton and glass roof and old lanterns. She wandered through the shops with Owen and then they watched the holiday lights switch on, giant yet graceful green and silver peacock feathers twinkling across the arches.

In the nearby park, trees were all wrapped up in rainbow lights. There was a holiday market there, little wooden chalets with pointed roofs, all covered with gingerbread hearts and glittery paper stars, pine garlands and tiny ruby poinsettias. They ate waffles sweet with sugar and strawberries, drank hot chocolate that burned the back of their throats while they looked at ornaments painted with tiny Cherwell skylines and ceramic platters with swirly blue flowers.

She stopped Owen at a stall selling earrings made of sea glass, held them up to her ears in the mirror, envisioned the way the ocean spent years tumbling those broken pieces. Smoothing their sharp edges.

Angela bought a pair and tucked them safely away in her pocket, then turned to Owen. His face was flushed with cold, his hair messy beneath a knitted hat. He was smiling, though, the night singing with the smell of cider and cinnamon, behind him a blur of children running, laughing in puffy winter coats. Everything under a canopy of lights as bright as an entire universe.

She wanted to say something but she forgot all the words.

"What?" he asked. Like he sensed it.

And now she'd been looking at him for too long without saying anything. She touched his arm, turned him to the luminarias leading away like a path of fallen stars instead. "Look."

They followed, walking down streets of townhouses covered in carved flowers and curls, icicles hanging from the windows like jewelry. Snowbanks all over the city. On the quiet sidewalk next to Owen with snowflakes on her lips and crystals on her lashes, she tried to feel less like she was watching everything from a distance.

***

Angela stayed home alone on New Year's Eve while her parents went to Cherwell instead of hosting their annual party. Somewhere in this town her old friends were wearing red lipstick and dancing. Drinking stolen champagne. Posing for pictures outside, arms and legs bare amidst silvery snowdrifts. Stars like confetti in the sky above them.

On TV she watched fireworks rain over cities where it was summer, where it was already a new year and she fell asleep on the couch long before it was midnight in Westview, dreaming of the sun.

***

All she could see as she drove was snow and trees.

She was about to text Owen to make sure she had the right address when she turned a corner and there it was, across her entire vision as suddenly as breaker waves. A mansion, pale limestone gleaming with icicles. His car was parked in the circular driveway.

"I can't believe I forgot about this. I was obsessed with this place when I was younger," she said, getting out of the car. Her voice left fog in the air and she shivered. "I used to make my parents drive by to see their Christmas lights ... I always wanted to go inside."

"The owner died last year," Owen said. "She left it to the Historical Society. They're working on some minor refurbishments and it's going to be open to the public as a museum later this year."

Ochre Mansion used to be one of the most talked-about places in Westview. It was modeled after one of the Gilded Age mansions perched along New England coastline. Renata Ochre, the last remaining member of another old Westview family, had lived here for as long as Angela could remember hearing about her, always surrounded in rumors because no one seemed to really know her.

Once every few years, she'd hosted an extravagant party for all the important people in town. Angela's parents were always invited. The invitations would arrive in the mail just a few days in advance but from what she heard, everyone always cleared their schedules immediately to be there, and then they spent weeks discussing the delicate purple of edible flowers on canapés and vines etched on crystal champagne flutes and the cloisters in the courtyard, carved like a canopy of roots.

Angela remembered hearing about Renata's death but was surprised that she hadn't heard anything about the mansion's fate given people's fascination with it. Another reminder that maybe she didn't know as much about this town as she thought she did. She didn't know if she liked that or not.

"So what are we doing here?" she asked.

Grinning, Owen held up a set of keys.

Her jaw dropped. "How did you get those?"

"The Historical Society sent me to take pictures of the library for something we're working on."

"They just gave you the keys to a mansion?"

Owen laughed. "They gave me keys to the library, which is its own separate building, and made me promise not to touch anything. I just finished taking the pictures but you need to see this."

She followed him down the path that had been cleared out alongside the mansion, into the backyard. Wide stairs spilled out into a snow-covered garden. Angela could see a fountain and a hedge maze and statues shaped like goddesses. The library building was at the back of the garden, the same light limestone as the mansion and bigger than Angela's entire house. She started to walk toward the front door but realized that Owen was walking to the other side of the building, to a staircase that led up to a balcony several stories up. It looked like the walls were made of blurry stained glass.

The balcony looked out onto water and trees. She could see the sun and sky hitting the reservoir, ice all over the water like a chasm of pearls.

"Okay, close your eyes," said Owen.

She did, echoes of white sky playing against her eyelids. She could hear him unlocking the door and flicking on a light switch.

"Careful, there's a step here." He took her hand and helped her inside, closed the door behind them. The room smelled like winter cold.

They kept walking, her eyes still closed, the sleeve of his jacket soft against her hand.

"Okay," he said, stopping, and she opened her eyes.

They were standing in a massive three-dimensional stained-glass globe, on a walkway that connected the opposite sides of the room. There was nothing else inside, just oceans and landmass and dotted lines marking continental drift all the way around the walls, high above her head, far below her feet. She had the outlines and colors of countries reflected all over her.

"This is amazing," Angela said, gazing up at the brilliant blue of the ocean over her head. She realized she was still holding Owen's hand and let go, feeling her face heat up. They were both quiet for a moment, looking around. "I wonder what she was like."

"Did your parents know her?"

"They went to all of her parties but I don't think they knew her very well. I don't think anyone here did, really. They just liked coming here for the story."

She thought of all those people coming to see this house and be seen at a party, the status of it all more important to them than the person. Once this place opened to the public, she knew they'd all show up and act like they'd known her but they would really forget all about Renata Ochre.

She sat down on the equator line walkway with Owen and pointed out all the places she wanted to go someday. Far away from here. Wondered how she always ended up in rooms made of maps with this boy. They were in the middle of the world in the middle of nowhere. She couldn't see outside. They could have been anywhere.

***

For weeks afterward, it was always summer in her dreams. Street signs and shades of green passing by. The smell of dirt, sun-soaked. Grass blades poking her bare shoulders and the buzzing of bees sweet in the air. Sunlight in her body. In her bones and in her blood. She could feel it in her hair. The color of the sky in her eyes. She could control the clouds with her fingertips. Go anywhere she wanted, as if time and distance didn't exist.

Warm every day when she woke up. Then her feet hit the morning coldness of her bedroom floor and she remembered that she was in Westview, in the middle of the longest winter.

***

She spoke to no one at school because everyone there was still talking about her. At home, everything was mostly silent but sometimes she could hear her parents making plans, figuring out how to win back Westview's heart.

When the roads were cleared, re-salted after the latest snowstorm, she spent a Saturday wandering around Cherwell with Owen, walking uphill through a neighborhood of red-brick rowhouses with black shutters, gas lamps gleaming delicate light onto narrow cobblestone lanes.

He was trying so hard to cheer her up today, like he knew she wanted to shut the world out. He wouldn't let her.

She pretended it was working, giving him forced smiles as they walked, leaving their footprints on the snow-dusted sidewalk. She knew he didn't believe her. She saw his eyes get a little sadder when he thought she wasn't looking.

"Are you okay?" he asked. They'd reached the top of the hill now, overlooking the rest of the city.

She nodded. Didn't know how to explain how it felt to drown when she wasn't even in the water, moving through each day without really living in it.

Cherwell looked like a painting from here. One of those New England winter scenes you sent on cards to people far away who couldn't feel the screaming of the wind or the scent of the cold. The park spooled out beneath them with skaters twirling across the ice, scarves flying. Rows of brownstones with green wreaths, the golden dome of the State House. Spires and skyline in the distance. Snow all over everything.

They rented ice skates and she wished she could soar across the rink, fast enough to feel like she was flying, escape her body. Owen wobbled on the thin blades. Grabbed the side of the rink, shuffled across the ice for a moment. Kids half their size were weaving backwards, skates singing extravagant patterns to shiny ice as they cut around hesitant skaters. They seemed so unafraid of falling. She wished she could remember how that felt.

"Come here," she said, reaching out her mittened hand.

Owen let go of the wall. He tried to move toward her. Stretched out his arm, hand landing safely in hers.

And then they were falling, almost tangled on the ice. And she was laughing, for the first time in weeks, even though everything hurt and the cold was soaking into her clothes.

Ice on the road made her car swerve a little on the way home. She turned up the sound of an old playlist, focused on yellow lines and white trees until her heartbeat returned to normal.

***

In the summer she used to drive around aimlessly. Windows down. Play music that made her feel alive. She drove past Westview fields and old barns, through roads that seemed to grow out of the woods. She drove to places where everything was sea salt and watercolor. To lookout points that could have been the end of the world. Boardwalks. Miles of highway and blue sky and backroads and paths that ended with the ocean.

All those roads filled up with snow now, so high they couldn't leave the house for days. Everything white and gray forever. Icicle columns grew from the roof. Electricity flickered.

She stayed in her room. Started working on a new dress to make herself feel something, the reality shows she used to watch with Cassie blaring in the background, but none of it made her as happy as it used to.

She wished all the snow would stop. For springtime. Every day was blinding white and then night was sudden, pitch-black ink flooding the neighborhood.

She got her letter from Harcourt on the coldest day. Air so bitter it screamed at her skin.

We regret to inform you.

She couldn't tell anyone.

She closed all the shades in her room on this town where winter was never going to end. Where everything was buried under infinities of white and there was a thin coat of ice freezing over the space where homes and hearts used to be. She was going to drown in winter.

That night, she looked in her closet at all the clothes she'd made and saw nothing but mistakes in every stitch. She ripped them all apart. Seams popped and buttons clattered on the floor, the song of tearing fabric the loudest sound in the house as she ruined everything and tried to start over.

***

Owen started texting her lists of all the things he was going to do when the snow stopped. All the places he wanted to go.

I'll go with you, she promised, then added her own. As long as no one else in Westview knew.

***

When everyone else in town was inside, hiding from the cold, he showed her all the secret places by the reservoir. Footprints instantly covered up by fresh snowfall.

She told him some of her secrets. About Harcourt. That her house felt even more lonely now. That she didn't know what to do, didn't know who to be.

He didn't tell her the things he was carrying around. Not yet. But some things she knew from the way he looked at her. She didn't tell him that every time she saw that look, heard his voice, had the darkness of her room lit up by a midnight text message, she could slowly feel tiny pieces of her heart unbreaking.

All those hours in between school and sneaking away with Owen, Angela cut fabric into dress shapes and sewed them into something whole, something her own, until it started to feel like magic again.

***

Again and again, they lingered in the parking lot at Gracie's. Slush all over their boots. Faces pink in the cold.

She always drew out the conversation in those last minutes. Not ready to go home. So many times, under January skies and February stars, she thought they would finally kiss. They always did in her dreams.

***

It snowed, snowed, snowed forever all winter and her entire world was blizzards and reworked patterns and Owen, and then it was almost the end of March and the sunlight slowly started to melt everything into the earth to reveal months-old holiday decorations buried under snowbanks. Forgotten, like a time capsule. The sky was blue again on the first day of spring and she wore the new dress she'd been making, the color of snowstorms and lilies.

20

Do you want to go to Hampshire Hills tomorrow?

There was a thud next to him as Lucie and Max set down their backpacks. Owen closed Angela's message quickly and started looking through his folders for the paper he was supposed to be submitting today.

"Hey," said Max. "Do you want to come over after school tomorrow? We were thinking of having a movie night. Declan and I want to watch—"

"I just agreed to cover a shift at work," Owen lied.

Lucie frowned. "You've been working so much lately."

"I need the money."

"We just miss you," Max said. "I feel like we never see you outside of school anymore."

"I can't remember the last time you were at trivia," Lucie added.

"I'm sorry," said Owen. "I'm going to try to come soon, I promise."

He felt the usual knot of guilt in his stomach as class began. He *was* working more lately—he'd been picking up extra shifts whenever he could. Decisions from the Westview

Scholarship Fund were due to come out in a few weeks and it helped to keep busy instead of thinking about how his fate was probably already decided, waiting for him in an envelope somewhere. But mostly, he'd been spending time with Angela. She didn't talk to him at school but she didn't talk to anyone. When he wasn't at work, they spent hours together after school, on the weekends.

Last weekend they'd gone to that little flea market in Cherwell Lanes that he'd found with his friends in the fall. She'd loved the stall selling vintage clothes and jewelry. She bought herself a long necklace with a pale blue stone that matched her eyes. She'd been so happy that entire afternoon. His stomach and heart did backflips every time she laughed and he would have given anything to bottle everything about that day. The whole city felt alive again, sun and pastel chalk on the sidewalks, yellow flowers on every corner. Everyone shedding winter coats for lighter fabrics. They'd walked through the park, around the pond where little turtles sunbathed on the rocks, to a view of the whole cityscape smudged with pale pink blossoms. If he could, Owen would keep that afternoon forever, share it with her whenever she was drowning.

Angela met him at Hampshire Hills, a popular hiking spot outside of Westview after school the next day. She was dressed in what looked like all new workout clothes, her long hair pulled into a high ponytail that swung as she walked.

"Have you ever been here?" she asked.

"No."

"I used to come here all the time with Naomi. There's a great view at the top."

They started walking into the forest, reveling in the energy of early spring. The sun was shining all over the new leaves and the sky was vivid blue.

"Have you decided on a college yet?" she asked after a few minutes.

The gossip about the Witneys had quieted a little lately, maybe just temporarily, with everyone talking about college as the deadline to decide approached. Lucie had already sent in her deposit to Enfield, Max to another school a few hours out of state. Declan was planning on staying in Westview and working instead. And from what Owen had heard, all of Angela's old friends were going to Walcott.

"Not yet. I'm waiting to hear back about a scholarship. Walcott is my first choice but even with financial aid, I can't afford to go there without one," he admitted, feeling the ever-present stress start to intensify.

"Oh," Angela said softly. The expression on her face made Owen wonder if she thought he resented her for not taking her practically guaranteed opportunity to go to Walcott, for never having to worry about money.

Then she smiled at him and it felt like his heart was going to burst. "I have a feeling you'll get it," she said confidently.

He hoped so, more than anything. But the part of him that was always reminding him that he wasn't good enough whispered that of course she'd say that; Angela was used to getting everything she wanted.

Everything except Harcourt. He still didn't know what she was doing instead and was afraid to ask. The last time he'd made the mistake of bringing it up, he'd watched her walls go up again and worried that he'd ruined everything.

"Do you still think you're going to major in history?" Angela added.

"Definitely."

If someone had told him a year ago that Angela Witney would remember this detail about him, he wouldn't have believed it. And he wouldn't have believed the rest of it either, that he'd told her what he knew about her family, that she'd kissed him. That they'd spend stolen weekend moments and late nights at Gracie's together. That she'd tell him her secrets and he'd tell her some of his.

The path narrowed and their hands brushed as they moved closer together, the way they always seemed to lately.

When they reached the summit, they had it all to themselves. Green for miles, blue hills in the distance. Owen took out his phone and took a few pictures of the view. Angela sat on a rock, quietly looking at the treetops. He wondered what she was thinking.

She turned around and looked at him, smiled as if she could read his thoughts. Patted the space beside her. He sat down.

"I love it here," she said, closing her eyes and breathing deep.

They sat there in silence for what felt like the best kind of forever. Around them, the early spring air was sweet with the scent of wildflowers and the sound of birdsong. Owen wished they never had to leave.

The spell was broken as the sun got lower, as a group dressed in shorts and Enfield T-shirts joined them on the summit.

"Would you mind taking a picture of us?" one of the girls asked.

"No problem," Owen said. He took her phone and they all smiled, arms around each other.

"Thanks so much," the girl said once he'd taken the picture. "Do you want me to take one of the two of you?"

Owen glanced quickly at Angela.

"Sure," Angela said. Owen handed his phone over and Angela put her arm around him.

He looked at the picture afterward. Their faces, smiling together on the screen. Her eyes were bright and happy and their hair was a little windswept. A few strands had escaped Angela's ponytail and curled around her face. Owen realized this was the first picture he'd seen of her in a while where she wasn't wearing that fake smile he'd seen so many times this fall.

He held out his phone to her so that she could look and at the same time, a text from Lucie popped up at the top of the screen.

We miss you. Wish you weren't working.

He knew she'd seen it. She looked at him and there was a hesitant expression on her face. "Can you send that to me?" she asked.

The picture didn't send until they were back in the parking lot, where the signal was better. And it didn't occur to him until afterward, when he was in his car, Angela already gone, that maybe that wasn't the question she'd wanted to ask.

***

He was covering a break at work in the jewelry department when he saw a familiar-looking woman gazing at a display of earrings.

"Would you like to try anything on?" he asked. They were supposed to be encouraging customers to look at their new stock of designer bracelets with enamel patterns but he noticed she was already wearing one. He recognized most of her outfit from this store, the pink linen dress currently on the mannequin in the window, the sunglasses he'd sold to two other women today.

She looked up. "Could I look at these?" She pointed to a pair of sapphire teardrops.

Owen unlocked the display and handed her the earrings.

She held them up to her ears. "Something blue for

my wedding," she said, glancing away from the mirror for a moment to meet Owen's eyes. She smiled, features shifting into something even more familiar and he realized who she was.

"You should ask your sister," he blurted.

Vanessa looked back at him, clearly trying to place him.

"Sorry," he said. "I'm Owen. Lucie's one of my best friends."

He glanced around quickly to make sure none of the managers were nearby and took out his phone. Scrolled through his pictures until he found one of him standing with Haley in the living room before the Tricentennial Gala. He zoomed in to focus on her bracelet and showed her the picture. "She's really talented. She made this for my sister. She's barely taken it off since."

Vanessa looked at the picture with an unreadable expression on her face.

"She also made these earrings for my mom for her birthday," he added, showing her the picture Lucie had sent him last summer as soon as she finished them.

"Lucie made these?"

He felt a little prickle of annoyance, a tiny spark of hurt and defensiveness on Lucie's behalf. *How do you not know?* he wanted to ask. How had she and Lucie once been so close but drifted so far apart?

He nodded instead, gave Vanessa his best customer service smile, wondering what else she'd missed.

"Wow. They're gorgeous," she said, still looking at the picture.

"It's probably not my business but I think it would mean a lot to her."

Vanessa looked up, nodded. "Thank you."

She placed the earrings she'd been holding back in

Owen's hand. He put them away for someone else to buy as she left, all those teardrops in jewel tones glimmering behind the glass. He wondered what she would say to Lucie, then worried that he'd done the wrong thing. Maybe he shouldn't have interfered. Maybe Lucie would be annoyed to have more work, another wedding-related task while Vanessa was distant as ever. But Lucie was so good at creating art that perfectly captured everything about the person it was for, better and more meaningful than anything you could buy here. He'd seen it every time his mother and Haley wore their jewelry from her.

He spent the rest of the night at the main register, ringing up summer dresses and sandals, placing them carefully into gift boxes and blue bags. He tried to concentrate on folding. He tried to memorize all the words of the songs that played on a loop all night. He tried not to think about all the lies he'd been telling lately, all the secrets he shouldn't be keeping.

21

The angle of the sunlight across the dining room made Angela pause as she walked into the house. There was a coating of dust all over the chandelier, she noticed, standing alone in the door-way. She could imagine the way a single footprint on the floor above it could send all that dust flying through the air. Break all the crystal, make the ceiling collapse. Everything falling apart like petals wilting from a flower.

The house was silent now, like it had been for months. She still didn't understand how you could live in the same space as someone but live in different worlds. All winter, while she was busy trying to be invisible, her parents had been paint-ing their name even louder all over Westview and Walcott. They hosted fundraisers at the country club, red dress and red tie bright against all the snow outside the windows. They gave money to sports teams and community projects, putting their names on even more plaques across town. They tried to smile their way back into this town's heart as the ground thawed, cut ribbons to return to its inner circle.

It was slowly starting to work.

There were people in this town who would never let them forget what happened, keep their reputation forever tarnished, but others were getting bored, moving on to the latest scandal. It was only a matter of time until the Witneys were close to the top again. It made Angela feel sick.

But she knew this was all happening less quickly than her parents would have liked.

Angela still only talked to Owen. Outside of school where no one could see them. In places where no one could overhear her secrets.

She thought about him while she did her homework in her room, filling up the silence with one of Cassie's old playlists as usual. The fact that they were each other's secret again. All the places they knew where no one would ever find them. All over Cherwell, all the small towns that surrounded them. They spent hours by the reservoir, in cozy coffee shops, wandering the city, and none of the Westview whispers followed her around. No expectations. For a while, she could feel less sad, ignore everything she was uncertain about. It was almost perfect.

The only problem was that he seemed so quiet lately, as if constantly lost in his thoughts. She wished she knew what he was thinking about because it seemed so unfair that he had to carry all her secrets, too. But whenever she asked, he just smiled and said everything was fine.

She was hungry by the time she finished her homework so she went downstairs to the kitchen. Her father was sitting at the table, working on his laptop. She hadn't heard him come home over the sound of lyrics that took her back to summer nights of sparks and starlight and the taste of saltwater on her lips.

"Hi," he said, glancing up from his laptop. "How was school?"

"Okay. I had a math test," Angela answered, not sure why she was even telling him this. But at least he was trying a little. More than he had in a long time. She thought of Dillon and Owen's families and the way everyone laughed and chattered as they prepared meals and kept each other company in all the in-between moments and felt a little sting of jealousy in her chest.

"Do you think you did well?"

"It was fine." Angela opened the refrigerator and took out the food she'd made yesterday. "Do you want dinner?"

"Sure." Her father closed his laptop and walked over, taking out two plates from the cabinet. "Do you have some time to talk right now?"

"Okay," she said nervously, wondering what this was about. She ran through all the possible scenarios in her head as she watched the food circle around in the microwave.

"So I want to apologize," her father said once they sat down. "I'm sorry that we just assumed Walcott was what you wanted and made you feel like that was your only option. We didn't realize how much pressure we were putting on you. And I'm sorry we didn't have this conversation earlier."

Angela didn't even know what to say. This was not the conversation she was expecting. She didn't know how to explain it, that it was more than her parents putting pressure on her. Sometimes she couldn't tell where her thoughts ended and Westview began.

"That being said," her father continued, "you have to make a decision about next year soon. What do you think you want to do?"

"I don't know. I didn't get into Harcourt," Angela admitted. She still hated hearing those words out loud.

"Did you apply anywhere else?"

She shook her head, feeling her face burning. She'd been so confident, so sure she'd get into Harcourt because she never failed anything. She always got what she wanted.

"I think it's too late to apply anywhere else," she said quietly, not looking at him.

"Do you still want to do something with fashion?"

"Yes." She could feel herself getting defensive, remembering how dismissive he'd sounded when she first told him, how her mother's eyes had flickered across the clothes she'd made, wordless.

But he opened his laptop again and turned the screen to her. "What about this? They're accepting applications until the end of this month so you still have some time."

Angela looked at the website, feeling her pulse quicken. It was a two-year fashion design program at a school she'd never heard of, the Kennett Institute. She scrolled through the course offerings, internship opportunities, photographs of current students, then clicked to see where the campus was located. It was on the opposite side of the country, all the way on the West Coast.

Ever since the day she'd been rejected from Harcourt she'd felt her world shrinking again. Everything smaller and duller as blizzards wept white and gray all over town and sent silver whispers through the wind to remind her that she would always be anchored to this place.

This made everything feel brighter. Full of possibility. It was the same feeling she had when she'd realized how much she wanted to go to Harcourt.

"You really think I should do this?" she asked.

"If you want to. I think it would be a good opportunity to get some experience and then see where you want to go from there."

She hesitated, feeling an uncomfortable combination of relief and nervousness. "How does Mom feel about this?"

"She's warming up to the idea," her father answered. He sighed. "We just don't want to lose you."

"Having a life outside of this town doesn't mean I'm going to disappear forever." She wished people could understand that. She felt like she lost another part of herself with every fake smile. If she spent her life in this town trying to be perfect, she'd be slowly drained away until she was just a paper doll. She thought about the infinity of Angelas in studio mirrors. The girl who practiced perfection in the silence of her bedroom. The girl who always smiled at parties, talked to the right people. She wished she could go back in time and tell her to stop.

"I know," her father was saying.

She didn't answer.

"Do you really hate it here that much?" He looked sad. And she could understand that a little. That it was hard to fathom that someone you gave everything to could hate the place so intertwined in their family's story.

But she hadn't always felt that way. She'd loved Westview for a long time.

"Sometimes," Angela said. "I don't like that I always have to be perfect."

"You don't have to be perfect. It's okay to make mistakes. We all do."

But she remembered how it felt to have all those eyes and voices on her. How she and her friends did the same thing. How they made it so easy to fall for being less than perfect, constantly pruning out their social circle the way all the adults did here. She thought of her parents, still trying to climb back to the top, how they could get close but probably never all the way back to where they once were. And the question that had been nagging at her for months.

"Can I ask you something?"

"Of course."

"Did you know the truth about the reservoir all along?"

He sighed again. "I knew something wasn't right. I used to think a lot about whether it was worth trying to find out the truth. I decided I was better off not knowing."

"Do you think you would have told anyone if you had?"

"Honestly? I don't know."

She let his words hang in the air for a moment, a little uncomfortable, even though she knew she didn't really have a right to be. Because she hadn't told the truth for the right reasons, and if she'd learned it any other year, she knew she would have figured out a way to destroy Owen's reputation instead so that no one else would ever learn the real story.

She hoped that part of her was gone now.

"Anyway, if you decide to do this," her father continued once they'd sat there in silence for slightly too long, "there would be some conditions. First, you need to get a job from now through the end of the summer to help pay for the program and living expenses."

"I can do that," Angela agreed.

"And we'd like you to rejoin the Tricentennial Committee."

She sighed. She didn't know how she could face them. She could imagine what they all must think of her now that the truth was out.

Her face must have given away her thoughts. "It's just a few months," her father added. "It's important for you to remain involved in the community, especially now. I spoke with Jan and she said you can take the lead on the time capsule project this summer."

"Okay," Angela said. "I'll think about it."

Later, she spent midnight at Gracie's with Owen

again. Looked around at all the photographs on the wall. For the first time, she didn't feel trapped by it all.

Their hands touched as they both reached for the door at the same time. She thought again about telling him everything she felt. About how it would feel to kiss him again. But the words were frozen at her lips. Alone in her car, she let out her breath, her thoughts like dandelion wishes.

As she drove home past sleeping shops and old houses lit up by green lights and street lights, she drew a map in her mind of all the places these roads continued on to. At their intersection, one traveled past old fields and painted curves along the coast. The other crawled west, all the way across the country, weaving through cities and state lines to eventually trace the footprints of the gold rush. Both of them stretching miles and miles away from white signs that welcomed people to a place they either lived in or drove through. Tonight she could imagine herself driving away, leaving those welcome signs behind.

22

Owen had an email from Walcott in his inbox. A reminder that the deadline to make his decision was approaching. It had been there all week, taunting him.

He clicked on it again even though he had it memorized. When he closed his eyes, he could still see the pictures of the campus, all the smiling students. He could still hear the sound of his classmates celebrating their acceptances at school.

"Owen, are you home?" He heard laughter, the front door slamming.

He went into the kitchen, where Haley and Lucie were holding cups with the Insomnia logo.

"We brought you coffee," Haley said, handing it to him along with an envelope and a postcard. "And these came for you in the mail."

"Thanks." Owen put the coffee down on the table and flipped over the postcard. It was from Enfield, another reminder about the deadline. He opened the envelope as Haley and Lucie walked past him into the living room.

"Owen," Lucie said a moment later.

He didn't answer because he was looking at the letter and his stomach was plummeting. All he could see were the words *We regret to inform you* and the Westview Scholarship Fund's logo swimming across his vision. All the air was gone from the room.

"Owen?" she said again and he walked over dazedly. And then he realized she was standing in front of the computer with the email from Walcott still bright on the screen. He'd never seen her look so betrayed and Haley looked panicked and suddenly he was angry.

"Why are you looking at my emails?"

"We were just looking up—"

He couldn't do it. He couldn't be here. He turned and left the house, let the door slam behind him. Walked down the driveway and started running so he didn't have to think. So the only thing he had to feel were his feet on the pavement.

It was windy and rainy out and he realized too late that he was still holding the letter as the wind tore it from his hands, careening into gray skies like a paper airplane. He didn't bother chasing after it.

He kept running, running until he couldn't feel his body. He didn't even know where he was going, he just kept moving away from his house and the expression on Lucie's face. He wished he'd never pinned his hopes on Walcott. He wished he could stop feeling like he wasn't good enough for Westview, that he would never be anything more than the worst things people in this town whispered about him.

He'd reached the old grist mill now and the rain was falling faster. He approached the door and was surprised to find the lock broken. He pushed the door open and walked inside.

It was dark with a musty scent, machinery covered in dust. On a barrel in the corner, a stack of red cups and empty beer cans that looked like they'd been left here recently. His wet shoes left dark prints across the floor.

He thought he'd prepared himself for how this would

feel. He thought having a backup plan would save him from feeling like everything he'd worked so hard to rebuild was falling down around him.

He didn't want to be alone anymore.

He took out his phone and texted Angela, asking her to come here. She answered almost immediately.

Owen paced back and forth across the room until he saw her headlights outside, gleaming like two little moons in the downpour. He opened the door as she parked her car.

He watched her take everything in, the sense of stepping back in time playing out across her face as her eyes roamed over abandoned machinery.

"What happened?" she asked, turning to Owen.

And now the words were spilling out, everything about the scholarship and Walcott and Lucie, stopping just before he got to all the other things he couldn't say out loud like the way he felt about her and the memories haunting him. He pushed all those things back down before they could get out, buried them deep and safe again.

"I'm so sorry," she said. Her eyes were sad and she moved closer, wrapping her arms around Owen. She was so warm, shrouded in that gorgeous summer flower scent he dreamed about.

"It's okay," he said, even though it wasn't.

He remembered everything he'd told himself so many times in preparation for this possibility: that Enfield and Lenox were both good schools, that he was so lucky to have the opportunity to go to college at all. That just knowing he'd gotten into Walcott should make him happy. But he couldn't bring himself to say it out loud because he kept thinking of every other time this place made him feel like he wasn't enough.

"No," Angela sighed against his shirt, still hugging him. "It's so unfair."

He exhaled, breath shaky.

Angela let go and stepped back. Her eyes were electric. Burning, like he'd never seen them before. "Come on. Let's do something ridiculous."

She grabbed his hand, led him outside to the old waterwheel and manmade waterfall that long ago powered this place. Stood there in the downpour, eyes on him.

"There's a waterfall in the woods near school," she said. "Cassie and I always used to go there when we were upset about something and do this."

She tilted her head to the sky and started shouting, the sound disappearing into the noise of falling water. Owen saw something in her face change and he pictured it, two seemingly-perfect girls who were never supposed to be sad, screaming when no one was watching, where the rush of water was loud enough to hide their pain.

And then she doubled over, body shaking. Collapsed on the ground. He thought she was crying until she looked up at him and he saw all the laughter in her face.

"Try it," she said, still laughing. "You'll feel a little better."

He helped her back to her feet. Stood next to her and closed his eyes as he shouted to the sky too, their voices the opposite of harmony. They screamed at sky and water until their throats and lungs ached and then they dissolved into laughter.

"Wait," said Angela as they stumbled back toward the mill. She stopped at her car and took out the blanket she always kept there, along with a black bag.

Inside, she spread the blanket out on the floor, sat down with her legs crossed. She looked up at him and motioned for him to sit next to her and even though Owen hated today he wanted to keep this moment forever, that half-smile on her face, raindrops still sliding from her long hair like tears. He was starting to feel calmer now, even though the disappointment was still heavy in his head.

"Thanks for coming here," he said. "I'm sure you have better things to do."

Angela smiled. "No, I want to be here." She looked down at the floor. "Plus, you were there for me. Even though I ruined everything for myself on purpose. You didn't have to after everything that's happened between us, but you were."

"I wanted to."

Her cheeks were a little pink. "Thank you." She placed the bag between them. "So I have something to show you. I've had this in my car for weeks now and keep forgetting. I found these when I was cleaning out my room."

The bag was full of things from her childhood, things from that summer all those years ago. Toy cars and a disposable camera and the tangled-up embroidery floss bracelets she always used to wear. A little wooden case that opened up to reveal colored pencils and oil pastels and square watercolor paints.

She opened an old coloring book to reveal crayon scribbles crossing every line. Their signatures on almost every page. A pad of drawing paper filled with colorful stick figures and shapes, their names all over everything.

"I don't think my artistic skills have improved much since then," he said and she laughed.

Angela tore off a blank sheet of paper. She drew swirling turquoise lines in oil pastel, color gliding across the page. Then she picked up an empty cup and opened the window for a moment, collecting rain. Sat down again next to Owen, so close their legs were almost touching. He wondered if she could hear his heartbeat, faster and faster, louder than the rainstorm.

"Do you remember this?" she asked, dipping a paintbrush into the water. "I used to love doing this."

She studied the watercolor palette and touched the brush to the little square of ultramarine. She started painting while the rain slowed outside. The paint soaked into the paper but stopped each time it collided with oil pastel scribbles, creating little bubbles at every intersection of oil and water. When she finished, the whole page bled with shades of blue and she could have been holding a piece of an ocean or reservoir.

She placed it on top of a barrel to dry, then joined him again on the floor.

"All of this would have kept me entertained for days. It was so much easier to be a kid," Owen said as they sifted through a jumble of crayons and playing cards.

"Do you think we'll be saying that about right now in twenty years? Looking back on high school and wishing we knew how easy we had it?"

"Maybe."

Angela picked up a knot of colorful string, tried to untangle it. "People are always telling us to enjoy right now, that this is supposed to be the best time of our lives."

So many people here still defined themselves by who they were in high school. The former Prom Queen, the football captain, the valedictorian. Their glory days, everything gold and rose-tinted. It always annoyed Owen when he heard adults talking like that. He'd always thought those were things that didn't matter much once they left high school, not labels they were supposed to carry with them through life.

"I don't want this to be it," Owen said. "I want to be more than who I am right now. More than high school."

"Me too," Angela said quietly. He could feel her

watching him as he continued looking through the contents of the bag.

He handed her a package of glow-in-the-dark stars. "I loved these. I used to have them all over my ceiling."

"Me too. They always fell off, though, so I put them on my walls instead."

She looked around and he could almost see the idea form in her mind. She jumped to her feet, ripped open the package, and gave Owen a handful of stars. She scrolled through her phone and a moment later, music was flowing from its tiny speakers, stretching all the way to old mill walls against the sound of slow rain. Lyrics breathy and hopeful like starlight. She sang along to herself while she made the walls less empty. And then it switched to an electropop love song and Owen knew that he would never hear this chorus again without thinking of tonight, pressing plastic stars to wooden beams with a girl who could probably orchestrate supernovas with her fingerprints and rearrange galaxies in her palms if she wanted to. He wished he could change the way time was moving, keep right now forever in slow motion.

Afterward, they lay down on the blanket in the now-dark mill to admire their work. Their own little universe lit up with the neon glow of fake stars arranged into invented constellations and the real ones outside, dulled by stormy skies. Their hands together. And then nothing else mattered except her lips on his like gravity and his hands in her hair, still damp from the rain and the way the moonlight shone in through dusty windows, making everything silver, a little oasis of almost-perfect in the middle of all this disappointment.

23

"We need to talk."

For a moment before she was fully awake, Angela lingered in the sleepy glow of last night, kissing Owen under fake starlight, idling outside in the misty air to prolong going home, his fingers wrapped around hers, happiness warm in her chest.

Then she opened her eyes and sunlight was crashing through the windows. Cassie had just barged into her bedroom and was holding an iced coffee and an iced tea, which she set down on Angela's nightstand.

Her first thought was that Cassie had heard about last night and she imagined everyone here talking, all of them ruining everything.

But there was no way anyone else could know, she realized.

Unless Owen had told someone.

"When are you going to stop giving me the silent treatment?" Cassie asked. "This has been going on for way too long."

Angela didn't say anything. She'd missed Cassie so much lately. It felt so strange to watch her life unfold on social media, seeing the pictures of her new tattoo instead of holding her hand through it, scrutinizing her outfits from blurry videos of parties she wasn't at instead of getting ready together. The longer they went without speaking, the easier it was to convince herself that Cassie would eventually turn out to be just like everyone else in Westview. It was inevitable. And it would hurt less to continue keeping her distance.

Cassie sighed. "Come on. Can you at least tell me what's going on in your life?"

She was quiet for another moment, then relented. "I didn't get into Harcourt."

"I'm sorry." Cassie sat down next to Angela on the bed and passed her the iced tea. "What are you going to do?"

"I don't know." She reached for her phone and showed her the Kennett Institute's website. "Maybe this."

"This would be perfect for you," Cassie said, scrolling through the page as she sipped her iced coffee. "So you could be getting out of here soon."

Angela didn't answer.

"Which means you should make the time you have left in Westview fun. Make the rest of the year memorable. Start spending time with our friends again—"

"They're not my friends," Angela interrupted, irritated. "All those people just use each other. And they're using you, too. Do you really not see that?"

"They're my friends," Cassie said defensively. "Have you ever considered that I'm happy here? I know Westview isn't perfect but I like living here. I like our group of friends and being near our family. I'm excited to go to Walcott. Why is that so hard for you to understand?"

"Don't you want something more, though?"

Cassie exhaled. "I'm not any better or worse than you because I like the life I have here. We just want different things."

"That's not what I'm saying—"

"Yes, it is. You think I'm settling for this because it seems easy but I'm not. I'm making a choice that I'm happy with. I support whatever decision you make, whether that's leaving here as soon as you can or staying. Why can't you be happy for me?"

Angela felt guilt wash over her. She remembered all the nights they'd stayed up talking about how excited they were for Walcott. How they'd planned to be roommates. They were going to take classes together and have all the best parties; everyone there would know who they were. And Cassie was the only reason Angela had visited Harcourt, even though that deviated from the plan they'd made for themselves.

"I'm sorry," Angela said. "And I'm really sorry for everything I said before. I am happy for you. You're going to be amazing there."

She meant that. She could already picture Cassie at Walcott in the fall, running for student government and coordinating new clubs, simultaneously maintaining good grades and being the life of the party. Just like she'd always wanted.

Cassie smiled hesitantly. "I'm not going to make you spend time with people you don't like. But at least spend time with me? I miss you. Are you doing anything today? I was thinking of going to Cherwell, I haven't been in forever."

"How about this afternoon? There's something I need to do first."

Once Cassie was gone, Angela opened her laptop and finished her application. She pressed *submit* and sent her wishes to the sunshine.

And later, while they walked around Cherwell together, finally catching up on everything except for Owen, admiring the pale pink magnolias and cherry blossoms that had exploded all over the city, everything almost felt right again.

***

The chilly spring air carried the aroma of freshly fried clam cakes from the small purple shack at the beach's edge. Seagulls swooped between the rose and gold sky and cobalt waves. Angela reached for her jacket and wrapped it around her body, sinking her feet into the soft sand.

Owen was stretched out on the blanket next to her with his eyes closed. If he were anyone else, it would have annoyed her that his entire attention wasn't on her. She was always surprised by how content she was to sit quietly with him. With Dillon, if they were quiet for too long, she always felt compelled to fill up the space with meaningless words because somehow the silence felt louder.

They'd sat by the harbor earlier when it was warmer, watched white sailboats ebbing in the calm water while the air breathed magic all over their skin. Angela felt brand new, like she'd been washed in sunlight. When she inhaled, her blood was sea and salt and sun and she was calm. She wanted everything to stay like this forever, for it to never get cold again.

She touched Owen's hand and he opened his eyes and smiled. She wanted to keep this too, the two of them new and safe and secret so that no one's words could ever break them.

"I'm going in the water," she said.

"It's going to be cold..."

She didn't care. The waves were calling her and she'd been dreaming of saltwater on her skin all year. She loved the feeling of the quick shock of cold the first time the tide touched her. Whenever she and Cassie were near water, they'd always wade in for a few minutes no matter what time of year it was, just to feel that momentary surge of adrenaline.

"Come with me," she said. She shrugged off her jacket and pulled her shirt over her head, sliding her jeans off. She stood there for a moment, shivering on the sand in her new bathing suit while the late April breeze tangled her hair.

Owen was looking at her with an expression she couldn't quite figure out. She placed her hands in his again, brought him to his feet to pull him closer to the ocean.

She started running, stumbling through the sand toward the water. She waded through the tangles of salty sea-weed at the shore's edge and let the water tickle her feet. And then she fell, tumbling into the shallow water, laughing as muddy sand pasted fragments of seashells to her body. The water was icy against her skin but she felt completely alive in a way she hadn't in a long time, as if all she needed to wake up was nothing but water and sky in her vision.

Owen was laughing, too, reaching out to help her up but Angela splashed him and then he was in the water with her. Sunlight danced across the tide and he was kissing her again, under endless skies this time instead of plastic stars. He tasted like the ocean. Angela wrapped her arms around him as sand and water pressed against her legs.

The bubbly froth of a wave splashed over them suddenly, draping their bodies with seaweed and drops of saltwater, and still laughing, their lips parted.

"Remind me not to come back here with you again until it's summer," Owen said, shivering in drenched denim and soaked cotton back on the shore.

Angela wrapped the blanket around them. She could feel the sand all over her body. Strands of seaweed mixed with her hair.

"Can I ask you something?"

"Sure," he said.

"Can we keep this a secret?" she whispered. She moved his arm across her shoulders and rested her head against his chest so that she didn't have to see his reaction.

"Why?" She could hear the hurt in his voice and it made her heart sink.

"I don't want to ruin it," she said. She imagined everyone in Westview talking again, making her forget what was real. She wanted to keep this theirs. Safe.

He was quiet for a moment, then said softly, "Okay."

The last sunbeams faded away behind the curving waves and the sky slowly turned deep blue to reveal twilit stars. They stayed there, quiet, until the beach was completely dark and the spell of silence was shattered by college students building a bonfire and drinking beer.

They kissed in the middle of the smudgy, faded crosswalk on the way back to their cars while the streetlights created long, stretching shadows across the road. Again in the parking lot. For a moment, their kissing silhouettes were caught in the shine of passing headlights and when they were gone, the shadows melted, dissolving into darkness and cracked pavement and all that was left was her and Owen, nothing else in the world.

24

It was a perfect day for a wedding, Owen thought as he drove past Winthrop Farm on his way to work. White chairs were set up on the lawn. An arbor covered in flowers, positioned so that the endless stripes of the fields would feature in the background of every picture. Late afternoon sunshine all over the grass. The guests were starting to arrive, cars lining both sides of the road. He couldn't see her, but he knew that Lucie was there somewhere, rushing around to ensure everything went according to plan.

There was an ache in his chest that he couldn't get rid of. It had been three weeks since that Friday night of rain and stars and kissing Angela. He hadn't spoken to Lucie since then. She'd been long gone by the time he got back home, a thousand different thoughts tangled in his mind. He'd gone upstairs to his room and texted Angela all night, wide awake, and somewhere in all those messages, they were together now.

And then, later that weekend, she'd asked him to keep it a secret. She kept saying it was better that way but Owen didn't know if that was true. He hadn't told anyone anyway. He barely saw his friends anymore, even at school. At lunch, the only time all four of them were together, he slipped outside with Angela, to the fragments of reservoir down the street. In between classes, Max and Declan tried to put his friendship with Lucie back together. She didn't seem to want to. She wouldn't answer his texts. Moved to the other side of the room in the two classes they had together. Owen tried to fight the feeling that everything was fraying.

He'd decided on Enfield just before the deadline and every time he saw someone running through town in a Walcott T-shirt or heard his classmates talking about it in the halls, it hurt a little less. He'd signed up for Orientation this morning and scrolled through their website, through their social media, finding things to look forward to.

He thought about Angela as he hung up dresses left behind in the fitting room. The way she smiled at him in golden hour and let her laughter carry across sea air, harbor lights and lighthouse beams far in the distance. He wanted to feel like this forever, like he was floating in the ocean she loved so much, nothing but soft-gold sky above and eternal blue collected from daydreams. But the expression on Lucie's face that day kept coming back to him. He thought about how she averted her eyes every time they passed each other in the hallway. His heart sank, heavy, all the way to the ocean floor.

Customers asked for flowy sundresses in colors he knew they didn't have, shoes they'd sold out of last month. Owen escaped to the back room. Pretended to look for them and texted Angela instead. On his break, he tuned out a conversation about the premiere of a reality TV show and smiled to himself as he made plans with her for the rest of the weekend.

When he left the store, he was surprised to see a message from Lucie. A picture of her and Max, smiling with wedding flowers blurred in the background.

Actually having a lot of fun tonight. I miss you. Can we talk soon?

The wedding was almost over by the time Owen got back to Westview. From the road, it looked like they were all in a snow globe of gold, a little capsule of lights with nothing but velvet sky around them.

There were a few couples still slow dancing, shoes off, music drifting up to the spring stars. The antiques Lucie had spent months collecting were the centerpieces of every table.

She was wearing a pale pink bridesmaid dress and sitting with Max. They both waved when they saw Owen approaching.

"We saved you some cake," said Lucie, handing him a plate of cake with tiny flowers trailing across the icing. "I'm glad you came. Let's talk."

He crossed the grass with Lucie to a cluster of haybales that overlooked the apple orchard, surrounded by lanterns made of blown glass.

"Vanessa told me that she asked me to make her earrings for today because of you," Lucie said. "I just wanted to say I'm sorry. For everything."

"It's okay."

"It's not. I feel terrible for making you feel like you couldn't tell me." Lucie sighed, looking out at the shadowy apple trees. "I wasted so much time judging Vanessa for her choices. When she decided she wanted to go to Walcott and became friends with all those people from legacy families, it felt like we weren't good enough for her anymore. Like she was trying to be someone she wasn't. That was all I could see. I thought she was going to spend the rest of her life trying to keep up with everyone in this town and I hated that."

Lucie was quiet for a moment, watching moths flutter around the lanterns, wings painted copper in the firelight.

"We finally talked about everything a few days ago. She told me she did get a little wrapped up in it all and didn't realize she'd made me feel like she was pushing me out of her life," she continued. "But I never realized how hard she worked to get into Walcott and to accomplish everything she has since then. She has an amazing career and she's happy. And I really like Dominic now that I've gotten to know him better."

"I'm glad," Owen said. "And I'm sorry, too. I shouldn't have lied to you. I just didn't want you to feel like I was doing the same thing and I didn't know how to tell you."

"You should be proud of yourself for getting in. I'm really sorry it didn't work out." She put her arm around him, rested her head on his shoulder and Owen breathed a sigh of relief that they were finally okay again. "They don't deserve you."

"It's okay. At least we'll be at Enfield together."

"Max told me." She sat back, smiling. "Is it selfish of me to be happy about that? We're going to have fun."

"I know, I'm excited," Owen said. He took a bite of the cake he was still holding. "This is really good. It might actually be the best cake I've ever had."

Lucie laughed. "Did you expect anything less than the best bakery in Cherwell?"

"Of course not."

"No more secrets, okay?"

"Promise." Broken as soon as he said it. He watched the long, slow flicker of the flames inside speckled glass because he knew he couldn't look at her.

She grabbed his hand and stood up. "Come on, let's dance with Max."

They danced until the only music left was the sound of crickets. Fireflies sparked in the distance. This was supposed to be one of those nights he wanted to slow down and keep forever, the blur of the lights as he laughed with his best friends and drew shapes in the sky with sparklers, the taste of springtime breathing all over tulip and lavender fields. The freedom of school starting to wind down, summer on its way.

He hated having a secret that was only half his to tell.

Later, he drove through New England backwoods with Angela. Into sleeping small towns like theirs, houses with American flags fluttering from their porches and empty rocking chairs pendulating gently in the breeze. They stopped for ice cream at a roadside stand that was just about to close and afterward, they stayed in the car until their breath fogged up all the glass. Her lips tasted like caramel. Hands soft. Skin warm and heartbeats fast, and Owen felt like he was lying to her, too.

***

Owen and Angela spent all the latest and earliest hours together now, at Gracie's or driving around aimlessly, lighting up the reservoir with their headlights while the rest of the town slept. They'd go home as the sky paled to steal a little bit of sleep, shuffle into class with tired eyes, but all those moments were worth it, he thought. Something to keep for each time she looked away from him at school, pretending he didn't exist until they could sneak off campus during lunch and then this town was only them again, if only for a few minutes.

Owen always waited until his family was asleep to leave, but tonight, he realized too late that the kitchen light was still on and Haley was sitting at the table, studying for a test. She looked up, startled when she heard his footsteps on the stairs.

"Where are you going?" she asked, eyes flitting to the car keys in his hand. She sounded nervous, almost suspicious, and he realized what this probably looked like. All those nights he'd snuck out of the house and couldn't remember how he'd gotten back here when he woke up.

"I have to finish a project with Declan," he lied, feeling guilty. But he couldn't tell her about Angela. As much as he still hated lying about this, the tiniest part of him liked having something that was only theirs. Something no one else could ruin with whispers and questions and lies.

Haley studied his face and Owen hated himself for everything she must have heard back then when she should have been sleeping. She was barely old enough to remember their father, being forced out of dreamland by the sound of shouting or drunken stumbling, the sounds that made Owen afraid of the dark as a child. But she'd known what was happening every time Owen came home the same way and made everything around him seem fragile.

He wished he could take that all back.

"Good luck," she said after a moment and Owen wondered if she really believed him or if it was just easier to pretend, the way he always had.

He met Angela at Gracie's and she drove them away from Westview, narrow roads and wide skies blending into empty darkness. Followed welcome signs into neighboring towns that all blurred together.

She was happy tonight, talking about a new photography gallery she wanted to visit in Cherwell and the dresses she'd found at a thrift shop earlier that she was going to redesign. Owen tried to pay attention but he couldn't stop thinking about that nervous expression on Haley's face, the guilt gnawing inside of him. All this time, she'd seemed so happy. He'd never stopped to consider that maybe she wasn't always okay either, that she could be pretending, too.

"You seem distracted," Angela observed as Owen stared out the window. If he hadn't known Westview by heart, he would have thought they were still there because all the roads and houses looked exactly the same. The only thing missing was the reservoir, which was supposed to belong to one of these towns instead of theirs. He sometimes imagined all the different stories that could have unfolded if Westview was whole.

Owen tested all the words in his head before he said them out loud. Tasted them. Their weight, the way they'd sound in this quiet car with nowhere to escape. He felt like he was running out of air, running out of ways to hide. Hands shaking.

"I need to tell you something," he said.

He'd almost told her so many times, the truth burning at his lips. It always took him a long time to trust people, to show them all the worst parts of himself and believe that they'd never use it to hurt him. Once he'd been a glass storm, until he taught himself to hold all those pieces close, guarded. It seemed like that was less dangerous, but it turned out it just hurt in different ways.

She'd never asked, though. Never pushed him into talking about it when the conversation veered too close, like she was waiting for him to feel safe. She must have known, too, that there were some things you couldn't say in daylight, easier confessed on late-night roads beneath violet midnights and small-town starscapes. That when you gave someone those fragments, the secrets and fears that ached all the way to your bones, there was no going back.

"Okay," said Angela.

They were stopped at a red light now, just past the center of town. Her gaze flickered over to him and she put her turn signal on without saying anything else. When the light changed, she pulled into the empty parking lot of a store that looked like it had been closed for years. Turned off the car. There was a diner across the street and for a moment, Owen watched the sleepy movements of its little universe. A woman out front on her phone, cigarette smoke hazy under neon light. Inside, a group of teenagers just like them.

Owen took a deep breath. His mouth was dry.

"My dad died when I was eight," he said. "I'm sure you've heard all the rumors about what happened."

He remembered the pictures in the newspaper, a stranger's narration of his family's nightmare folded on the kitchen table. On TVs all over town but over time the story got distorted because people loved to speculate, rewrite the facts with their own theories and details. And so parts of it got less true, while others got closer to filling in the blanks than they'd ever know.

"I've heard stories," Angela admitted. She reached over and held his hand. He looked down at the delicate silver rings she always wore.

"He hit a tree on our street on his way home after he'd been out drinking one night," Owen continued. His voice sounded so matter-of-fact but that night was still seared into his dreams. The whole world blazing with blue and red when it was supposed to be dark out. Sirens and screaming. That place he never let himself look every time he drove past.

"I'm sorry," Angela said quietly and he looked at her now. Shadows soaking her face, eyes full of sadness.

"A few years ago, everything caught up to me and it felt like too much. I'd go out drinking with people from work all the time, make bad decisions. I didn't bother trying to do well in school. I didn't think about what I was doing. I just wanted to escape."

He stared ahead again, into the diner. All those people inside probably knew versions of each other's secrets, the stories of whatever little town they were sitting in right now. Unaware of the strangers outside in a car who knew absolutely nothing about any of them, trying to be more than the things their own place and pasts had written for them.

"My mom tried to get me to stop," he said.

She'd always give him coffee in the morning when he stumbled downstairs with his head and stomach aching, tried to reason with him until it turned into shouting and slammed doors followed by hours of silence that echoed just as loudly.

"One day when we were arguing, she just looked at me and said she was afraid of me turning into him."

The words he'd known everyone in town was saying about him, what they thought every time they looked at him. He'd never forget the way her voice sounded when she said it. Like she'd given up.

Her words hurt but they'd scared him, too. It was enough to make him realize how badly he'd messed up. How much worse everything could have gotten. That day, he'd made a promise to himself that he'd be as close to perfect as possible for her.

"That was the only time we've really talked about it in years. We don't talk about him anymore. We don't talk about anything that happened but I can't stop thinking about it and I feel like I have to act like everything's okay all the time now so that she doesn't worry about me," Owen said.

He couldn't look at Angela now. "I don't remember a lot of good things about him. I don't know what Haley remembers. But she definitely remembers me being that way. She caught me leaving tonight and she had this look on her face like she was afraid it was going to start happening again."

He felt like he was clawing for the next words, the thoughts he'd had over and over, so many nights screaming in his head, feeling so sick and alone his body couldn't remember how to move or see anything but tides of jade black. Making him beg to forces and gods he didn't believe in until he was almost praying to himself, pleading to the air for help.

"Every time things in my life feel like they're getting better, I get so scared that part of me is going to come back somehow," he said quietly. He felt Angela's hand grip his fingers more tightly.

"It's not."

The way she said it was like a promise. Like something she could make true. He wished she could.

"I don't want other people to be afraid of that, too."

"Do you think you should try talking to them?"

He shook his head. Didn't say anything. He didn't want to think about it, everything he felt right now loud and amplified among all the bad memories in their house.

"That's not the only part of you," Angela added. There was something protective in her voice he'd never heard before. "You're so much more than the bad things that happened to you or mistakes you've made."

Owen willed himself to believe that. For right now to be all that mattered, almost alone in the middle of nowhere, faith in nothing but the sound of her voice and the warmth of her hand on his. Almost all of his secrets sheltered inside this car as they drove away later with the darkness and woods and stars tucked safely outside the windows, reservoir water calling them home.

The inside of his body felt scraped up, like they'd been removing tiny shards of glass. Angela kept their hands together while she drove. He was starting to feel like he could breathe again. A little lighter now that he'd said those things out loud.

But there were still the parts he couldn't tell her. Couldn't tell anyone. That day he was six and it was hot outside and he was building a city in his sandbox, thirsty.

He remembered walking into the kitchen to find

water. The way the sunlight flowed in through the open window, framed by old curtains, painting angles of glowing gold across his mother's face.

His father, standing by the sink, wrapped in the stale scent of beer. Shattered at his feet, a plate, white with red flowers painted precisely around the edges. Stressed syllables leaving his lips with strings of spit.

And then, a movement that seemed to occur in slow motion, suspended seconds. His father's fingers curled into a fist, arching through stripes of light and graceful dust to collide with his mother's skin. The mark it left, red.

She stumbled back toward the counter, knocking over a bottle of wine. It covered the floor with pools and frantic lines of scarlet, sharp edges of glass glinting in the sunlight.

He wanted to run to her but he was frozen, skin still against the doorframe. And when his body finally remembered how to move, he ran away instead. Outside through the heat to collapse in the sandbox, crushing his carefully constructed city with shaking limbs. Shards of sand stung his eyes. He could taste its grit at his lips. The shouting was outside now, too, bleeding through the windows. Loud in the blazing sunlight like the sound could touch the sky.

And after that day, so many times until that winter night where siren light painted the snow like stained glass in a cathedral, he'd hidden away while it happened again. He couldn't ever move, tired eyes scared wide open in the dark. No one to ask for help when he saw her at her mirror in the mornings, blotting on makeup in stale sunlight to cover all the bruises. And now, he still didn't know how to live with himself for doing nothing, staying scared and silent, letting her get hurt. So he just kept running and running, all of it always so close behind, always chasing him in his dreams, down streetlight-less Westview roads drenched in black.

25

"Do we really have to go back to school right now?" Owen sighed.

They were at what had become their new lunch spot after almost getting caught at the reservoir last week, a small park at the top of the hill where Angela used to go sledding every winter. From where they were sitting, they could see cars soaring down Westview's main road.

"What if we don't?" Angela suggested, stretching out on the blanket she'd brought from her car. She kicked off her shoes and buried her toes in the grass.

"You mean skip class?"

"No one's going to miss us," Angela insisted. "It's too nice to be inside. Come on, let's be a little rebellious."

"I spent most of freshman year skipping class," Owen said, sounding apprehensive. "I think I've been rebellious enough."

She could see a little flicker of regret in his face and she thought back to everything he'd told her. Everything he was afraid of.

Until that night, she hadn't realized he'd been pretending, too.

She moved closer to him, wishing she could take every bad memory away. He was looking up at the sky now. Then he glanced at her and sighed, a small smile at his lips as she was about to tell him they could just go back to school, find someplace to meet up later.

"It is really nice out, though," he said, like he was actually considering it. "And you're right, no one's going to miss us, especially in study hall…"

"Okay." Angela sat up and took his hands in hers, arranging her face into an overly serious expression and trying not to smile. "I promise we'll go to every class for the three weeks we have left of high school. With the exception of the last day of classes because no one goes then. I've *never* skipped a class. Isn't that one of those things you're supposed to do before you graduate?"

He laughed. "Fine, you win. Where do you want to go?"

In Cherwell, they walked along the esplanade, holding hands. Past the tables of old books with orange spines, past painted carousel horses and trees threaded with blue lights. They went to the modern art museum and took the escalators all the way to the top, moving slowly through galleries that looked over the river.

"So I got into the Kennett program I told you about," Angela told Owen as he stopped to take a map of the museum from an information kiosk. She'd found out last night but wanted to keep it for herself for a little while. She hadn't told either of her parents yet.

"That's amazing," he said. "Congratulations."

"Thanks." She smiled. It felt so much more real, more exciting now that she'd said it out loud.

"So are you going to do it?" Owen asked.

"I think so." Angela led him into the next gallery,

where a large metal sculpture sprawled across the entire room. She hadn't been able to stop thinking about it. She didn't know how she could turn it down, even if it wasn't the exact plan she'd made for herself.

She didn't feel time passing as they worked their way through each gallery. The riverside was busy by the time they left the museum, the city partway through the evening rush as a stream of people in black businesswear left their offices. The bars and restaurants facing the water were slowly starting to come to life as people congregated at tables beneath striped umbrellas, sipping cocktails. Angela inhaled the energy of it all. Calm and chaos all at once, water lapping softly against the embankment and hundreds of conversations buzzing in the atmosphere, wildflower-bright. Stiletto footfalls and cell phone gossip and crisp fabric rushing past on their way to different destinations.

They stayed there until the flow of commuters slowed and the evening twinkled with a symphony of laughter and clinking cutlery.

"How do you feel about boats?" Angela asked. "Or heights?"

"I'm fine with either," Owen said. "Why?"

Angela pointed to a red tour boat gliding across the river, traced the water all the way to the Ferris wheel further along the bank. "Remember that list we made this winter? Do you want to do something really touristy?"

"Sure."

She bought tickets from the small booth by the dock and they boarded the boat. They stood on the deck, against the railing. Hands together. Ahead of them, the lights of the bridges stretched across the water like necklaces. There was a guide talking about Cherwell's history, pointing out all the landmarks. Beside her, Owen listened intently but Angela let herself tune out. Right now, she felt free, like the city was theirs, everything open to endless possibility. She imagined that this was what next year would feel like. New people and places, opportunities she'd been dreaming about all year. Far away from all the history that rooted her in Westview. Far away from people who thought they knew everything about her.

She caught Owen's eye and smiled. He wrapped his arms around her as the sun sank into the water. Angela closed her eyes and let this city have all of her, steal the air from her lungs, tear wind through her hair.

They disembarked in front of the Ferris wheel and floated all the way to the top in glass capsules like bubbles. They kissed high above the gold veins of the city, over the gentle tide of ultramarine that ribboned all the way across centuries-old gridlines to meet saltwater. She let Owen erase the entire world, one of those movie clichés she would never admit to wanting aloud. She smiled in the dark. All the things she felt tonight sang back to her in clear skies and city lights.

On the ground, she led him to an outdoor market in the shadow of a bridge where color and flavor sizzled in the air. She'd never taken Dillon here. They'd always gone to the fanciest restaurants, places people went when they wanted to be seen. Perfect places she wore her best clothes to, shielded her face with makeup because she thought if she looked perfect, too, no one could see everything she felt inside. She'd built castle walls out of all the words she didn't want them to say. Fed them sugar and venom to keep them close but not too close.

Tonight she didn't worry about that. She watched the city move from the stone steps of a quiet cathedral. People eating and laughing and lost in each other's eyes. Everyone in their own world but part of the fabric of this place, millions of stories and dreams intersecting. Tonight, her happiness could light up this entire city. Everything around her felt bright.

26

Owen's phone was ringing when he got out of work. Angela.

He knew she only liked to talk on the phone when she was lonely, to fill her big, beautiful house with sound. But when he picked up, she sounded excited.

"I got us tickets for the summer festival tomorrow," she said as he got in his car. "I thought we could go later in the afternoon, that's the best time to go."

"Oh." Owen hesitated. "That's a little far from here, isn't it? I have plans tomorrow night."

"What are you doing?"

He could hear just the smallest hint of hurt in her voice.

"It's Declan's birthday. We're having a surprise party at Max's house. I told him I'd go over early to help get everything ready."

Angela didn't say anything.

"You can come if you want to—"

Angela sighed. "I told you, I don't want anyone to know yet. And your friends don't like me."

"My friends don't *know* you."

He wanted to tell them. He was so tired of hiding this.

Now that he and Lucie were friends again, he knew it would be better to just come clean, instead of letting them find out from someone else. At this point, she'd be more upset to find out he'd been lying to her again.

"What if we just go for a little while? You can go to the party later. Please, it's a tradition."

It wasn't, he wanted to say. It was her friends' tradition. He saw pictures of them every year, posing on pale sand against pink sunsets, lounging on the lawn in their bathing suits, smiling from the deck of a beach house with plastic palm-tree shaped cups in their hands. He'd heard something about them all going to the Tremonts' new lake house this weekend, though, and realized with a stab of disappointment that she was only suggesting this because she wasn't worried about people seeing them together.

Sometimes he felt like all Angela ever wanted to do were things she used to do with her friends and a feeling of doubt crept into his thoughts. Sometimes he was afraid that she was just using him to escape, to kill time while she counted down all the minutes and miles until she was flying free from this town. He tried to push the feeling away.

"Okay," he agreed.

He could feel a sense of heavy exhaustion coming back to him as he hung up. He'd woken up in the middle of the night from another dream where the universe was tearing itself apart or maybe he was destroying it himself and then he was chasing ghosts and voices he couldn't find. After an hour of staring at his ceiling, wide awake in the dark, remembering all the glow-in-the dark stars that used to be there, he'd crept downstairs to make coffee and afterward, when he couldn't stand the thought of not moving, he went outside and started running. He ran until the sky burned pyrite and indigo and the sun bled daylight all over the fields. Even now, he still felt like he was trying to catch his breath. Slow his heartbeat.

He texted Max another lie, promised to stop by the party later. Drove home with a pit in his stomach.

"Welcome to the unofficial start of summer," Angela said the next afternoon as their feet touched the lawn. She threw back her head, spread her arms like she was trying to absorb the sun and sky. Her floppy straw sun hat fell off and Owen caught it before it hit the ground. She laughed as he put it back on her head and kissed her.

As she spread out a blanket on the grass, she looked so happy that Owen felt the last traces of annoyance dissolve. The park was full of people lying on beach chairs and blankets in their bathing suits. There was a stage set up at the front, with food trucks and artist shanties lining the park's perimeter. Across the street, flags shaped like sails and ropes of striped, colorful lobster buoys led to the beach. From where they were sitting, Owen could see a tiny triangle of ocean ahead, and to his left, a row of gray-shingled shops with sky-blue hydrangeas spilling over white picket fences.

"I love this band," Angela sighed. She took off her beach cover-up, revealing a turquoise bikini underneath, and lay down on her stomach. "I'm so happy right now. We're going to have the best summer. We can go to the beach all the time, we can do all the touristy things in Cherwell we've never done…"

"We should go to the Pier," Owen suggested.

"Definitely," Angela agreed. "I've heard that's fun. And we should come here for the fireworks on the Fourth, they're so much better than the ones in Westview."

"And Bismore Island," Owen added.

Angela smiled, eyes bright. "I love Bismore Island. We used to go there all the time. I can't wait until school's over. I want every day to feel like this. I feel so *free*." She reached for her bag, which was next to Owen. "Can you pass me my sunscreen? I think I'm burning already."

He handed the bag to her and she rummaged through it. Onstage, the band launched into a new song, happy and upbeat.

"I must have left it in my car. I'll be right back," Angela said after a moment, standing up and sliding her feet into her sandals.

Owen closed his eyes and let the warmth of the sun and slight breeze lull him into sleepy content. There was something about ocean air, he thought, even the air in their little reservoir town. He couldn't imagine being landlocked.

"Owen? What are you doing here?"

He opened his eyes and sat up. Brooke Marston was standing there, carrying a folded-up beach chair and cooler.

"Hi, Brooke." He hesitated and Brooke glanced at the hat and beach cover-up Angela had left behind on the blanket. Her eyes widened.

"Are you here with someone? That explains *so* much, Lucie was just saying you haven't seemed like yourself lately..."

His stomach plummeted. He wondered why Lucie was talking to Brooke about him.

Brooke was looking around the park and Owen hoped that Angela was still at her car because he couldn't do this right now; he couldn't have Brooke find out before any of his friends. "So who is she?" she asked.

He bit his lip. "I'm sorry," he said quickly. "It's really new and we're not ready to tell anyone yet ... can you keep this quiet for now? I promise I'll explain later." He hated saying that, hated how he sounded right now. None of his friends would have ever done this to him.

"Of course." Brooke glanced at her phone, curiosity still gleaming in her eyes. "I have to go now anyway but we'll talk later. I was just here with my family—we come every year. But I need to get back home before the traffic gets bad. I'll see you tonight."

"Tonight?"

"Declan's birthday. You're coming, right?"

He looked at her, confused. He'd thought tonight was just going to be the four of them. He didn't even know that Brooke and Declan were friends; he'd barely seen them talk to each other.

"Oh. Yeah, I'm going to try to stop by."

Brooke's eyes narrowed a little and her lips turned into a slight frown.

"Please don't tell anyone you saw me here," he added, feeling horrible as he said it.

"I won't," she said but her voice was a little less friendly now. "See you later."

He lay back down and closed his eyes again, feeling slightly on edge, until Angela came back with her sunscreen. She stretched out beside him and Owen let the sounds of the music and conversation wash over him. They watched people shuffle to and from the beach carrying totes and beach chairs, flow in and out of the stores along the street. Angela bought them a white paper bag of saltwater taffy from a pink-painted shop and they ate them while people danced by the stage. He kissed her, hands in her hair, warm from the sun. He tried to ignore how tired he felt. The way Brooke had looked at him and the tone of her voice when she left.

They didn't realize that they'd lost track of time until the sky started to turn dusky blue. He kissed Angela goodbye in the parking lot, got in their separate cars to go home to the same town. Sat in traffic for hours and watched the stars come up from a highway lane glowing with headlights for miles. Owen felt worse with every minute that dragged by.

When he got to Max's house, only his parents' car was in the driveway and all the lights were out. Owen thought about texting him to find out where they'd gone but exhaustion was aching behind his eyes and he felt sick.

He drove home in the dark by himself. Woke up at two in the morning after yet another dream about screaming skies and shattered planets. He looked at his phone to distract himself. There were pictures from the party. Declan walking into Max's living room, clearly faking surprise. Max, Sam and Theo, all smiling. Brooke and Lucie wearing party hats. A bonfire, all of them together in front of a red barn he didn't recognize with sunflowers painted along the sides. Another group picture on the back deck of a house Owen had never seen. Disoriented, he tried to figure out where they were. He thought about it until he fell asleep and when he woke up again he was glad he couldn't remember his dreams, but the heaviness in his head and heart was still there.

27

On the evening of Prom, Angela wore a dandelion-gold dress and diamond earrings, and styled her hair the same way she had for the Homecoming parade and Tricentennial Gala. She stood on the sweeping staircase inside Cassie's house like they always did, and then outside by the lilacs, smiling for their parents.

"Are you sure you don't want to come to Naomi's for pictures first?" Cassie asked once they were alone in the driveway.

"Actually, I don't really feel like going to Prom at all," Angela said nonchalantly, trying to act like this thought had just occurred to her.

"What?"

"There are some people from Cherwell who got into Kennett and we were thinking of meeting up tonight," Angela lied.

Cassie looked disappointed. "But it's our Senior Prom. Don't you think you'll regret not going?"

"I don't think so. I had fun last year. I'm okay with that being my memory of my last high school prom." She remembered it still, that blue dress floating around her like she was wearing the prettiest summer day on her body.

"It won't be the same without you, though," Cassie said.

Angela thought about how people always used to say those words to her, how it always used to make her feel important. The center of attention in every room, at every party. She shook her head. "You won't even notice I'm not there."

She drove away from Westview with her windows down and put on one of Cassie's old playlists, one from the beach last summer. When she heard it, she remembered the sight of the ocean from lighthouse windows and sunrise colors across sand dunes and nights where the stars seemed to go on forever. The feeling of flying.

Owen was already there, waiting in the train station parking lot.

"You look nice," he said, getting out of his car and leaning in through Angela's open window to kiss her.

She smiled. "Thanks."

"Are you sure you don't want to go?" Owen asked, gaze sweeping over her dress and she thought she saw a little longing in his eyes.

"I'm sure. It's too late to get tickets anyway," Angela said. "I just want to be with you. I'm just going to change quickly before we go."

In the backseat of her car, she exchanged her prom dress and heels for a sundress and sandals. She scrubbed off some of her makeup, left the diamond earrings on.

She'd always wanted to come to Cherwell Arts Night with Dillon but they'd never had the chance. Along the river, a series of pop-up galleries showcased work by local artists and she wandered through them with Owen, admiring everything.

When it got dark, a crowd gathered at the riverside and the notes of a slow, hypnotic melody warbled into the air. A procession of people carrying torches made their way onto waiting gondolas and one by one, each boat glided serenely toward a line of wood-filled cauldrons raised slightly above the current. As the music drifted across the night, somehow sounding like both hope and heartbreak, they lit each one until a mile of river burned bright with flames, the reflections shimmering amber on the water. If she'd watched from above, Angela would have thought the whole river was ablaze.

It all felt like magic. The night smelled like wood smoke, air perfumed with embers and cello notes. Water and fire electric gold, a collection of all the stars and sun and city lights burning and flowing in tides.

She glanced over at Owen, who was looking at his phone. In the firelight, she could see a sad expression on his face.

"What's wrong?" she asked.

"Nothing," he said quickly, erasing the sadness from his face as soon as he realized she was looking at him. He put his phone in his pocket.

She took his hand and they walked along the river, past dancers and performers. People drifting by in boats spun fire and tossed yellow roses into the crowd.

"I'm so glad we came here," Angela said as they crossed the bridge. She stopped to take a picture of the view on her phone. Plumes of fire smoldering over water, the city iridescent in the background.

The screen lit up with a notification from Cassie. It was a picture of her and Adam in the middle of a dance floor, both wearing plastic crowns. Familiar faces of their classmates blurred around them.

There was a twinge of regret she didn't think she'd feel, a sensation she was missing out on something she was supposed to be a part of. She ripped it up in her mind and tried to focus on where she was now, how she felt alive and electric here.

She realized Owen hadn't answered her. He was looking at his phone again and Angela saw a picture of his friends on the screen, all dressed up and smiling.

"Wait. Are you upset we're not at Prom?"

He ran his hand through his hair the way he always did when he was frustrated. "I just wish we didn't have to keep this a secret."

"It's better this way," she whispered. "Just us. No Westview."

He looked like he wanted to say something else but he didn't. He just sighed.

"Look," Angela said, pointing ahead toward a small square where paper stars hung from the trees, little lights inside them to make them glow blue and gold. She led Owen to the table where a woman was collecting donations, handed her wrinkled bills in exchange for glittery, counterfeit cut-outs of the galaxy. Passed one to Owen, watching it twirl on its string.

Angela remembered the first time she saw Cherwell at night, years ago. The first time she'd ever looked up at a clear night sky and not seen the stars there, couldn't find the familiar letter she'd always draw in the air with her finger. All the lights here were too bright, her parents explained to her back then. You couldn't see the stars. She'd hated that for the longest time, until the night she fell in love with city lights.

So now, years later, she hung up stars in a starless night with a boy she could be slow dancing with in a small town if she hadn't been so afraid of words. She kissed him there, under all the trees and paper stars in a city without constellations, in a universe constructed of manmade lights. Made him forget everything except her.

28

"What did you get for the last question?" Declan asked. "I think I did something wrong."

"I thought we agreed not to talk about finals right now," said Lucie. "We're supposed to be celebrating. We're officially done with high school."

"I don't think we're officially done until graduation," Declan said and Lucie rolled her eyes.

Owen sat down next to her and looked around the familiar restaurant. Breakfast at the Red Hen was their tradition after the last final exam of every school year. The décor around them was Americana amplified, all tin stars and patriotically painted barn wood secured to the wall in flag stripes. Rooster figurines and everything plaid, old paintings of horse-drawn carriages. This place looked like a cliché of what people probably expected to find when they came to a town like this, somewhere clinging to nostalgia, but Owen loved it here. The smell of home fries and freshly brewed coffee. It felt cozy, like home.

The door opened and Max walked in with Theo, followed by Sam and Brooke. Owen realized that Max and Theo were holding hands and he felt a rush of guilt, wondering how he could have missed that.

"Lucie, do you want to go shopping later?" Brooke asked, sitting on Lucie's other side. "I know it's early but I already found a sale on dorm supplies."

"Did you two get your dorm assignment already?" Declan asked.

"Not yet," said Lucie. "We just submitted the request to be roommates and we'll get assigned to a dorm later this summer."

Owen looked over at her, confused. The last time they'd talked about it, she'd been planning on living at home, turning Vanessa's old bedroom into a study space.

"Owen, are you living on campus, too?" Theo asked. "Maybe you'll all be neighbors."

"No, I'm living at home."

"I'm sure we'll see each other all the time," said Brooke but her voice was almost cold again, like it had been that afternoon at the summer festival.

Owen nodded and pretended to look at the menu even though he got the same thing every time they came here. Lucie and Brooke had moved on to talking about how they wanted to decorate their dorm room and he wondered when they'd all become such good friends. How he'd missed Max and Theo finally getting together. Had he really been that distracted? It was as if he'd forgotten that the world went on for everyone else while he was roaming around the reservoir and escaping to riversides with Angela.

He felt terrible now for missing all of those moments, not just the big moments they'd spent hours dreaming of around their corner table at Insomnia, but the little memories. Lunchtime conversations and sitting by the water until dusk, after-school coffee runs and wandering through town. He'd tried to convince himself that it didn't matter every time he lied to sneak away with Angela, that there would be another trivia night or movie marathon. But their lives moved on in all those moments, diverging a little every time he didn't show up.

"What can I get you all?" a server asked, approaching the table with a notepad, interrupting a conversation about something that had happened when they'd camped out in Brooke's backyard last weekend.

Owen placed his usual order, relieved to have a momentary break from sitting there with a fake smile on his face, pretending to know what they were all laughing about. He felt like there was a spotlight on him that no one was looking at.

He tried not to check his phone to see if Angela had texted him back from her first day of work at the vintage shop in the next town over. He could tell she'd been more nervous about it than she wanted him to know.

When their mugs were filled with hot coffee, Lucie tapped her spoon against her glass. "We need to toast," she said. "This has been the best year. Here's to finishing high school and to all the new memories we're going to make this summer."

They raised their coffee mugs and clinked them together.

Owen remembered all the times he'd looked at this group and thought they were everything keeping him together. He'd never wanted to break that but somehow, he had. Without even realizing it.

Their food came but he wasn't hungry. He pushed it around on his plate until it got cold, looked down at the paper placemats that were printed with ads for local businesses. Brooke and Lucie were talking about Lucie's upcoming art show and across the table, Sam and Declan were debating the ending of a movie they'd just seen, one Declan had promised to see with Owen back when they'd first watched the preview. Max and Theo were making plans for next weekend.

These were the only people he'd never felt alone around but he felt it now and knew it was his fault. He didn't even know what to say to them.

So much about today felt familiar. All of them cramped into this tiny restaurant with little tables pushed together, big plates of crispy bacon and eggs and fluffy pancakes drenched in sweet syrup, topped with bright berries and a snowy dusting of confectioners' sugar. The coziness of chatter and hot coffee, sunshine streaming in through checkered curtains. But he could feel a distance, a distance he hadn't even felt back when the rest of them were already knit together by years of friendship and he was just getting to know them all. He could feel himself fading away.

29

Angela hadn't expected to feel sentimental about graduation.

But they'd all been here together in this town for so long that it seemed like they knew the insides of each other's thoughts. Bonded by days of hopscotch in front of the brick elementary school and dances in the middle school gym and constructing high school Homecoming floats. It was getting harder to imagine a life without seeing these people every day because that was all she'd ever known, no matter how she felt about them now.

She crossed the stage, shook hands with the principal. Thought about how all those years of yellow school buses and math tests and damp, dreary mornings on the outdoor track were over now, all culminating with this moment in a white polyester gown with too-long sleeves.

On her way back to her seat, she saw a group of freshman girls, carefree, and remembered herself back then, when she loved Westview, when it seemed like everything she needed in the world was here and she'd never thought of leaving. When high school seemed infinite and things would never change and that was okay because the innocence of morning walks to the bus stop and late-night phone calls was enough.

At the end of the ceremony, they turned their tassels. Threw their caps in the air. For a moment the sky was gone and all she could see was photographs. Favorite memories frozen in color and glued to black mortarboards, careening through the universe, then raining down into waiting hands.

Angela took a deep breath and took it all in, the buzz of the parents on the lawn, the scratchy stitching of the gown's hem across her legs, and the breeze and the sunlight and the groups of classmates gathering for pictures as the ceremony ended.

"Angela, get in the picture," Cassie called, motioning for her to join the group standing in front of the stage.

For just a second, Westview didn't seem so bad. Angela put her arms around Cassie and Rose. Smiled, real this time.

It seemed like all week, people had been telling them that Westview made them who they were. Angela wondered if she would have been someone else if she'd grown up in a different town, with different people. If she would have wanted to fly far away from other places too, higher and further until they were only blue and green and then gone, so that she could scatter pieces of her heart elsewhere.

***

The air conditioner at work was broken and the store was uncomfortably warm already, summer heat burning bright through the windows. She'd been here since they opened this morning and it had been mostly quiet since then. The only other person working was Rayne, a local college student who had trained Angela last week.

Angela wiped down the register yet again just to have something to do. The radio switched over to a beach traffic update, then into commercials. She flipped through the channels until she found something she liked. A song she'd blared in her bedroom last spring while she got ready for Prom with Cassie and Naomi.

"These are great," Rayne said. She was holding Angela's phone, looking at the pictures of the latest clothes she'd been working on. "I love this purple dress."

Angela felt pride spread through her. "Thanks."

"Is this your boyfriend?" she asked, scrolling to the next picture, Owen and Angela smiling, wind and Cherwell lights in their hair.

Angela hesitated, then remembered that Rayne wasn't from Westview. They didn't know any of the same people. She smiled. "Yeah. That's Owen."

"What's he doing next year?"

"He's going to Enfield College."

Rayne handed her phone back. "Do you think you'll stay together when you leave?"

"Why wouldn't we?"

Rayne leaned against the counter and shrugged. "You're going to be on the other side of the country, right? Think of everything you'll miss out on if you're still with someone here. My best friend's boyfriend moved halfway across the country for college and she stayed here. They tried long distance for a while but it didn't work out. She really regretted not just ending it before he left."

Angela pictured the few people she'd known who left this town, always returning to the places they'd left behind. Everything felt cold now.

Something in her face must have looked panicked, because Rayne quickly backtracked. "Or maybe you'll be fine. It's just a year or two, right? You'll be back here soon enough."

She thought about that at home while she got ready to go to the beach with Owen. She put on her bathing suit and a sundress but hated how it looked when she saw her reflection in the mirror. She tore through her closet, left clothes all over the floor. Nothing seemed to look right.

She suddenly realized exactly which dress she wanted, the seafoam-colored one she always used to wear around Dillon's beach house. She dragged out the boxes of clothes she'd pushed to the back of her closet last fall and started taking them out, hanging them all up again until she found it. She put on the dress, looked in the mirror, and smiled. It looked perfect.

***

After they left the beach, they climbed to the top of a nearby stone tower. From one side, all they could see was water; from the other, miles of small towns. She remembered that night on the Ferris wheel in Cherwell when she could see endless light. Here it was just houses and lives like hers on the horizon, the sky a canvas of pink and purple.

Angela didn't tell Owen what she was thinking, Rayne's words echoing across her thoughts. She didn't want things to change right now. Didn't want to know his answer.

Instead she told him she needed to go home and they kissed goodbye in the blue hour. As she drove home to old songs, the realization kept creeping back into her thoughts as suddenly as burned-out streetlights on midnight roads. She'd spent so much time dreaming of running away that she'd forgotten it might only be temporary. Forgotten to think about what came after. She hadn't realized that if she failed, she too would be flying back here, this place magnetic in her bones.

30

"That looks good," Angela said, peering over Owen's shoulder at the flyer he'd just finished making to advertise the remaining tricentennial events. "I think we can print them now. Where's the paper Jan wanted us to use?"

"I think it's downstairs."

"I'll go get it," Angela offered.

She went downstairs and Owen stood up, taking a quick walk around the quiet library to the bathroom. He'd barely slept last night and in the mirror, his face was pale and puffy, purple-gray shadows under his eyes. He splashed some cold water onto his face.

As he returned to the computers, he saw Lucie standing at the circulation desk.

"Hey," he said, walking over as the librarian took a stack of books off the shelf and handed them to her.

"Nice to see you," Lucie said coldly, sliding the books into her tote bag.

"What's wrong?" Owen asked, startled by her tone.

"Where were you today?"

He tried to remember what else he was supposed to be

doing today but his head felt like it was underwater. "What are you talking about?"

"The art show. We were all texting you, trying to find out where you were. I can't believe you didn't show up. You knew how important this was to me."

Owen's heart dropped. He reached into his pocket to take out his phone, then realized he'd left it downstairs earlier. "I'm so sorry," he said. "I was—"

"Don't," she said. "Don't tell me you were at work. We were all at the mall last week when you said you were working and we stopped by to visit you since we never see you anymore but they said you had that day off. And Brooke told me she thought you were lying about why you missed Declan's party."

"I promise, I just forgot the art show was today—"

"You've missed so much, Owen. I don't know what's been going on with you but you've been drifting away all year. I thought you were just busy with school and that's why you were never at lunch and stopped coming to trivia. But I feel like you always have an excuse not to be around us. The last time we saw you other than graduation was when we got breakfast after finals and you barely talked to anyone."

"I'm so sorry. I honestly just forgot and didn't have my phone on me. I know that's a bad excuse but that's the truth."

Lucie sighed. "I have to go."

"Lucie, wait—"

She was already leaving. Owen slumped into a chair by the computers, the feeling in his head even worse.

"I couldn't find—what's wrong? You look sad," Angela said, coming back up the stairs. She placed his phone on the table. "You left this downstairs, by the way."

He got up and turned away from her, pretending to

look at a display of new books because he didn't want her to see his face right now.

"Owen," she said softly and the sound of his name made him feel like everything was burning. She touched his arm and then she was kissing him, the way she never did when they were somewhere in Westview where people might see. Her lips were soft and she tasted like wintergreen. But the world didn't disappear like it usually did. He was too busy thinking about Lucie, who had only showed up to the gala because he'd helped plan it and always practiced for school presentations with him. She'd made beautiful jewelry for his family and decorated their friends' lockers on their birthdays every year. And he couldn't even remember to go to her art show.

"Are you okay?" Angela asked, lacing their fingers together.

He was so angry at himself, disappointed. He couldn't even look at her.

And then he heard Lucie's voice again at the circulation desk. "Sorry, I just left my—"

And then their eyes met and she was walking toward them. Angela was still holding his hand and the moment she realized what was happening, she jumped back like she'd been scalded.

"Owen. Are you serious?"

"I'm going to go," Angela said quickly, giving Owen a panicked look.

Lucie didn't even look at her as she brushed past. "What happened to no more secrets? Is she the reason you've missed everything?"

He sank into a chair, face in his hands. "I'm sorry. It's complicated."

"No it's not," Lucie said and he hated that she didn't even sound angry. She just sounded sad, which made him feel even worse. "You just don't value our friendship enough to tell the truth about anything. We've been drifting apart for so long. Maybe it's just better to let that happen."

It hurt to breathe. Lucie was walking away again and Owen considered going after her but his body felt like it was tearing apart from the inside. The room was blurry, computer screens bright blue and book spines angry stripes across his vision. All the silence was hurting his head, her words screaming in his thoughts over and over even though she hadn't raised her voice. Her sadness turning him to dust.

He tried to breathe. Closed his eyes and pressed his fingers to his eyelids. He went downstairs to look for the paper so he could at least do one thing right today. Angela was there.

"Please don't," he said when she started to say something. He didn't want to fight with her, too. He turned away and started searching through cabinets and drawers. They were all labeled wrong, and frustrated, he slammed one shut harder than he meant to, cringing at the loud clanging noise it made. Something about that sound, all his fault, made him want to break down, dissolve right there.

"Owen, I'm so sorry."

"Not now," he said, the words catching in his throat. He finally found the paper and grabbed both reams even though it was more than he needed. His head was still spinning. There wasn't enough space for everything he felt right now. Everything was falling apart. Everything was gone. All their inside jokes and adventures and plans for next year.

"Okay," Angela said quietly.

Upstairs, he printed the flyers. The bright red of the paper stung his eyes. He drove home. Everywhere he looked it hurt. Reservoir everywhere. He had memories mapped out all over this place, so many of them with Lucie. Without her, this town felt like nothing but empty pages.

31

Angela loved summer mornings. She loved the color of the sky when she woke up, the warmth of sunlight all over town, the stillness of the neighborhood. She stood on the diving board of the pool, savoring all the quiet, and jumped in.

She opened her eyes underwater and saw nothing but ripples and blurry tiles. She emerged when it felt like her lungs would burst, floating on her back. Watched a plane soar across the sky, leaving behind contrails like contour lines on a map. She thought about what Westview must look like from up there. More blue than green.

She'd booked her plane ticket this morning and her heart raced every time she thought about it. Rayne's voice still lingered in her head, along with the feeling she'd had driving back from the tower when she realized what failing meant. All of that tangled with the longing she felt when she looked at pictures of other places.

When the water felt too cold, Angela got out of the pool and showered. Snipped the tags off a flowy white eyelet sundress she'd bought at a boutique last summer when she was staying at Dillon's beach house. She left with her hair still wet. As she backed out of her driveway, she paused to take a picture of her house with the instant camera Jan had given her to document today.

Tonight Westview was filling its time capsule, which was going to be kept in the library and opened a century from now. Angela wondered what this town would look like then, if all the places she knew by heart would still be there.

She drove around and took pictures of the green-trimmed shops downtown and the old grist mill, ash-colored, with all the plastic stars still hidden inside. The prettiest part of the reservoir and the fields and the view from the top of Pembroke Hill. She stopped at Walcott and photographed the wrought iron gate with its little gold flowers and the reflection of the chapel in the fountain. Took a picture of the library on her way inside.

In the basement, she spread out all the pictures across a table and started writing the name of each location across the bottom until Owen walked in with a large envelope and a cup of coffee. He sat down next to her but didn't say anything.

"What did you bring?" Angela asked, desperate to cheer him up. He'd been distant all week, his fight with Lucie polluting everything. She tried to smile like there was nothing wrong.

Owen emptied the envelope onto the table. There was a copy of this week's local newspaper and a coaster from Gracie's. A printed map of Westview and colorful flyers advertising all of the tricentennial events throughout the last year. One of the bottle stoppers they'd given out as favors at the gala, with the words *Westview Tricentennial* and little evergreen trees etched into it.

"What about you?" he asked. It sounded like he was asking more out of politeness than actual interest and Angela hated that. She wished they could go back to when the world was only them, like summer all the time.

Angela pointed to the small pile to their left and Owen looked through it. She'd collected magazines over the last few days, a combination of local and national publications, laughing a little when she thought about people reading century-old celebrity gossip and news that seemed so important now. On her way out of the house, she'd added the Westview Seniors T-shirt from Spirit Week with the names of everyone in their graduating class printed on the back. A copy of Trent Prescott's article about the Witneys and the reservoir, which Owen glanced at with a slight frown.

"What's this?" he asked, holding up an envelope.

"Open it."

He did, revealing the picture from that afternoon at Hampshire Hills, both of their faces bright with happiness in the fresh spring air.

She'd been expecting him to smile, for the tension that had lingered between them for the last few days to fade away. But instead, his frown grew deeper, eyes almost stormy.

"What?" she asked.

He put the picture back in the envelope, didn't answer.

"Have you talked to Lucie yet?"

Owen sighed. "No. But I don't think she's going to tell the whole town, if that's what you're worried about. She's not like that."

"I'm really sorry," Angela said. She hated how bitter his voice sounded. She reached for his hand, traced her fingers across his skin.

He flinched away. Didn't look at her.

"Owen," she said quietly.

She didn't want him to be mad at her. But she didn't want him to say what she knew he was thinking, that they should just tell people; everyone was bound to find out soon anyway.

She wasn't ready for that.

"Can we not talk about this right now?" he said.

"Okay." She felt a guilty sense of relief in avoiding this conversation for now even though she could feel the questions he didn't want to ask heavy in the air between them, making the room feel small and stifling.

They sat there in silence for a moment. Owen still wouldn't look at her, staring ahead at the photographs on the table with his jaw clenched. Behind all the storminess, Angela could see exhaustion in his face.

"You look tired," she said.

For a second, he seemed to forget he was mad and closed his eyes, rested his head against her shoulder. "I can't sleep."

Angela put her arm around him and felt him take a deep breath, relaxing against her. She reached for his hand again and this time, he wrapped his fingers around hers.

She hated ugliness, unhappiness. She wished she could make it all go away. Wished she knew what to say to make everything perfect again. She thought about the stars and the beach, midnight drives, just them, all alone and content, and tried to conjure up that feeling.

If she could get that back, make him feel that way again, maybe everything would be okay.

There were footsteps on the stairs and startled, Angela jumped to her feet and started gathering the photographs into a pile.

"There you are," said Jan. "Dave just got here with the box we're going to use for the time capsule if you want to bring all this upstairs." She took a few photographs off the pile.

"These look great. Make sure you take some pictures tonight so we can include them."

"Okay," Angela answered, making her voice sound cheerful. Beside her, Owen was trying to smile but she could see all the hurt, all the sadness, and her heart sank.

Upstairs, she and Owen were the first people to put their items into the time capsule, covering the bottom with pictures and newsprint.

The committee had spent a lot of time debating how to run this event. Some people wanted it to be almost ceremonial, another occasion to get dressed up for. But every time Angela pictured it, she'd imagined it to be informal, people coming and going, mingling and chatting about the items they'd brought with them. The way everyday life was in Westview, where everywhere you went, you ran into someone you knew. She felt a little warmth in her chest now as she watched it all unfold, like she always used to when she walked into a room and saw her entire world there.

Cassie walked in and Angela waved her over.

"What did you bring?" she asked.

Cassie held up the group picture from graduation and a picture of her and Adam in their prom crowns. She dropped them into the box and they watched them land on a layer of letters and favorite books and family pictures.

"So my parents are taking their anniversary trip early this year," she told Angela. "I'm thinking of having a party that weekend. I'll send you the details later."

"Okay."

Angela stayed at the table with the time capsule after Cassie had left, watching what felt like the entire town, each of them depositing memories for people to find in a century. Took pictures of everyone and had them write their names and little notes on them, scattered them inside the box.

When the rush of people around the table slowed down, she looked around the room. Owen was sitting in the corner, talking to Max and Declan. They all looked unhappy and she wondered what they were talking about. A group of her former teachers were standing together, talking. She saw her neighbors laughing at a story Jan was telling.

Her parents were here now.

She remembered the PTO fundraiser, when the room was loud with whispers, all eyes on them. That didn't happen this time.

Instead, the groups of people who were no longer speaking to them tightened the circles they stood in, pretending they weren't there. Angela watched her parents stop to chat with a few of their old friends, people who had moved on to the next scandal. But they didn't seem to stand as tall as they used to. Didn't seem to burn as brightly.

They were still trying to win Westview over and watching it made her feel empty, imagining them like this as long as they lived here.

They'd only brought one thing, the family picture from the Walcott Young Alumni awards. Her mother placed it in the box and then they left, not staying to socialize like they would have before.

And then Dillon walked in.

His eyes met hers across the room. He walked over, smiling, and she felt a tiny pinch of sadness. Not missing *him*, exactly, but when everything was uncomplicated. When her mind wasn't crowded with all these conflicting emotions, when everything in Westview was enough and she didn't have to worry about failing.

"How have you been?" he asked. Like they were friends, like their last conversation wasn't Angela breaking them apart in the rain outside her house.

"Fine," she said.

He was everything she used to be. He had all her old friends, her old life, and he knew that.

"We're staying at the beach for a few days next week," Dillon said, adding a picture of the football team to the time capsule. "If you want to come."

She flashed back to those days for a moment. The heat of summer clinging to her skin like a dress. Jumping off the dock into water colored by the sunset. She remembered how free she felt there, how time ceased to exist. Part of her wanted that back, even though she knew it was all too late now, too far away.

"Maybe," she said anyway and immediately wished she hadn't. She could see Owen watching them, frowning a little.

She walked over to him once Dillon was gone. "We need your help with something," she lied. He followed her downstairs and she kissed him in the archives, surrounded by centuries of old documents, all that ancient cartography.

This town had made her so good at faking smiles that when she left the library to drive around places just like this one in the dark with Owen, she almost forgot the truth. She couldn't even admit it to him. Every night now she counted down the days she had left here. And now, despite everything, she was terrified to leave.

32

The lighthouse was red and white and from the top, every-thing, everywhere was blue. Angela was smiling but it didn't look real.

All day, ever since they got on the ferry to Bismore Island, Owen had felt like something was wrong. She'd been talkative the whole way from the harbor but it seemed like her thoughts were far away. Like she was just speaking to fill space. When she kissed him, it felt like she was trying to escape from something else.

He watched her smile start to slip away once they were back on the ground, as they made their way down the street toward the path that led to water. She wasn't talking now, all quiet and cloudy.

Owen felt like he was putting on a facade, too. He still hadn't spoken to Lucie. When he saw Max and Declan yester-day, all they'd known was that he'd missed her art show. So his secret with Angela was safe, still in their hands. He tried not to think about what it meant that they weren't telling anyone, still weren't talking about it to each other. He didn't want to be the one to bring it up.

Everything suddenly seemed so fragile.

The path cut through overgrown bushes and pink wildflowers to an empty beach. He followed Angela onto the sand. The water was sapphire, the biggest waves Owen had ever seen. Wind-sculpted dunes the color of moonstone across the landscape.

Owen thought back to that day on another beach when they were both happy, when he'd kissed her in the water, on the shore, in the parking lot. He wanted that feeling back. Right now he felt like it was all spilling away, sand in an hourglass.

"Do you want to go swimming?" he asked and Angela's shoes were already off, dress on the sand. Running to the waves in a striped bathing suit, hair flying in the wind.

He followed her. The cold shocked his skin.

For a moment, surrounded by sea and sky, Owen thought maybe it would be okay. And then he realized she was crying.

"What's wrong?" he asked.

She shook her head.

"Please talk to me," he whispered. He didn't even know if she could hear him over the sound of the tide.

He put his arms around her and led her out of the ocean. They sank into the sand. Saltwater everywhere. From her eyes, at their feet. He didn't understand where everything had gone so wrong. How everything seemed to be falling apart at once and he didn't know how to fix it. He watched the ocean as they sat there. All the sunlight and clear tides and bright skies didn't feel right today. It felt like they should be watching lightning storms instead, ultraviolet lines cracking open the atmosphere, turning the sky and water heartsick shades of navy blue.

***

It was the Fourth of July and they were waiting for fireworks.

They were at the beach like they'd talked about at the summer festival, humidity heavy in the air. Deep blue twilight was washing away the orange stains of the sun's slow downfall beyond the horizon.

Angela seemed more like herself today. In the morning, they'd snuck onto the dock of the yacht club before it opened, jumping into the water, splashing and seagulls the only sounds for miles. She kissed him there, their own little harbor, surrounded by white masts and fluttering nautical flags. Sky and ocean interchangeable. Afterward, they spread towels on the beach and let the sun warm their skin. And Owen tried not to think about anything but right now. Tried not to think about all the things they should be talking about.

"Oh, I almost forgot," Angela said, sitting up now and reaching into her bag. She took out snacks and a plastic bottle full of something that clearly wasn't water. Passed the food over to Owen, then opened the bottle and took a sip.

She held it out to him. "Fourth of July tradition. Want some?"

He shook his head. There was an uncomfortable feeling in his stomach as he watched her take another sip.

"Look," she said, pointing at a group of kids playing with sparklers along the shore, the light fizzing golden in the heat. She smiled. "I'm so happy we're here. This is perfect."

It sounded like she was saying that to convince herself it was true because something seemed off now. He felt like the evening had shifted, the voices around him a little too loud, the smell of grill smoke over-strong. He kept glancing over at her, at the slowly dwindling liquid in the bottle, as they sat there for an eternity, waiting for the fireworks to start.

She hadn't had that much to drink but he could see it

in her eyes, a little in her voice. Owen could feel tiny sparks of panic igniting inside of him. He didn't understand why she needed to do this right now, why little pieces of her old friends' traditions suddenly seemed so important.

"I think I should drive you home," he said when he couldn't hold the words inside anymore. "I'll bring you back here to get your car tomorrow morning."

"I'm okay." She moved over and kissed him. Liquor like lipstick on their mouths. The strap of her dress was slipping off her shoulder and he reached over to fix it, gently brushed her hair away from her face.

"Angela, please let me take you home." He could feel panic pounding through his bloodstream now because he could still picture it, looking out the window, the color of sirens against the snow. The crumpled car and so much screaming and he couldn't let the same thing happen to her.

"I'll be fine." She opened the bottle and poured the rest of its contents out on the sand. "Look, I'm done. I'm sorry."

"Please," he said. "You know why."

He was starting to feel sick and panicked, body ice-cold and jittery. He wished he wasn't in the middle of a crowded beach. He wanted to run. He didn't want to feel anything but the wind on his skin, cold in his lungs. He could feel a familiar ache starting in his head that he hadn't felt in a while. It felt like it was pressing up against his skull from the inside and it was going to drag him down into darkness for days, make him move through the world like he was stranded in mud and storm clouds. Make him forget what it felt like to taste. Make him lie wide awake forever, even though he was so, so tired.

Angela reached for his hand and he realized his fists were clenched so tightly his nails were cutting into his palms.

He tried to take deep breaths, stop all those feelings from taking over.

"Can we just go home?" he asked.

He caught a flash of an expression that somehow looked defeated, which he didn't understand. "Okay," she said finally.

He held her hand as they walked back to his car. Bought her some water at the tiny, empty gas station at the main intersection in town.

The fireworks lit up the sky on their way back home. As he drove, hands tight on the steering wheel, he couldn't stop himself from constantly looking over to make sure she was okay. When he couldn't stand the crackling of fireworks and the sound of his own shaky breathing anymore, he asked her to pick the music.

Every song she picked felt poppy and loud and fake cheerful. Out of place tonight, in this car.

Angela's parents weren't home so he went inside with her. Her house was enormous and beautiful but it was showroom-shiny, like no one actually lived there. Her bedroom walls were blank. He thought about all the maps on his own walls at home and pictured one that might be better suited here, where she could see the place she was going to fly away to. Far away from here, far away from him.

"Owen, seriously, I'm fine," she said and he knew she was. Her voice was back to normal and she just looked tired now but he could still feel all the panic and sadness swirling in his blood.

"I'm sorry," she added. She sat on her bed and reached for his hands. Pulled him close to her, kissed him, and then they were sinking into the pillows and her fingers were at the hem of his shirt.

"I have to go home," he said, moving away from her.

At home, he lay on his bed, staring at the ceiling. Sat up and stared at all the maps. He wished he could sleep. Wished all these feelings would go away. He remembered the night he told her almost everything, when he felt safe. Fading now. Because even though Angela was always so afraid of the way this town whispered, there was a part of her that could be so careless. Didn't think about consequences.

There was a knock on his door.

"Come in."

He hoped it wasn't his mother. He couldn't imagine telling her how he felt right now, how he could hide it from her. He needed her to think he was okay.

Sometimes he felt like they were all trying to survive by never talking about the past. He didn't know how he could do that anymore. But he didn't know how to tell her the truth either, because everything was so fragile and painful he felt like he'd just start screaming or crying and never be able to stop, shatter all the glass in this town with his broken heart and fraught words.

Haley and Sophia stood in the doorway, still dressed up in stripes and stars from the Westview fireworks. This was the first year Owen hadn't gone with his friends and he remembered how they would always sit together along the sidewalk and share a pint of ice cream while glittery colors burned above this little snow globe town.

"Owen," Haley said. Her eyes were bright. "Is it true you're dating Angela Witney? The entire town's talking about it."

33

What Angela should have known by now was that it was impossible to keep secrets in Westview. They were all bound to come out somehow. This town was too small.

According to Cassie, Rose and Jocelyn had seen her and Owen together at the beach, waiting for the fireworks.

Before they'd even left, everyone knew.

She knew her parents had heard. She knew they wanted to say something. But they didn't. The house was silent again. The way it always was, while outside they pretended to be perfect and held up masks Angela knew all too well. So she framed the pictures she had of her and Owen together and hung them up all over her room.

Everywhere she went, people looked at her. Everyone was talking.

***

And now they were alone by the reservoir and it still seemed like the talking wouldn't ever stop. Angela imagined it going on forever, ringing in her ears even when she was far away from this place. Waiting for her at arrival gates, written all over the wooden white signs that welcomed people here.

"Why do you care so much about what people think?"

Owen asked as they walked, everything around them foggy and gray. Sticks cracked under their feet. He looked at the ground and his next words were so quiet Angela almost didn't hear. "What's so bad about me that you didn't want people to know?"

All the hurt in his face broke her heart. She shook her head, trying to find a way to explain how this was easier when it was just them, without rumors and opinions and judgements she'd overheard slinking into her head, making her doubt everything. How now that her family's secrets were out there, she'd liked having one thing no one could touch.

"It's not you."

He sighed.

"I just liked it better when it was just us. When we didn't have to worry about how people could ruin things or what they'd say."

"But life doesn't work like that," Owen said, frowning. "You can't control what people think or what they say about you."

But for so long, she had.

Angela thought about the football game back in the fall when she was happy to flaunt Owen in front of other people because it didn't actually mean anything. All the lies, all the rumors, that was how she distracted from the truth and kept people far away.

And she'd been so good at it that she'd even been lying to herself. Every day she tried to tell herself that she didn't care what people in Westview thought of her. That it didn't matter. But just like her parents, she cared. She cared too much.

"What happens to us next year?" she asked, finally voicing the other words that had been haunting her thoughts.

Owen took a deep breath. "Honestly, I was hoping we could make it work. But if you care more about what people think in a town you're not even going to be living in, maybe we should just—"

"No," she said, grabbing his hand, trying to keep every moment with him from falling away. "It doesn't matter what people think."

She would make that true, she promised herself. She would make herself not care. Whatever people said didn't have to ruin them. She didn't have to listen.

Owen looked at her for a long time without saying anything.

"Please," Angela continued. "Come to Cassie's party with me this weekend. I'll show you, it doesn't matter."

He hesitated.

"Just for a little while. We can leave if you're uncomfortable," she promised, feeling guilty as she remembered the expression on his face when they'd left the beach, then in her bedroom when he'd walked away.

Owen sighed. "Fine."

She kissed him. Made Westview disappear again. At home, she posted their pictures on the Internet, let the whole town know too late.

***

Angela was wearing her favorite dress, black and silky and perfect even though perfection wasn't supposed to matter anymore.

She took a deep breath, prepared herself for all the rumors, speculation. For the ribbons of whispers about to follow her down familiar hallways.

It didn't matter, she tried to tell herself, because soon she'd be rewriting her life somewhere new, far away from Westview. Far away from small-town secrets and scandals.

But as she parked her car in Cassie's driveway, Angela thought of something her mother always said about Westview.

"Here, you're guaranteed to succeed," she'd told her so many times, as they drove down streets where maple leaves blazed like rubies, as they sprayed expensive perfume on their skin before black-tie galas.

Every time she thought about failing, she wondered if it was a mistake to give that up.

And then she remembered what Owen had said the last time she complained about all the people who never left this town, who she thought didn't want to change their lives.

"I think it's unfair to assume that no one's life is going to change," he'd said thoughtfully, taking a sip of his usual coffee order from Gracie's, all those pictures of the rest of the world hanging behind him. "They'll be going to school or getting new jobs, learning new things, meeting new people. Having new experiences. Just because they're still here doesn't mean things won't change. It's just a different type of change than what you want."

And now she understood. All this time, she'd been dreading failing, coming back to this town to all the things that never seemed to change. The drama, the whispers everywhere. The way unhappiness seemed to be the biggest sin. But she was just as afraid of the things that *would* change here. That while she was miles away, changing her own life, everyone else's lives would move on, all of them here together without her, and the next time she came back there wouldn't be a place for her.

She walked into Cassie's house.

Nights like these were familiar. Cassie was already dancing out of sync to the music blasting from the speakers. Adam and Rose were making up a new drinking game. Naomi and Paige were laughing on the floor, eyes glossy and teary. Jocelyn was kissing Nolan Everitt outside on the patio.

Angela got a drink she didn't want, just to have something to do, something to hold. She watched everything for a moment, then sat down on the couch alone, inexplicably missing it all, when she wasn't torn in all these opposite directions. When the people and place she knew best weren't close to becoming unfamiliar. Every time she thought about getting on a plane her heart sped up and she felt sick.

And there was Dillon, walking in from the backyard. He smiled when he saw her.

"Hey," he said, squeezing onto the couch next to her and putting his arm around her. He smelled like smoke. Summer and the sea.

She looked into the full cup in her hands instead of at him.

"I miss you," he whispered and she knew it wasn't true.

"I miss you, too," she said but she didn't really mean it either because now, she wasn't thinking about real things, just the fact that his hands were warm through her dress and her head was spinning with confusion and Dillon's voice was soft, whispering all the right words into her ear. All the things she wanted to hear. She remembered how easy it was to be with him, how he made this town okay. She couldn't have all the things she really missed but he always reminded her of how she felt back then.

They stood, holding hands, walking toward the dark hallway.

Just one kiss. Just one, to take her back to being that girl in the soft blue dress the color of summer, happy and tipsy because everything in Westview belonged to them. The girl in a crown under small-town skies, when the whole world was gone except Westview, a storm of confetti, the smell of popcorn in the air. That girl made up of summer. And then she could leave all this behind.

34

The first thing Owen noticed as he drove through the center of town was that all the streetlights were out, casting the roads in the same darkness as his neighborhood. He parked his car at the end of Cassie's driveway, so long it could be its own street. The girls walking ahead of him were complaining about the lack of light, bitter about this being "typical Westview," which didn't mean anything, Owen thought, because the lights were always on here. On the street and inside, showing off houses like display cases. On the way here, he'd been able to see inside every house he drove past, all marble and hardwood and everything gleaming, pristine.

He should be at Max's graduation party right now. They were probably building a fire, flecks of gold painting even more stars into the summer sky, turning this town magic. They'd end up at the reservoir as night softened into morning, the way they always did. The place they'd shared so many secrets and fears while the sky changed color across the water, sometimes laughing, sometimes pasting fragments of a broken heart back together as best as they could.

But the four of them didn't exist like that anymore. Lucie was still mad at him; Max and Declan were awkwardly in-between. They all had their new friendships with Theo, Sam, and Brooke, a whole new language of jokes and memories that Owen wasn't part of. And he had everything with Angela that felt so messy and complicated now, on the verge of burning up, but all his feelings for her were still so strong.

He imagined his friends, the spell of July, crickets and trees whispering into the clear night. Usually, this time of summer still felt new, free, the best kind of endless. But this year, the days seemed to be going by so quickly, every sunset a reminder that this wasn't forever. Everything was already changing. As soon as they'd graduated, Declan had started working full-time at the bank; in just over a month, Max would be moving out of state for school and Lucie would be unpacking her dorm room with Brooke. It hurt to think about seeing her on campus, walking past each other like strangers. It wasn't supposed to be that way; they were supposed to be making new memories, adding to all their Westview traditions. Owen hoped he could find a way to fix it.

Now, on the other side of town, he walked into Cassie's house. It looked like every other one on this street. Like no one actually lived there.

He could see people watching him, whispering.

The music was loud, syncopated sound spilling out into the crisp night air through open glass doors. Outside, a small group was gathered around a fire pit, drinking and laughing.

He'd been hearing stories about Cassie's parties for years, snippets of secrets in the halls on the first day of school. He thought about his friends in Max's backyard again and wondered if he was making a mistake by coming here.

He stood there awkwardly until he felt a hand on his arm and turned to see Cassie, clad in a black bikini top and short skirt. She was clutching a drink, her wrists glittering with bracelets. For a moment, he was struck by how much she resembled Angela, face fragmented by the flickering lights. The same profile, wide-eyed and straight-nosed, silky hair falling past her shoulders in seemingly effortless waves.

"Hi, Owen," said Cassie. He could smell rum all over her breath. "Do you want a drink?"

"No thanks. Do you know where Angela is?"

"Yeah, she was just there," Cassie said, pointing to the couch. She frowned. "Wait." Her eyes widened and she grabbed Owen's arm, steering him outside into the backyard.

"What's wrong?"

"Stay here. I'll go find her," Cassie said, stumbling a little as she tried to stand between Owen and the doorway.

"Cassie, what's going on?" he asked, feeling cold with dread.

"Just wait. I'll be right back."

Owen hesitated, then followed her inside. "Cassie—"

And then everything happened in fragments.

Angela and Dillon, standing close together in the dark hallway. She was holding a red cup, her back to Owen. One of Dillon's hands tangled in her hair. The other reaching up to her face, leaning in to kiss her...

And then she pushed him away. Stepped back.

She turned around to walk away and when she saw Owen and Cassie, her face froze.

"Owen," she whispered and his name somehow sounded harsh. She grabbed his hand. She was wearing a black dress he would have loved if he wasn't afraid she was about to break his heart in it. Her hair smelled like smoke. "Nothing happened. I wasn't thinking. This town—"

Pain twisting deep in his chest. Flooding through his body.

He couldn't breathe. He stepped back, trying to push

her hand away and the words rushed out, sharp and bitter. "You can't blame this town for everything."

His voice was so loud, louder than he meant it to be, and he hated that. He remembered the way loudness used to turn on all the lights in his house in the blue-gray stillness of early morning, when the world was supposed to be silent. He thought of all the planets breaking, sunlight inside and red sky, but that wasn't who he was, *it wasn't it wasn't it wasn't…*

Tears filled her eyes, catching on her lower lashes, making him feel even worse. He was faintly aware of Cassie grabbing Dillon's arm, leading him back to the party so that it was just him and Angela in the hall, her face shiny with tears.

"I wasn't thinking," Angela repeated. Crying, stumbling over the words. "I got scared about leaving and he was there and I just wanted to escape for a minute and then I realized I was making a mistake…"

He wanted to believe she was telling the truth. He didn't want to hear the sound of his own voice shouting again. But everything hurt, the thought of what could have happened. He didn't want to be here anymore in this picture-perfect house with too-loud music and too many people. Didn't want to think about how the first time he'd kissed Angela, she and Dillon were still together…

He thought about their conversations at Gracie's over mismatched mugs and on dark roads with no destinations, when they spent hours talking about everything, all the little details of each other. Afternoons, her laughter, the sun in her hair, the city stretched out before them. The feeling of the ocean and summer and her lips on his. Everything gold, everything blue. Hands together, safe, patterns of sailboats and paper stars.

"Have you just been trying to escape with me, too?"

He didn't know what he'd do if none of that was real.

Angela shook her head.

He breathed out, relief dulling the tiniest bit of hurt. He sank to the floor and so did she, kicking off her shoes, strappy and sparkly.

"What about when you kissed me when you were still with him?" he asked quietly.

Angela's face clouded over. "I shouldn't have done that."

He didn't answer.

"I'm really sorry," she whispered.

Her eyes were red and her makeup was smudged, watery black lines trailing down her face. Owen's heart felt like it was cracked in pieces beneath his skin. Above them, he could see framed family pictures along the walls, Angela smiling in so many of them. The noise of the party was getting louder. A song he hated, people cheering as they started playing a new drinking game. His head hurt.

"I shouldn't have asked you to keep this a secret. I'm so tired of revolving my life around what people might say or think. I'm really done with that now, I promise." She looked at her shoes, tangled together on the floor in front of them. Sighed. "I used to think all I had to do to be a different person was change things like the type of clothes I wore or where I live."

"It's not."

It had to be more than that. You had to change yourself if that was what you wanted, Owen knew, otherwise you were just the same person in different cities and different clothes. He thought of everything he'd done to try to reinvent himself. To escape from his past, try to be a better person. How even now, it still didn't feel like enough.

"I know," she said, tears sliding down to her chin. "I'm trying."

He reached over and wiped them away.

"Please," Angela whispered. "I'm so sorry."

That feeling of exhaustion was coming back, the heaviness in his head. All he wanted was to go home and not think about anything right now. He stared at her teardrops on his fingerprints.

He reached for her hand. Looked down at the silver rings she always wore. There was a new one, a tiny drop of opal in the middle.

He didn't want this to end now, not like this. But the hurt was still there, waves cresting and falling with every word. He wondered if they could ever be like sea glass, all their jagged edges transformed by storms and slow tides.

"I need some time," he said finally.

"Okay." In her eyes, a mix of disappointment and hope.

"We can talk tomorrow," he promised, trying to keep his voice steady.

Angela squeezed his hand, let go.

Outside, the night was liquid around him. So dark, but the stars were burning so bright he could be close enough to touch one, close enough to hold it in his palm and turn it into a supernova with his sadness, paint the sky with celestial colors that didn't exist in this town.

He couldn't see the moon.

Owen got in his car and shut out all the stars. They laughed at him against the windows, glittered.

He felt so alone right now.

He wished he could go to Max's but he couldn't face his friends like this. He couldn't go home yet. Couldn't risk letting his mother see how sad he was, the pain making him erode.

Everything reminded him of Angela. All the stars in

the sky and the way the air felt. She was all over this car, her hair elastics and a pack of gum in the cupholder. The smell of her perfume, her shampoo. He could remember every time he'd kissed her here. Every secret they'd shared.

He closed his eyes. Saw violet on his eyelids.

So tired.

He kept playing it in his mind. Angela, so close to Dillon. His hand in her hair. What could have happened but didn't. His memory distorted it every time, pushed them together when she'd really pushed him away.

And the sound of his own voice over and over, angry and loud. The same as the voice he'd tried to forget but his dreams always remembered, forever familiar with the pitch of every syllable, exactly what his father sounded like even when nothing else made sense, when ink was raining from the sky and he could cut up the clouds.

And now that voice belonged to him, even if only for just a moment.

Owen forced himself to open his eyes.

It was starting to sound like the crickets were screaming, constellations rearranged.

He felt like he'd been running and running without stopping for months, chasing a false promise that if he just kept going, he'd reach a point where it was all far enough away but now all the air and energy were gone. Like he'd known all along it would be, someday. He was going to collapse, like the inside of his body had spent too much time reshaping itself to contain every painful word that couldn't leave his lips, and tonight, everything ached from simply trying to hold his skin and bones together.

Just go home, he told himself, trying to remember how to breathe, trying not to scream his hurt to the sky. It didn't have to be like this anymore.

His mother was probably getting ready to go to bed soon, leaving the front lights on for him, so tomorrow, he promised himself, he'd tell her everything he'd been trying to hide for so long. Maybe they could start to figure out how to be okay again instead of just pretending.

He turned on his car. Practiced the words in his head.

A car hurtled down the driveway. Past him, down the street. Too fast.

Angela.

She was driving past the turn that would take her toward her house. Where was she going?

And then he remembered the cup in her hand.

No no no no no no

He tried to call her. No answer. He was panicking now, hands shaking.

He lit up the road with his headlights.

She was already so far ahead of him, tail lights getting fainter, fading away.

He drove faster. Heart racing.

He thought about their summers. The innocence of being five years old, toes in warm earth while a girl spun from sunshine danced in the sprinkler. Last year, the end of August when she showed up on his doorstep with a little more darkness. Their lips together at the top of a city and all their wishes whispered throughout small towns. And this was what it came down to: running red lights on backroads that wound around water, chasing after a girl whose fate he was afraid of, running toward everything that scared him the most because he couldn't let their story end here. Couldn't live with himself if he hid away again, if something happened to her because he was afraid.

Because the streetlights were out, Owen didn't see

the deer skittering across the street until it was too late. He swerved.

He saw its shadow in the headlights just before its body and the car collided with a thud.

The last thing he saw before his car careened into darkness was the shattered windshield, a pattern like unraveled lace all over his vision.

35

Angela woke to a white morning, sunlight streaming bright through the frothy fabric of her curtains. The house was heavy with silence.

She stared at the ceiling, snapshots of last night filling her mind. Standing in the hall with Dillon, that moment everything was so familiar, his eyes, his hands, the way he smelled, and she realized what she was doing, that she couldn't keep trying on different worlds like clothes without consequence, couldn't keep running away to the past when she had so much to look forward to.

And then. Owen's eyes, a sad shade of sterling. On the hallway floor with him, hoping this wasn't the end of them. After he'd left, she'd sat there in the dark, all alone at a party she'd begged him to come to. So she'd shut off her phone, threw away her untouched drink, and left without a word. Drove to Gracie's just a little too fast. Stayed there for hours, staring at the pictures of other places on the walls, thoughts reeling until traces of deep blue slowly returned to the sky, still awash in summer stars.

She wondered what he'd say to her today, what she could do to fix everything.

It hurt to think about it. Heartache stabbing at every synapse.

She got out of bed. Last night's clothes hung wrinkled from her tired body, the dress she'd thought was perfect.

Angela paced downstairs to the sunlit kitchen, turning on the small TV on the counter as she boiled water to make tea. The anchor, white teeth and cabernet-colored lips, was reporting a late-night car accident on a nearby road. Angela cringed and muted the sound. She watched the silent syllables escape the anchor's mouth for a moment, then turned to pour her tea. The first sip stung her mouth.

She moved toward the kitchen table, fingers wrapped around warm ceramic. She glanced again quickly at the TV.

A familiar picture stretched across the screen with white letters blurred across the bottom. She stood still, stared.

The smooth, glossy mug slid from the pale laces of her fingers, splattering her hands with hot tea. She heard shattering. She had the same picture upstairs on her nightstand, frozen smiles caught by the camera, trapped behind glass and the curves of a black baroque frame. Angela had been cut out of the picture on the TV screen but she could see her arm wound around him, the edge of her own shoulder tucked safely into Owen's half-embrace. His smile was captured mid-laugh.

Frantically, Angela stumbled up the stairs, toes tangling in the indigo fringe of the rug in the hallway. Her footsteps matched the panic in her head, a short frenzied pattern of *no no no no no no*.

She turned on her phone and called Owen because this had to be a mistake, it couldn't be real.

The call went straight to voicemail.

She sank to the floor.

Hands shaking, Angela called his mother next. The photographs on her walls began to fade to black-and-white blurs. A sound like screaming echoed in her head with each unanswered ring.

"Angela?" Valerie, voice unsteady.

Owen's name was the only word Angela could say, in a broken breath, nearly unrecognizable. She squeezed her eyes shut, clutched her phone.

"Angela ... did you hear..."

The sound of sobbing echoed in her ear. She felt like her body was curling in on itself, collapsing. She couldn't speak.

"Angela ... are you there?"

"What happened?" Angela whispered.

"Owen was in a car accident last night." His mother's voice reached Angela's ears in fragments. "Near your neighborhood ... he hit a deer and veered off the road."

Angela heard her inhale shakily, exhale. The silence before her next words seemed infinite. "He died before—"

Without thinking, Angela flung the phone across the room so she didn't have to keep hearing that fractured voice put words to the newscaster's silently moving lips downstairs.

Today, they were supposed to talk. They would have met someplace like Gracie's, their usual table, sunshine through the windows and the scent of warm coffee, and maybe this wasn't how it ended, maybe she could make it okay and they'd make plans for all the long summer days ahead, all the places they still wanted to go. Blue skies and saltwater, the taste of heat, skin sun-drenched.

Or maybe they would have driven home to different parts of town with broken hearts, all this to fade out of each other's life again as summer melted into fall.

Not this.

Over and over, she pictured Owen's car spinning off the road like a ballerina dizzy from a violent twirl, skidding tires leaving black-ribbon stains on the pavement. Jagged petals of shattered glass glittering on the ground. Headlights flickering under country starlight.

She wondered if he saw his life ending as the car spiraled, or if his world went black before he realized what was happening. She hated the thought of him clinging to consciousness so close to here in the solitude of shadowy trees, waiting for blue and red lights to dance across the winding road. Sirens racing, staggered breaths and slowing heartbeats. She wondered if he saw the ambulance arrive, hands reaching out to help him, one last comfort before his eyes blinked shut, or if anyone was even there to call for help and she wanted to wake up now so that none of this was real.

She saw blood, so bright through all the tears in her eyes. Her foot was bleeding, cut open by a broken edge of the fallen mug.

She let it bleed. On the floor, she closed her eyes to the image of a car in its fatal pirouette.

36

The church was warm. Sunlight and stained glass made constellations all over the floor. The fragrance of flowers and incense so strong she felt sick.

She didn't want to cry. Stared instead at her shiny black shoes. Scraped their points against the ground, dulling them.

She shut her eyes to hymns and couldn't stop seeing Owen's car spiraling across the road. She was afraid to sleep now, haunted by harmonies of skidding tires and sirens and the fear of forgetting his voice.

She couldn't stop thinking about that night. Running through every moment, rewriting every scenario in her mind so that they ended with Owen still alive.

Her entire life, everywhere she looked in Westview, there was reservoir. And now, there was something new: black lines curving across the road. Grass, flattened, still sparkling with shards of glass. A makeshift memorial of flowers and pictures. And even when that was all gone, cleaned up or wilted or washed away by rain, every day she had left here, she had to drive past it, that lonely stretch of road where Owen's life stopped. As familiar now as the layout of streets and water in this town. Memorized when she closed her eyes, like the shape of the Cherwell skyline, the sound of the ocean.

Afterward, everyone wanted to talk about him. They all shared memories she wasn't there for. Jokes she didn't understand, favorite places she'd never been.

She didn't want to talk. Didn't want to give away their winter nights and summer skies. She kept him for herself, every detail folded up in her heart, tiny paper airplanes that would never take flight.

***

The night before Angela left Westview, Owen's mother let her into his bedroom. It was in disarray, as if he'd only left temporarily. Books open on the floor. Broken shards of setting sun glowed against the bright white pages. His bed was unmade, sheets wrinkled. She thought about all the nights he came home safe to this room, how he must have left it this way with plans to clean it up in the morning.

The edges of some of his maps were starting to curl away from the walls. She found one of Westview, took it down. With a red pen from Owen's desk, she drew little symbols, Westview in miniature. Her house, Owen's house. The high school, Gracie's. Ochre Mansion and the library, then Town Hall and their spot by the reservoir. Pen-sketched stories and lives among colored lines that led to other places.

There was a box for her here. He must have planned to give it to her before she left. A thin shoebox with a piece of tape stuck to it. Her name in red marker. Angela. His handwriting was precise, pointed.

She sat on his bed for a while, holding the box in her hands, memorizing each line and curve of the crimson letters. Its presence was comforting, something to focus on while the space around her was wild with the memory of his movements, the sound of his voice. His bed smelled like him. She let it seep into her hair, her clothes, close against her skin for the last time.

She knew what was inside the box before she opened it. She removed the cardboard lid carefully, as if it was breakable, her fingertips grazing his invisible fingerprints. The box was mostly full of pictures. The ones he'd promised to show her almost a year ago, when her voice carried boredom and disinterest. The once-bright ink had faded slightly. There were ticket stubs from the movie theater, from the Ferris wheel in Cherwell. A pin from the modern art museum and a glow-in-the-dark star. Pictures from this year that hurt too much to look at now.

She looked through the old pictures slowly. She could almost hear her five-year-old laughter, Owen's footsteps swishing through long, green grass. Their Popsicle-lined smiles and crooked teeth were featured in every picture, and if she looked hard enough, they were still the same.

Angela placed the map on top, closed the box, and watched the dying rays of summer flash slightly against the streaky glass.

37

He'd left his sweatshirt in her car and she wore it to the airport. It still smelled like him.

All the seatback screens on the plane displayed maps as she sat down, New England all zoomed in. Dotted lines dividing it into states, little stars on the capitals. The Westview reservoir was there, labelled, and Angela jabbed at the screen until it was zoomed out far enough that she couldn't see it anymore.

She closed her eyes as they ascended so she didn't have to watch what it all looked like as it disappeared. Fell asleep as the sun set over all the places she knew by heart.

When she woke up, the moon was shining gold over the Pacific Ocean.

***

She thought she saw Westview everywhere.

Her mind turned every familiar feature into someone from Westview for brief moments until she realized they were all strangers who had never heard her name. In the hall, a girl whose eyes and nose could have belonged to Cassie but the color of her hair was all wrong and she blinked, confused, as she became a stranger again. At the coffee shop across the street from her dorm, a tall boy with messy hair that was just a little too long—there was Owen!—and her heart jumped until he turned and the shape of his nose wasn't right and her eyes filled with tears.

She hung a map in her room of the place she was now and thought of him, then tried to forget. Marked all the places she wanted to go with tiny stars.

On the first day of Orientation, she wore a dress she'd made herself. Deep blue, the skirt light and flowy like a summer breeze.

She had a moment of panic as she walked into the room, searching for an anchor, someone who knew her. Took a deep breath.

"Hi," she said to a girl sitting at an empty table. "Do you mind if I sit here?"

"Go ahead." She gave Angela a friendly smile.

"Thanks." She sat down and smiled back, aware of the nerves in her voice. But that was okay, she reminded herself. She turned to introduce herself for the first time in a long time, to this girl who had probably never heard of Westview, didn't know her story. "I'm Angela."

***

"This is gorgeous," Cassie said.

Angela smiled. "Wait until we get to the overlook."

Cassie had only arrived this morning, but Angela had already taken her to her favorite vintage shop, introduced her to some friends who hadn't left for the holidays yet, and spent hours talking at her favorite café, the one with turquoise tiles and citrus trees in a hidden garden.

She knew her life looked close to perfect again and it wasn't fair. Wasn't fair that she had all this and Owen was gone and couldn't have any of the things he'd been looking forward to.

"Your parents told me they liked spending Thanksgiving here," Cassie told her as they walked, winter sun shining all over them.

Angela shrugged. It had been a little uncomfortable but at least they were trying. At least no one was pretending anymore. She hadn't taken them here, though, the place she always came alone when she was sad.

"This way," she said, leading Cassie up a steep path, almost all hidden in green.

They were overlooking a small cove, the brightest blue waves crashing against a shore covered entirely in sea glass. Drops of every color, each one sculpted by the water.

She'd brought her camera with her so they took some pictures, then sat down, kicking off their shoes, breathing in the scent of sea salt. She let Cassie tell her all the latest West-view news: the internship she was starting next semester, the new shop opening on Main Street. The scholarship Owen's friends were starting in his memory and the plaque they'd hung with his name in the high school hallway outside the history classrooms.

She could feel Cassie looking at her once they'd been silent for a few minutes and the only sounds were birdsong and the movement of the ocean.

"I know you didn't want to talk about it before," she said. "But can you tell me how you're doing now?"

The sun was setting, glittering over rainbows of polished broken glass. Turning palm trees into shadows. And because she was done pretending, Angela told Cassie the truth as they watched it, as the world turned carnelian. How much she missed Owen, how some days it felt like she would never be whole again and others, the pain had dulled into something more manageable, and still others, it came rushing back in sharp focus in moments she wasn't expecting. That sometimes she felt guilty for being happy. Afraid of moving on, but scared she wouldn't, either; terrified that someday she'd realize she'd forgotten the way it sounded when he laughed. And that she didn't know if waking up in a place thousands of miles from anyone who knew him made it harder or easier.

She hated that things were forever unfinished between them. That she didn't know what he would have said when they spoke on a day he never got, that she spent so much time wondering how much of that night was her fault, trying not to drown in what-ifs. That this was always going to be part of her story.

Later, back in her room, she showed Cassie the projects she'd spent the semester working on.

"What's wrong?" she asked, noticing the slight frown on her lips.

Cassie looked up. "They're good," she said. "But don't take this the wrong way ... they don't really seem like *you*."

Angela sighed. "I know."

She'd spent all semester trying to create something she was excited about, something that stood out and captured who she wanted to be, but she just felt empty. She'd followed the instructions for every assignment but everything she made seemed dull and insignificant, like something in her had burned out.

She thought about all the time she'd spent in her bedroom in Westview, trying to make something that could take her far away until all the red lights and evergreens there were just a memory. And now that she was here, she didn't remember how that felt.

She stared at the ceiling while Cassie slept. After what seemed like an eternity of imagining constellations across it with her eyes wide open, hugging Owen's sweatshirt that didn't even smell like him anymore, Angela got up. Took out the box from Owen she kept under her bed. She hadn't looked at it since the night before she left Westview.

She touched the letters of her name, his handwriting. Remembered the sound of his voice. His laugh.

She opened the box. The map of Westview she'd taken from his wall was on top, their story charted by her in red pen at the end of summer. Her eyes roamed over familiar roads.

And then she found a blank page and started drawing. A dress, blue silk that flowed like reservoir water. Another, green for all the trees that protected it, the same way she used to build walls around herself. All over their insides, she drew that map of Westview, everywhere she'd been with Owen marked, so faintly you could barely see but it was there. Because the truth was, she hadn't forgotten she was from Westview. She remembered it all the time. Couldn't erase it from herself, no matter how much she wanted to or how hard she tried.

She heard Cassie moving and glanced up to see if she was awake but she'd just rolled over. On the wall above her, the map of the Pacific Coast, the tiny stars on dream destinations glinting a little.

Angela kept drawing until sunrise turned the sky gold. One more dress, a blur of colors this time instead of just one, a sea-glass beach. Inside, the Pacific Coast map, some lines incomplete, some spaces empty for everywhere else she had left.

Resources

If you or a loved one have been affected by issues raised in this book, please don't be afraid to ask for help or talk to someone you trust. The following organizations can provide advice and additional information.

Abuse and domestic violence
Men's Advice Line
Website: mensadviceline.org.uk
Helpline: 0808 801 0327
Email: info@mensadviceline.org.uk
Refuge
Website: refuge.org.uk
Helpline: 0808 200 0247
Email: helpline@refuge.org.uk
Women's Aid
Website: womensaid.org.uk
Email: helpline@womensaid.org.uk
Bereavement and grief
Cruse Bereavement Care
Website: cruse.org.uk
Helpline: 0808 808 1677

Email: helpline@cruse.org.uk

Other mental health information and resources

Mental Health Foundation
Website: mentalhealth.org.uk

Mind
Website: mind.org.uk
Information line: 0300 123 3393
Legal line: 0300 466 6463
Email: info@mind.org.uk

The Mix
Website: themix.org.uk
Helpline: 0808 808 4994

YoungMinds
Website: youngminds.org.uk

Author's Note

The town of Westview and its story are fictional but like Angela and Owen, I grew up in a "drowned town" that was partially razed and flooded in the early 1900s to create a reservoir that now supplies drinking water to over 60 percent of the state of Rhode Island. While doing research for this book, I was surprised by the number of other places throughout the US with similar stories—small towns chosen as locations for water sources, completely transformed by the rapid growth of nearby cities. Some of these towns were relocated, others were partially flooded, and still others were disincorporated, disappearing underwater. Some residents opposed the construction of these dams and reservoirs in their communities; many families were compensated for the loss of their homes and property. It's easy to imagine how this could change a place in so many ways beyond just geography, and in creating this story and its setting, I was interested in exploring what the culture of a community might look like if this happened in a town where it was never supposed to, if the story you'd grown up hearing was really about the most powerful people's need to control a narrative, and how that could trickle down, even generations later.

Library Booklists (librarybooklists.org) maintains a list of books and other information about real drowned towns, for readers interested in learning more.

Acknowledgements

To my parents, Robert and Marita Pierce, thank you for everything— for all your love, support, and encouragement, for always helping me find ways to pursue my dreams. Kathryn, Christopher, and Michael; and the entire McKendall family, I'm so incredibly lucky to have a family as supportive as you all.

Zack, thank you for all the adventures and endless encouragement.

Cate, thank you for reading every version of this book and believing in it since day one.

This book was written in part during my time at Wheaton College. I'm so grateful to every workshop group I worked with there for their thoughtful feedback and critiques, and to the Creative Writing faculty, especially Deyonne Bryant, for your guidance and mentorship, and for helping me become a better writer.

Thank you to Xander Cansell, Anna Simpson, Julia Koppitz, Becca Allen, and the rest of the team at Unbound for your patience, support, and enthusiasm. Editors Sarah Forbes Stewart, Dushi Horti, and Philippa Hudson, thank you for making this book better with your valuable insights and suggestions;

and to designer Mark Ecob for bringing it to life with the gorgeous cover.

To the Unbound Author Social Club, it's been a pleasure to be part of such a supportive community of writers; thank you all for your wisdom and encouragement over the last few years.

Finally, to all the Unbound patrons who helped make this book possible, thank you so much for your generosity.

Unbound Supporters

Unbound is the world's first crowdfunding publisher, established in 2011.

We believe that wonderful things can happen when you clear a path for people who share a passion. That's why we've built a platform that brings together readers and authors to crowdfund books they believe in – and give fresh ideas that don't fit the traditional mould the chance they deserve.

This book is in your hands because readers made it possible. Everyone who pledged their support is listed at the front of the book and below. Join them by visiting unbound.com and supporting a book today.

Casandra Archetto
Tim Atkinson
Kelly Austin
Matt Bond
Alyssa Bostrom
Richard WH Bray
Louise Brown
Alaina Carnevale

Sue Clark
Charlotte Cockle
Charlotte Cockle
DE
Roberta Desiderio
Jeanne Durfee
Dave Eagle
Alys Earl

Eamonn Griffin
John H.
Chelsea Haynes
Courtney Hulbert
Charles Humerickhouse
Gill James
Samantha Jennings
Elena Kaufman
Dan Kieran
Shona Kinsella
Beth M.
Helena Markou
Caitlin McCutcheon
Ray McKendall

John Mitchinson
Carlo Navato
John-Michael O'Sullivan
Chris Pierce
Michael Pierce
Tom Plante
Justin Pollard
Ilene Riley
Ian Robinson
Solitaire Townsend
Lisa Vinas
Alex W.
Joshua Winning